The Brazen Altar

Holy Land Mysteries

Book II

S. E. Thomas

The Brazen Altar
Holy Land Mysteries Book II

A Novel

Published by The Dramatic Pen Press, L.L.C.

Lolo, Montana

Table of Contents

Dedication

Table of Contents 4

Map of First Century Jerusalem 7

Map of First Century Samaria 8

Map of First Century Judea 9

Darash's Home 10

Jesus the Messiah 11

Chapter One: Night Terrors 13

Chapter Two: The Road to Samaria 23

Chapter Three: The Wine-Maker of Gophna 31

Chapter Four: Strange Things 39

Chapter Five: Change of Plans 47

Chapter Six: Shechem 53

Chapter Seven: Claiming Territory 61

Chapter Eight: Samaria 69

Chapter Nine: Simon the Sorcerer 75

Chapter Ten: The Woman of Sychar 83

Chapter Eleven: The Leatherworker   89

Chapter Twelve: Straying   95

Chapter Thirteen: The Mandrake   103

Chapter Fourteen: Whispers of the Past   111

Chapter Fifteen: The Sign of Molech   119

Chapter Sixteen: The Acropolis   125

Chapter Seventeen: The Power of Guilt   133

Chapter Eighteen: The Brazen Altar   139

Chapter Nineteen: The Substitute   145

Chapter Twenty: The Romans   151

Chapter Twenty-one: Soothing Samaria   159

Chapter Twenty-two: The Road Home   165

Chapter Twenty-three: The Suspicious Traveler   171

Chapter Twenty-four: Gone   177

Character Descriptions   185

Going Deeper: Discussion Questions   189

Glossary   219

Research Bibliography   223

6 | The Brazen Altar

Map of First Century Jerusalem

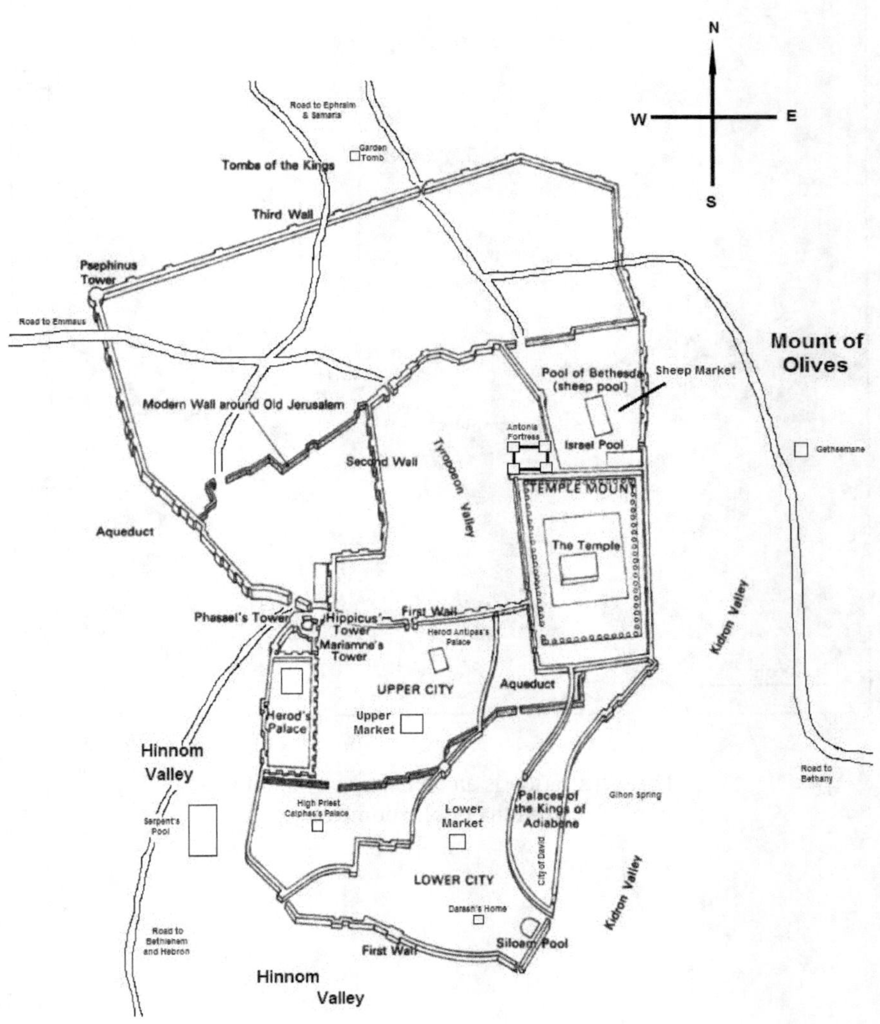

This illustration is an adaptation of an image
from the public domain.

Map of First Century Samaria

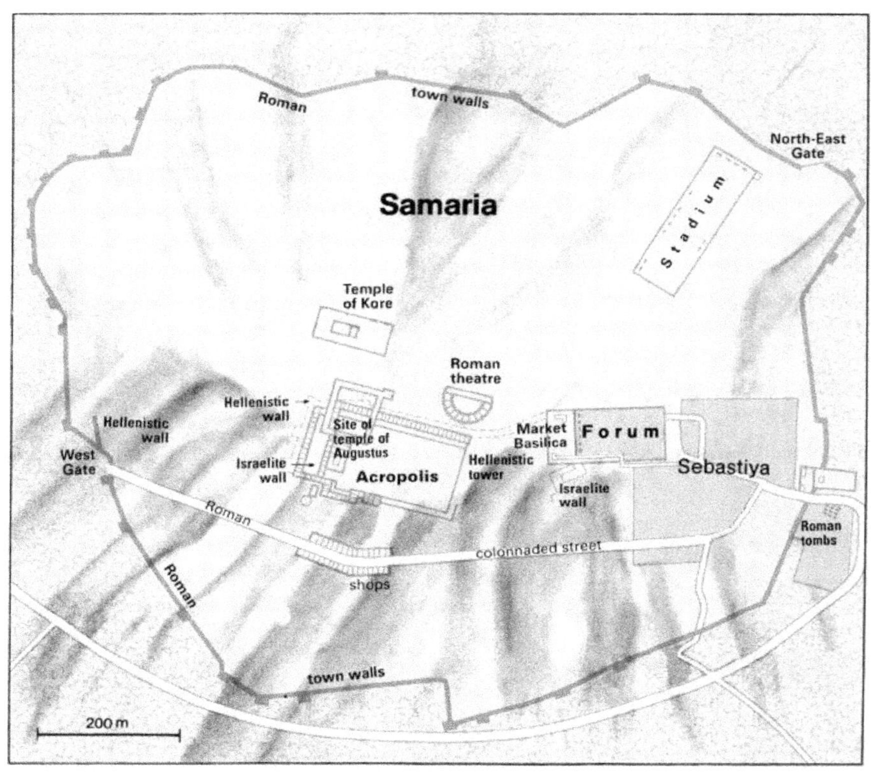

This illustration is an adaptation of an image
from the public domain.

Map of First Century Judea

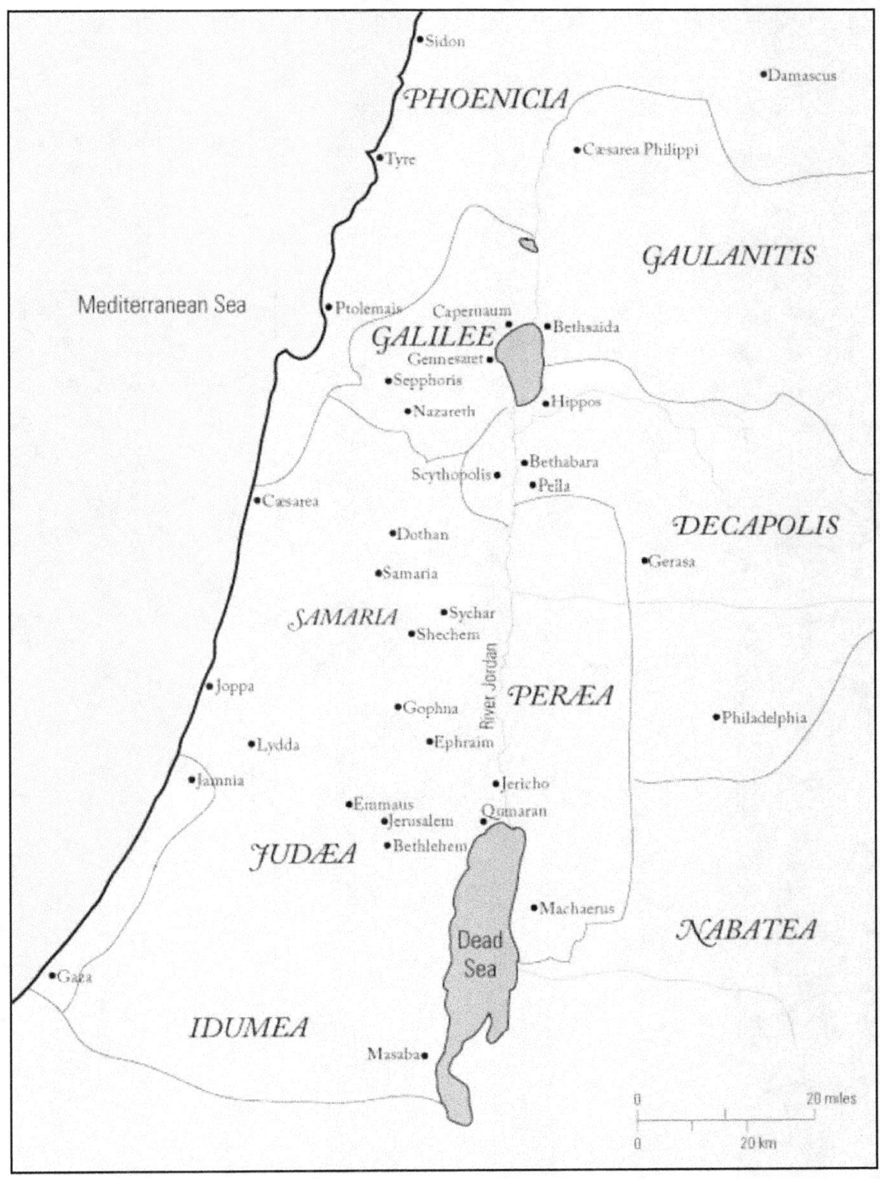

This illustration is an adaptation of an image
from the public domain

Darash's Home

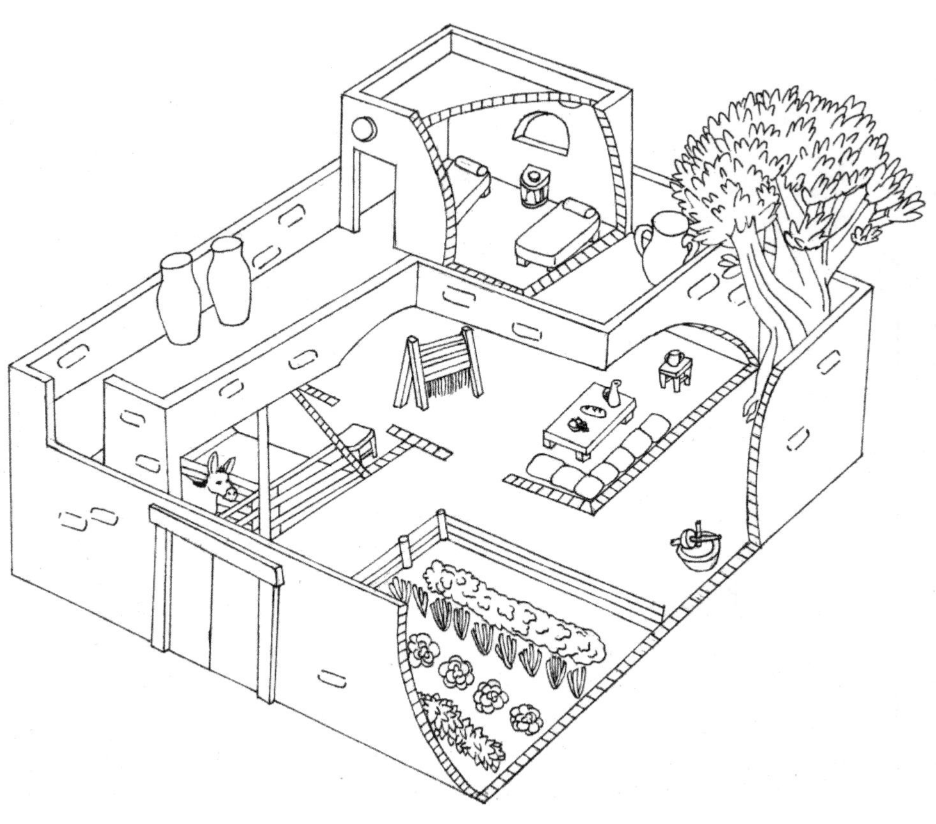

Then you will know the truth,
and the truth will set you free.

~ Jesus the Messiah

I

Night Terrors

Hazaiah swept his four-year-old son, Ikaiah, into his arms and deposited the child on a large sack of grain in the back of their cart. Taking a small carving of a sheep from his belt, Hazaiah placed it in his son's hand.

"You can sit on this soft sack," he told the boy, "and play with your toy. If you get tired, you can lay down across these three bags of grain. It will be like a little bed for you." He smiled. "What do you think about that?"

Ikaiah patted the sack next to him and nodded. "I want my blanket."

"Your imah has it. She is still inside the inn. I will fetch her."

Hazaiah turned toward the inn but nearly bumped into Bagad, one of the other guests.

"Oh, forgive me," Hazaiah apologized.

"You are leaving quite early," Bagad said. He was a tall, Jewish man with a thin, patchy beard. "I wanted to say good-bye. I admit I am sorry to see you leave."

"Uh… yes, well, we have a long journey before us. We did not want to disturb you." Hazaiah took a step back from Bagad as he spoke, for the man had an odd and unpleasant smell about him.

"Oh, it would have been no disturbance. We are friends, are we not, brother?" Bagad smiled, but his eyes were hard.

"Oh, uh, of course, of course." Hazaiah forced a smile. He glanced toward the inn, wishing his wife would appear and rescue him.

Bagad swept past Hazaiah and moved to the back of the cart. "Shalom, Ikaiah," he greeted the child, leaning on the cart railing nearest the boy. "Did you sleep well?"

Ikaiah nodded.

"That is good." Bagad placed long, possessive fingers on the boy's arm. "I am sad to see you go. We are friends, right?"

Ikaiah smiled and nodded.

"Would you like to come see me some—"

"Eliana!" Hazaiah called loudly toward the inn, unwilling to leave his son alone with this man.

"Here I am," Eliana said, appearing at the door of the inn, carrying the remainder of their belongings.

Hazaiah rushed to help her unload a bag and two bed rolls with blankets into the back of the cart. He then gave her a hand up so she could sit on the front bench with him for the first part of this day's journey to Jerusalem. Hazaiah returned to the back of the cart where Bagad now whispered something to Ikaiah.

"Here is your blanket," he told Ikaiah, pushing himself between Bagad and his son. He tucked the blanket around Ikaiah and turned to Bagad, keeping his body between them. "Shalom, Bagad, and farewell. May Adonai bless you. It is unlikely we will meet again."

"Oh, one never knows," Bagad said. "We may yet have the good fortune of finding one another again."

"Well, good bye," Hazaiah said. He returned to the front bench of the cart, climbed up beside his wife, and slapped the reins on the rumps of his team of mules.

As they drove away from the inn onto the open road, Hazaiah gave a sigh of relief.

"I admit, I am glad to be rid of that place," he confessed to his wife.

"I, too," she said. "That man is strange."

"Indeed." Hazaiah glanced back at Ikaiah who sat comfortably on the sack of grain, playing with his toy sheep and humming a tune to himself. "But we are on our way now, and soon we will be with family." He smiled at her. "All is well."

סֶ לָ ה

Eliana opened her eyes to the sound of moaning and the acrid smell of smoke. She rolled to her side and tried to sit, only to be hit with a wave of nauseating pain emanating from the left side of her skull. Moving her hand to the place, she brought back fingers smeared with blood.

"Hazaiah?" she said, finding her voice as the terror returned. "Ikaiah?"

A moan.

Eliana turned to see her husband lying next to her groaning through barely parted lips. An ugly patch of blood soaked his tunic over his abdomen.

"Hazaiah! Oh, no! Hazaiah, my husband! What have they done to you?"

She placed a hand on his cheek and patted lightly to rouse him, but he did not open his eyes. Eliana's attention turned to her son.

"Ikaiah?" she said, looking around. No response. "Ikaiah!"

Eliana fought against the pain and pushed herself to her feet. She took a wobbly step forward and surveyed the devastation. Their two servants lay nearby in pools of blood. Hazaiah's mules lay slain, still attached to the overturned, smoldering cart.

The cart!

"Ikaiah!" she cried again, her voice desperate, haunted.

She raced forward and circled the blackened wreckage. When she saw the place where her little boy once sat and played, she lifted a hand to her mouth and screamed.

סֶ לָ ה

Darash jolted from his sleep, heart beating wildly. He held his breath, listening for the sound. Something had happened. Something terrible. He searched his fragmented memory, separating dreams from reality to search for the terror that had awakened him.

A scream.

He heard it again. A terrified, helpless sound. Desperate for escape. Desperate for rescue. It sounded like….

Tsarah!

Darash jumped from his bed, ignoring the stabbing pain in his chest from the wound that refused to heal. A quick search told him Tsarah, indeed, was missing from her bed. He ran barefooted from the upper room they shared, along the roofline over the stables, and down the cracking stone steps. A few long strides brought him to the front door.

He heard the cry again, this time closer, clearer.

"Tsarah!" He called.

Darash pushed inside the main room and followed the sound of weeping cries to his mother's bedroom. The sight before him brought him to an abrupt halt at the room's threshold. He caught himself with both hands, one on each side of the entrance. His chest burned with pain.

His mother, Revayah, who he called "Imah," sat on her bed holding a girl in her arms. But the girl was not Tsarah, his eight-year-old sister. Tsarah sat at the foot of the bed, hugging her knees, deep worry lines crossing her brow.

And Darash remembered.

The girl cradled in his mother's arms, hair askew, wails ripping from her tiny frame, was known only as "Amah," meaning female slave. She was about thirteen years old, he guessed. He had purchased her from an evil Greek man named Pertho and brought her home two nights ago.

Revayah had expressed her doubts in no uncertain terms about the wisdom of brining Amah into their home, but Darash had appeased her by suggesting that Amah would make a good servant who could replace their beloved maid and cook, Huldah. Huldah had left shortly after Abba's death because they simply could no longer support her. Now, witnessing Amah's crippling fear, Darash wondered if he had done the right thing by bringing her here. Revayah no doubt had also realized by now that the girl would be little help with the chores.

Revayah's eyes met his. They darted to a blanket in the corner of her room, then back to him. He understood.

Darash retrieved the warm, wool blanket, woven with strands of blue against white, and opened it. The girl still wailed.

"Please," Revayah whispered, telling Darash with her eyes to spread it across the girl's back, fearing to release the fragile, unpredictable girl.

Tsarah, eager to finally be able to help, moved from her huddled position to grasp one side of the blanket while Darash pulled the other edge up and around both the girl and his mother.

Revayah snuggled the terrified child to her chest like a newborn babe as she whispered soothing sounds into Amah's hair. Darash sunk to his knees, and Tsarah returned to her former position, each feeling the stabbing sorrows brought with each cry, each sob, each ragged gasp.

But soon Amah began to calm.

As the wailing turned to weeping and the weeping to whimpering, Revayah's voice emerged into the space left behind.

"Be still. All is well. Adonai has rescued you. We are with you now. And you are with us. You are safe."

סֶלָה

"You look terrible. Did you sleep in the street last night?"

"Shalom, Valad," Darash greeted the cheese-seller with whom he shared the little corner of the alley off the market square.

Darash tied his donkey, Nekoda, to a post and began fumbling with clumsy fingers to untie a sheaf of hay from her back. The fifteen-year-old yawned widely, not caring who saw.

"Ah, Darash!" Nib'haz, the blind basket-weaver, called to him.

Nib'haz, an elderly man, had become like a father to Darash since Darash's own father had been murdered earlier that year. Shortly thereafter, Darash lost the family shop to his father's former business partners. They had forced him out due to some clever but dishonest trickery, claiming Darash's father, Tuwr, owed them money. Though this year had been the hardest of Darash's young life, Nib'haz had provided the encouragement and wise insights Darash needed—not only to deal with his grief, but also to learn to support his mother and sister without yielding to the temptation to cheat in business.

"I was beginning to wonder if you would make it today," Nib'haz added. Then, to Valad, "Move your cheese. Darash is here."

"No, leave it," Darash said. "I am not staying long. I simply came by to ask Ibnei'ah if he needs any bitumen this week."

Some weeks earlier, Darash had helped Ibnei'ah, a local mosaic artist, with a problem he had relating to his daughter. Afterwards, Ibnei'ah had promised to only buy bitumen—a tar-like substance necessary for tilework—only from Darash. This arrangement had become Darash's only reliable source of income, though it did not bring in enough to support his family.

Darash dropped a pile of hay before Nekoda, who wasted no time rooting through it with her round snout.

"Then why did you bring your donkey? And why are you feeding her?" Valad wanted to know.

"I am feeding her because I got up too late to do it at home this morning and she is hungry." He yawned again. "And I brought her because, if Ibnei'ah needs nothing from me this week, I am going to Gophna. There is a metalworker there who—"

"Oh, good!" Valad interrupted. "While you are there, find that no good brother of mine and tell him he still owes me three and a half denarii and, if he does not return it by next week, I am going to come up there and—"

"Peace, Valad," Nib'haz said, one hand in the air. "Be still and let the boy alone. He has no share in your family's troubles." He turned toward Darash's general direction and said, "This is your first trip out of town since your injury, and it is a full day's journey. Is it absolutely necessary?"

"Injury!" Valad interrupted. "You say that as if he tripped and stubbed his toe. The boy was stabbed in a dark alley by a murderer!"

"Yes, Valad," Nib'haz said, "we know. Let us not relive it." He turned back to Darash.

"But it is the best story I have right now…." Valad muttered.

"Perhaps someone could go to Gophna in your place," Nib'haz suggested to Darash. "Perhaps Valad could go."

"Wait… what?" Valad said.

"No, Nib'haz," Darash responded. "I appreciate your concern, but if I do not purchase more merchandise soon, I will have nothing left to sell. I need to make the selections myself—know what I am buying. Gophnan wine and cookery can be had for little and sold for a good profit to the travelers who come to Yerushaláyim."

"Wait," Valad said. "Why are you in such a hurry? Where is the reward money that Grecian, Barus, gave you for finding his daughter's killer?"

"I, uh...." Darash lowered his eyes. His black bangs fell over his forehead as he turned back to Nekoda. He stroked her long ears. She twitched them, preferring not to be disturbed while she ate.

"Oh, no! Do not tell me you spent it all already!"

"No! ...Well, not all of it...."

"Darash!" Valad cried. "I cannot believe this! That was at least a year's wages! Gone in a matter of days?"

Darash took a deep breath and turned to Valad. Sweeping his hair from his eyes, he said, "I bought Amah."

"Who? You bought a slave girl?"

"No..." Nib'haz said in his low, guttural voice. "Not a slave girl. He bought the slave girl."

Valad opened his eyes wider. "Ahhhh.... Ah!" He slapped his skinny thigh. "Amah! The Amah! That little mud flower you took such a liking to!" He bellowed a laugh. "Boy, you must be out of your mind!" He laughed again. "I knew you liked her, but—I never imagined this! What are we to do with you, Darash? Ah, ha, ha, ha, ha!"

"My mother needed a servant."

"A servant? A servant! Do you know nothing? Boy, that girl is a prost—"

"I think it was an excellent purchase," Nib'haz interrupted, speaking more loudly than usual. "No amount is too large to free a Jewess from slavery. Do you not agree, Valad?"

Valad was laughing so hard that tears ran down his cheeks making tracks in the thin layer of dirt that resided there. "Of course, of course, but... ah, ha, ha, ha!"

"Thank you, Nib'haz," Darash said. "Can I leave Nekoda here while I go look for Ibnei'ah?"

"Yes, my son. Go. Go now."

סֶלְה

Twenty minutes later, Darash led Nekoda through the lower *shuk*, the southern market in Jerusalem's Lower City, called the *agora* in Greek. The moved through the smell of cumin and diced onions that stung his eyes into a cloud of red clay dust created by a man sweeping out his pottery stall. Darash sneezed and turned a corner, heading toward the

Upper City to begin his journey. As he passed the dyer's booth at the northern edge of the shuk, he overheard a loud lament.

"What are you going to do about it, Magistrate?" It was Millah, the dyer's wife. Her voice, normally flowing with choice gossip interspersed with sales attempts, now flowed with complaints littered with accusations. "How are we supposed to keep our business running without our son? How could he leave us like this—without even a word! And now his father is ill! He might even die—not that you would care about that! Then what will become of me? Alone and widowed? You must do something, Magistrate! You must do something now!"

"What time did he leave?"

Even before rounding the corner, Darash recognized Magistrate Quintus Arrius's voice. The Roman official had been deeply involved in in the incident involving the murder of Barus's daughter—that is, he became involved after Darash discovered that the killer was a Sadducee named Ratash. Though Magistrate Quintus Arrius had once threatened to have Darash thrown into prison for interfering, Arrius had been among those who rescued Darash from Ratash when Ratash tried to take Darash's life, as well. Afterwards, Arrius decided Darash had done the city a service—despite that he was a destitute, no-good, Jewish teenager.

The magistrate now stood before the colorful dyer's booth, surrounded by a flock of disinterested chickens and interested customers.

"How am I supposed to know when he left?" Millah demanded, her voice rising further. "Sometime in the night! We awoke to find his bed had not been slept in and his belongings missing."

"Do you have family in the area? Perhaps he simply went to visit a relative."

"Our closest family is in Gophna, but why would he want to go there? They never speak well of him."

"Would he have reason to want to leave home? ...Perhaps you and he were not getting along."

Millah sucked in her breath and put her hands on her ample hips. "What are you suggesting? That I drove him away?"

The magistrate sighed. In that moment, his eyes landed on Darash.

"Where are you going?" the magistrate asked Darash. "You should be at home recuperating."

"I must take a trip out of town for supplies," Darash answered.

"A trip? Are you sure that is wise? Where are you going?"

"Just out of town."

"But where out of town, Boy?"

Darash swallowed.

"To Gophna."

סֶ לְ ה

Darash kicked at a pebble as he led his donkey beyond sight of the Northern Gate along the newly constructed Roman road.

"I should have kept my mouth shut," he chided himself. "I should have said I was going to Bethany instead. Then he would not have insisted I chase down Millah's backward son for her. And what am I supposed to say to him, even if I do find him?"

He stepped to the side as three Roman soldiers passed, riding horses and heading the opposite direction, toward Jerusalem. The men looked hard in his direction. Darash kept his head down, hoping to avoid any trouble. The law stated that any Roman soldier could force a Jewish man or boy to carry his load for him in any direction for up to a Roman mile of one thousand paces. Thankfully, these men, being on horseback, had nothing to gain from Darash or his small donkey.

As the sound of hooves against stone and the jingling of the horses' metal fastenings died away, Darash returned to his complaints.

My chest hurts, and I am only a few hundred paces from the Northern Gates. How am I going to make it all the way to Gophna? Why did I not offer Pertho less for Amah? He surely would have taken it. Now we are out of money again and I am the only one who can get more!

He thought of his mother, Revayah's, recent borrowing from Nakal, Darash's enemy, and how hard it had been to pay the man back.

Nakal and his business partner, Hathal, had once been the business associates of Darash's father, Tuwr. When Tuwr died they refused to give Darash his father's share and, instead, claimed Tuwr owed them money—something Darash knew to be a fabricated lie. But Darash could not disprove the men's claim, so he had been forced to relinquish the shop into the possession of Nakal and Hathal and find a place for his small mercantile business on the ground in an obscure alley of the lower shuk—the marketplace in the southern, less affluent section of Jerusalem. The only good to come of it, in Darash's mind, was meeting Nib'haz.

If Imah borrows money from Nakal again we may never crawl out of this hole! I have to spend this week earning money for my family—just to keep us out of debt, but now Magistrate Arrius expects me to find Millah's strange-looking, odd-mannered son! What a waste of time!

Darash trudged on, allowing his foul mood to warm him against the cold morning air. It was still winter in Jerusalem, but the days had begun to grow warmer and the rain had let up. Darash did not want to leave Jerusalem—not only because his stab wound still caused his chest to burn with pain—but because he worried about Amah. He did not believe he could do much for her himself, but he hated not knowing what was happening at home.

Darash's mind returned to the night he had been stabbed, as it often did when he had little else to think of. The dark alley, the heaviness of Ratash's body on his, the struggle… and then the pain.

Darash stopped walking, gasped, and held his chest. He bent over, trying to still his heart and catch his breath. The pain in his chest refused to subside. Darash knelt on the side of the road, clutching the front of his robe.

Nekoda, who generally liked frequent stops to loll in the grass, tossed her head in impatience.

"Just a… short break, Nekoda," Darash promised her, gasping. "We will get there… eventually."

The sound of shoed horse hooves moving fast across stone echoed toward them from the direction of Jerusalem. Soon four horses with riders galloped into view. Darash recognized three of them as the men he had passed earlier. Only this time they were being led by someone he knew. Magistrate Quintus Arrius.

"Whoa!" Magistrate Arrius called, pulling his horse to an abrupt halt when he spotted Darash sitting in the grass alongside the road. He raised a hand. "Hold up a moment, men. I know this boy. Darash, what are you doing here? You should have been nearly to Gophna by now."

"I will make it… eventually."

The magistrate considered for a moment. "Change of plans. You are coming with us."

"What? But I—"

"Let the lad ride with you," Arrius said, turning to the smallest of the three soldiers—a man who stood head and shoulders taller than Darash once dismounted. "And you, Sergius, secure his beast of burden to your horse." Though the soldiers immediately moved to obey, they looked as confused as Darash. Arrius explained, "The boy has helped me before, and the people at the inn are Jews. Perhaps he can be of service."

II

The Road to Samaria

The smell of smoke found Darash's nostrils before the sight of the smoldering cart met his eyes. They had traveled past Gophna and continued north toward Samaria until they reached a lonely stretch of road bordered by a rocky hillside on the west and a stretch of desert and scrub brush on the east.

As they approached the wreckage, Darash saw several Roman soldiers already at the scene, cleaning up debris and loading bodies onto the bed of a horse cart.

"What happened here?" Darash asked his Roman escort—a man named Artorius. These were the first words he had dared speak since Artorius had lifted Darash onto the horse to sit in front between hairy, thickly muscled arms.

"Do not ask questions," Artorius barked. He pulled his steed to a halt and laid hold of Darash's right arm. The soldier roughly lowered Darash to the ground before dismounting. "If the magistrate wants you to know something, he'll tell you himself."

Magistrate Quintus Arrius approached one of the men at the scene.

"Bandits?" he asked.

"I believe so," one man responded. He was shorter and stouter than Arrius, with a scruff of dark brown beard beginning to show. "According to the Jew, Hazaiah, they were attacked last night at dusk. He said there were at least three of them. They stabbed Hazaiah and his three servants, and they knocked his wife unconscious. Then they killed the animals."

"Odd.... Did they take anything?"

"Some sacks of grain and a few other supplies. Nothing of real value. Oh, except the Jew says his son is missing."

"His son? Have you searched the surrounding area for another body?"

"We are in the process now. Nothing so far. No blood trails, either."

"Perhaps he wandered off in all the commotion," Arrius mused.

"Doubtful," the soldier responded. "He was only four years old, and we searched the area and found no child's footprints. The attackers' prints disappear into those rocks over there." He pointed toward a rocky incline about a stone's throw from the road. "I have two men over there now, trying to pick up their trail again."

"Then the boy was carried off," Darash said, drawing a look of annoyance from the Roman soldier.

"Perhaps," Arrius said, moving toward the scene of the skirmish. He examined the four blood stains in the road, the carcasses of the mules still secured in their harnesses, and the empty, burned-out cart.

Darash approached, careful not to come in contact with any blood in the road. *Four blood stains. One for each of the three servants and this smaller one must have been where Hazaiah lay.... But the boy's body is simply missing.*

"Do you know the Jew, Hazaiah?" Arrius asked Darash.

"No," he responded. "Where is he from?"

"He is of Dothan," the Roman soldier, to whom Arrius had been speaking a moment ago, responded, but he kept his eyes on Arrius. "According to Hazaiah, he and his family were coming to Jerusalem to visit family. They passed through Samaria and stayed at an inn near Neapolis—which the Jews call Shechem—night before last." At this he gave Darash the barest glance. "Yesterday morning they set out early and were ambushed here. They are at an inn in Gophna now, waiting for word of their son."

"I doubt we will be able to tell them what they want to hear," Arrius said. "The child is likely dead." He rubbed his chin and turned toward the slain carcasses of the mules. "But why kill the animals? Why not steal them, along with the rest of the goods?"

"They did not even take all the goods," the soldier added. "We found a small box in the cart with a pouch of silver still in it. We think perhaps something startled the bandits before they could take everything. But we have not been able to locate any witnesses."

"That still does not explain why they killed the animals."

"They must have wanted the boy," Darash said. "And, since he was not killed here, he must still be alive. At least, for now."

Both men looked at him as if suddenly remembering he was there.

"What would anyone want with a child?" the soldier asked, incredulity evident in his voice.

"They could have been slavers, I suppose," Arrius said, but then shook his head. "But a four-year-old is of little value as a slave."

"Slavers would not have killed able-bodied men," Darash added, glancing toward the cart where the dead bodies of the slaves now lay heaped, with their bloodied feet dangling off the back.

Darash's continued interference in the conversation elicited a scowl from the soldier, but Arrius simply followed Darash's gaze.

"Yes...." Arrius said. "Slavers would have wanted to take them alive." He shook his head in frustration. "It simply makes no sense! Who would attack a whole company of travelers just to get one small child?" He rubbed the stubble on his chin. "We must speak to the family."

"We have already spoken to them, Magistrate," the soldier said.

Arrius glared at the man. "Are you a Jew?"

The soldier scowled and spat. "No! I am no dog!"

"Then what makes you think these Jews would speak to you openly?" He shook his head in disgust. "Even dogs communicate best with other dogs. It is clear you are incapable of running an investigation. I will remember that next time your name is considered for an increase in rank." He glanced at Darash. "We will go speak to the family again. Boy, go get on my horse."

As Darash moved to obey, Arrius turned to his men. "Artorius, you men wrap things up here. Make sure to get the wreckage off the road and dispose of the mules. Take the bodies on to the chief priests in Jerusalem. Let the Jews bury their own dead. And give me that silver you found. I will return it to the family personally."

סֶלָה

"This is the third killing along this road this year," Arrius told Darash as they rode southward toward Gophna. "Every couple of months they call me up here to help sort things out."

Darash sat in front of Arrius this time, with Nekoda tethered behind. Darash would have ridden her if she had not been laden down with supplies. He had packed her with items he hoped to sell, as well as with empty bags and baskets to fill with new inventory.

"Have you discovered who is committing these killings?" Darash asked.

"Bandits, usually. Zealots, Sicarii, and the usual criminals encamped in these mountains. They hide among the rocks and attack travelers for their silver, supplies, and animals. We go in and root out some of these bands each year, but more come. And they move around. Reports often arrive long after the information is useful. They are a constant thorn in my flesh."

"Have you ever heard of them stealing children before?"

"No." Arrius sighed. "Which is why I suspect the child is dead. They tossed his body somewhere among the scrub brush. The men will find it eventually. Normally bandits take the animals—to sell or, perhaps, to eat. They do not kill them. And they never leave silver behind."

Arrius led his horse down a slight slope off the main road and around a wide bend. A long stretch of vineyards spread before them, empty of laborers for the winter season. As they passed beyond an outcropping of boulders and massive, gnarled olive trees, a series of stone and clay buildings came into view. The town of Gophna lay before them.

The third building on the right was slightly larger and had an enclosed courtyard attached. The front gates stood open. A dormant apricot tree grew in a patch of earth just outside the gate, and two old women sat beneath it wrapped in blankets, talking together. They stopped their conversation when they saw the Roman magistrate approach, but their eyes soon landed on Darash.

"Is this the inn?" Arrius asked them, drawing his horse to a stop on the road before the open gates.

One of the women nodded and gestured toward the building. The magistrate secured his steed to a post and led the way inside.

The inn consisted of a large, open room on ground level with a stone staircase along the eastern wall leading to an upper level. As it was winter, the lower level doubled as a stable for the family's four mules, two milk cows, six goats, and about a dozen sheep. Those who could afford it slept upstairs, away from the cattle's filth. Darash would not be so lucky.

A middle-aged man with thick sideburns greeted them as they stepped inside. He came from the shadows into the sliver of light created by the open door.

"Shalom," he said to the magistrate with a bow of respect, but his voice trembled as he spoke. "I am Ira, the innkeeper. We have room here in our inn, if you would like to stay. I have a nice spot on the upper level for you."

"I will not be staying," Arrius responded, not bothering to make eye contact. Instead he glanced around and peered into the shadows. "I am looking for a Jewish couple. The man was stabbed by bandits along the road yesterday. Are they here?"

"Oh, yes," Ira responded quickly, no doubt relieved that the Roman official had no interest in him. "They are right over there."

Ira pointed toward a dark corner on the lower level where a woman sat on the ground next to a man, his head in her lap.

"The woman is Eliana and the man is Hazaiah, her husband."

As Arrius and Darash approached them, a different woman, wearing a sage green tunic with the sleeves rolled up to her elbows and, carrying several items, knelt at the man's side and pulled back the blanket to reveal a bloodied bandage over his stomach. She removed the old bandage and went to work to clean his wound. It had already been stitched closed, but the gash still oozed blood.

"This is my wife," Ira said, following behind them. He gestured toward the woman in green. "She is the town midwife, skilled in medicine and tending wounds. She has done her best to repair the injury and is keeping the wound clean so it will not rot. We expect the man will survive, thanks to her ministrations. ...Of course, we have not yet been paid for our—"

"You will be," Arrius cut him off. "My men found that some of their silver had been left behind by the bandits." He pulled the pouch of silver from his belt and handed it to Hazaiah's wife, who had been watching them with interest since they walked in the door.

"What is your name?" Arrius asked her.

"I am Eliana," she answered. "My son—have you found him? Have you found Ikaiah, my son?"

Darash noticed that she held a small carving of a sheep in one of her hands, rubbing it with her thumb in nervous agitation.

"I regret that we have not," Arrius said. "He is likely dead."

Eliana sucked in a breath and a small cry escaped her lips. She put a hand to her mouth, but dropped it a moment later to push on. "But you have not found his body. Perhaps he still lives! He was taken. I know that man took him!"

"What man? Of whom do you speak?"

But Eliana no longer looked at Arrius. She buried her face in her hands and wept. Though Arrius questioned her again and again about the man she mentioned, she refused to speak to him. Arrius let out a groan of annoyance and turned to Darash.

"Boy," he said. "See if you can get them to talk. Meet me outside when you are through."

The magistrate strode from the room out into the sunshine, leaving Darash with the distraught couple. Seeing Eliana holding her possibly dying husband brought back painful memories of his own mother's grief at losing his father. Darash swallowed hard and took a step forward. He dropped to one knee and then squatted next to Eliana. The innkeeper, Ira, stood nearby, looking on with interest, as did his wife, who still knelt at Hazaiah's side cleaning his wound.

"Shalom, my aunt," he said to her, giving her the respect of a Jewess of her standing—a respectable, married woman.

Eliana wiped her eyes and looked at Darash. "What are you doing with that Roman?" she asked. "Are you his slave?"

"No. Well..." he shrugged, "at least, not yet. I am a merchant's son. My father was killed many months ago, so I must find a way to support my mother and sister. I helped the magistrate find a killer before, so he has asked me to help you, as well... if I can."

Eliana's face softened. "I am sorry for your suffering."

"And I am sorry for yours. However, perhaps, if you tell me everything you remember about the man you spoke of, we might be able to locate him and find out if he knows anything about what happened to your son."

Eliana nodded, a spark of hope in her eye. "We met a man at the inn near Shechem. He struck up a conversation with Hazaiah. He was very friendly to us, but seemed mostly interested in our boy. He wanted to hold him and play with him—to the point where I had trouble getting him back."

"What was this man's name?"

"I… I do not remember."

Hazaiah muttered something then they did not quite catch, and weakly raised his right hand.

"What is it, my husband?" she asked him.

"His name… His name was… Bagad."

"Bagad?" Darash asked. "Do you happen to know his father's name or his tribe?"

"No," Hazaiah whispered.

"Can either of you describe this man to me?"

"He was a Jew," Eliana said. "He was tall for a Jew, though, with sunken cheeks and a hooked nose. He said he was new to the area, but did not say where he was from. He had a thin, patchy beard and long, skinny fingers. He wore a long-sleeved robe of gray and white over his tunic. It looked old and… he had an odd smell about him, as well…. I do not know how to describe it."

"Please try," Darash said.

"He smelled of… of…." She paused, considering. "Sheep, hay, and… I think… I think it was… blood." Eliana put a hand over her mouth and closed her eyes against tears. "I think it was blood I smelled," she wept.

Darash swallowed and glanced at the innkeeper. Ira fidgeted with his robes, and his wife stopped cleaning Hazaiah's wound to look at Eliana and then at her husband. After a moment Eliana opened her eyes again.

"And there was something else," she said, looking at Darash again. "Another smell… something sweet."

"Something sweet?" Darash asked.

"Yes. I do not know what it was."

"And your son. Can you describe him for me?"

"His name is Ikaiah. He is only four years old. Black hair and dark brown eyes. He is about this tall." She indicated a place with her hand that landed at about the innkeeper's hip.

Darash sighed.

She could be describing any four-year-old Jewish boy.

Eliana sensed his frustration and added, "He has an unusual birthmark on his right arm."

Darash perked up. "Where on his arm? What does this mark look like?"

Eliana pointed to her forearm.

"Right here," she said. "He has a dark red birthmark. It is fat at the top," she pointed to the place two inches beneath her wrist, "and skinny at the bottom." She drew her finger three inches down her arm. "It looks like a club." She paused and dropped her arm. "People are so superstitions…. We mostly keep it hidden beneath the sleeves of his tunic. Few people know about it aside from us."

סֶ לָ ה

As dusk settled on Gophna, Darash located a place near the fire to unroll his sleeping mat. Magistrate Quintus Arrius had returned to Jerusalem to report what they had discovered, which was not much. Despite Eliana's fears, there was no evidence the man they had met in Shechem had anything to do with the attack and no way to track him down. The magistrate could do nothing but wait to hear if his men had any success locating the child's body or a sign of the culprit.

After the magistrate left, Darash approached the innkeeper. Ira had taken a seat on a small, three-legged stool near the outer gate to watch for possible late-comers. The women who had been sitting beneath the apricot tree earlier had gone, and few people remained on the road.

"Pardon me, good sir. What are the charges for a week's stay?"

"For your lodgings on the lower level, the charge is a half *as* per day. Food is extra, of course, and so is the space for your donkey. Bread and a pint of wine is one *as*, meat is two. Use of the upper room for bathing and necessaries is a quarter *as*. If you pay me two denarii up front, you can eat two meals a day and use the upper room as liberally as you like all week, but you will still have to sleep on the lower level."

"I cannot yet afford to pay you for the entire week," Darash admitted with regret.

"You may pay me at the close of each day, then," Ira said. "If you want something to eat, my wife will be serving a meal shortly."

Ira was a short, stout man of about forty. He wore a new, long-sleeved robe that bore smudges of dirt and animal dung around the hemline. He wore no head-covering to hide his receding hairline. Unusually long, flowing sideburns draped from his cheeks along his jawline to match the straight, black hair of his beard, which swayed with his movements. The effect reminded Darash of a mountain goat who had acquired his full winter coat.

"Thank you," Darash said with a slight nod. "Might I inquire of you further?"

Ira nodded without bothering to make eye-contact. He kept his eyes on the road, looking for travelers as he scratched at an itch along his beltline.

"Have you, by any chance, met a young man named Nimrah, son of Obed and Millah, the dyers of Yerushaláyim? He left home yesterday and his family does not know where he went. They think he might have come here to visit family."

"Hmm…. No. No one by that name came to my inn yesterday, nor have I heard any word of it. I know of Obed and Millah. I believe Obed has a brother who lives at the other end of the city, in the house between the winepress and the apricot orchard. His name is Zephath."

"Thank you. I will visit them in the morning."

"Wait until the afternoon," Ira cautioned. "That man is a heavy drinker and his foul mood each morning is best avoided."

"Ah, I see. I will follow your advice, then." Darash leaned against the doorpost of the outer gate and joined the man in scanning the road.

"That Roman magistrate friend of yours does not know what he is up against," Ira said after a long pause.

Darash looked at the man with interest and waited for him to continue.

"I suppose it is just as well that he has given up on searching further."

"Why do you say that?"

Ira looked Darash in the eyes. "Because that child who went missing… he is not dead. But he will be. And soon."

III

The Wine-Maker of Gophna

The next morning, as the first rays of dawn filtered through the cracks in the inn door, Darash rolled to his side and sat up, glad to have an excuse to rise. Most of the others still slept, but Darash had struggled throughout the night, thanks to the snoring of the other guests and the constant sounds and smells emanating from the cattle. His chest and back ached from sleeping on the hard ground, for he was used to his raised bed and straw-stuffed mattress. And at some point deep in the night, he had been awakened by the sound of a mule relieving itself and a cry of disgust from one of the travelers as the man searched for a spot farther away from the beast and the river of filth it had created.

Darash located the communal wash basin, dumped the brown water on the ground outside the front door, and refilled the bowl with fresh water from a clay jug. The cold water revived him somewhat. He slipped out the front door and asked a servant to unlock the outer gate. Once on the street and in the fresh air, his hunger returned. Darash dug into his belt for the small pouch of bread and cheese he had brought with him from home. He had no wine to drink, but he hoped he might be offered some at the home of the metalworker this morning.

Darash left Nekoda lodged with the other animals at the inn and headed toward the center of the village of Gophna. It was the fourth day of the week, Yom Revee'ee. He would find the well and marketplace, the shuk, to see who might be about.

Gophna was not a large community. No more than a few dozen families lived here together—mostly vineyard and olive orchard owners. Another hundred or so young men lived and worked here seasonally to tend the vineyards and olive orchards. Since it was winter, most of them had moved back with their families.

The shuk was nothing compared to what Darash was used to in Jerusalem. He had no trouble locating a place amongst the five ramshackle booths near the well where he could spread out a cloth and sell his wares, if he decided to fetch them from the inn.

He approached a young man, not much older than himself, who lounged on a stool in one of the booths, eying Darash as he approached. Bowls of various grains and spices—nothing exotic—sat haphazardly about the table—millet, cumin, dried dill, and the like. The young man also offered a small selection of preserved edibles—raisins, dried figs and apricots, fig cakes, and raisin cakes.

"Shalom," Darash said.

The young man nodded, but did not move.

"Could you tell me where the metalworker lives?"

"I only give information to customers."

"Ah, I see," Darash responded. "I will ask someone else."

Darash felt the eyes of the surly young man on his back as he moved to the next booth. A gray-haired woman sat on a narrow, wooden bench stitching together two lengths of cloth, making what appeared to be a child-sized tunic. Before her the table bore various sizes of cheap-looking tunics and robes in blues and browns. She looked up and smiled at his approach.

"Shalom, grandmother," Darash said, shooting her a smile and using the familial term to honor her advanced years.

"Shalom, my child," she said, baring five graying teeth. "Are you well on this fine morning?"

"Very well, thank you. I came from Yerushaláyim last night to see the metalworker."

"Oh, yes, I know. My sister and cousin saw you come. They told me all about you."

Darash recalled seeing two elderly women sitting near the outer gate beneath the apricot tree. Darash was not surprised. In a town of barely three hundred people, news of any visitor would travel fast—especially in the winter when there was little else to occupy one's mind.

"The metalworker is my nephew. He lives in the house next to mine—just down that path and to the left." She pointed with her chin toward a narrow road between two houses. "There is an olive tree by the gate and the forge is in the yard."

Darash smiled again and nodded in thanks. He turned toward the direction she had indicated. Before he had taken his third step, the woman called to him in a voice much louder than the distance required, "He has a daughter about your age. She is not very beautiful, but she is a very good seamstress!"

Darash glanced back to smile again—pretending to appreciate the information. He caught the smirk of the young man in the booth of spices and cakes. Darash's cheeks flushed with embarrassment as he headed away from the shuk, his eyes trained on the ground and his stringy, black hair falling before his eyes. But, by the time he got to the house of the metalworker Darash had regained his composure.

What does it matter if the man has a daughter of marriageable age? What is that to me? I am not looking for a bride.

The image of Amah flashed before him for a moment. Unkempt hair, skinny arms, frightened, brown eyes.

I hope she is doing better this morning.... I hope she had no nightmares last night.

Darash stopped outside the outer gate and clapped loudly to get the attention of those inside. Someone on the other side removed the locking plank, and the gate easily swung open on freshly greased hinges.

A broad-shouldered man wearing a black-smudged apron greeted Darash.

"Shalom," Darash responded in kind. "You must be the metalworker. I have come from Yerushaláyim to see what I might acquire from you to sell there."

The man opened the gate wider and stepped to the side. "Come in, come in," he said sweeping his arm toward the interior courtyard. "I have much to show you—fastenings of various kinds, excellent metal cookery of all sizes, nails and tools, even jewelry."

The metalworker welcomed Darash into the yard. As Darash followed the man through the yard toward the house, he noticed the forge and was surprised by the sheer size of it. It was far larger than a town of this size should need.

סֶ לָ ה

After a morning spent over a meal shared with the metalworker's family, haggling over prices, Darash took his leave, promising to return with Nekoda. The daughter, an awkward girl of fourteen, had silently peered at him from side doors throughout his entire visit. She would have followed him to the gate, but her mother pulled her back. Though Darash felt the visit was a successful one, he was glad to be leaving.

Following Ira, the innkeeper's, advice, Darash waited until later in the day to search out the winemaker in an effort to find Millah and Obed's foolish son, Nimrah, as a favor to Magistrate Arrius. As the sun rose high in the sky, Darash located the winepress where Ira told him it would be. He moved to the house next to the large, stone winepress, which had to be the home of Zephath, Obed's brother. His clapping, however went unnoticed for so long Darash wondered if anyone was home. He banged on the wooden outer gate, making one last effort to be heard.

If Millah wants to find her wayward son, she should come up here and look for him herself.

Darash turned to leave but noticed a man coming toward him. The man looked and dressed like a Gentile, possibly of Greek descent. He passed Darash and went to the very gate where Darash had been waiting, and clapped loudly.

"I do not believe anyone is home," Darash ventured. "I tried to raise someone from inside, but got no response."

"Oh, there is someone here, alright," the man said. He pushed on the gate, and it opened easily before him. "I am Luke, the physician," he said, glancing at Darash. "Come with me. I will take you to Zephath."

Darash followed Luke inside. They passed the withered remnants of a garden and a stable of skinny mules. They approached the house. The physician did not bother knocking on the door. He simply opened it and stepped inside. He found an oil lamp, lit it by a lamp on a small side table that was always kept burning, and then gestured to Darash to enter as well.

"Is the man ill?" Darash asked, thinking better of his decision to visit.

"Not exactly," Luke answered. "Do not worry. It is quite safe. Zephath is a drunkard and, when he drinks too much, he sends his servant to fetch me. There is little I can do for him, but he insists, so I come."

"You live in Gophna?" Darash asked, finding it strange that a town this size would have a Greek physician as well as a trained midwife.

"No. I have a sister who lives here. She is recuperating from an illness. When she was sick there was no one to tend her, so I have been staying with her this winter."

"What about the innkeeper's wife? She is a midwife, and trained in medicine."

"Ira must have told you that." Luke shrugged. "She does well enough, I suppose, but she is not—" He stopped mid-sentence and grimaced as they stepped into the dank interior of the home—the smell of urine and decaying grapes heavy in the air.

"Where is the servant?" Darash coughed, also caught off-guard by the smell.

"I know not. After delivering Zephath's message to me, he said he had other business and disappeared. I suspect he simply did not want to be around during my visit. The man is incredibly lazy." The physician moved a stool out of the way and pulled a tattered curtain back from a darkened doorway. "I end up barking at him to clean up the whole time I am here."

"Does Zephath have a wife?"

"Yes. That is why he drinks."

Darash followed the lamplight into the bedroom and stood awkwardly in the corner between piles of filthy garments. The physician knelt next to the bed where a heavy-set man lay. Darash put a hand to his nose. This room smelled worse than the other. The scent of body-odor mixed with the odors of fermented grapes and human excrement from a chamber pot that had not been emptied.

"Ah, good," Zephath said, his words thick, "you are here. I think I may be dying this time."

"You are not dying. You drink too much," Luke responded brusquely. "Stop drinking. Go find your wife. Here," he fumbled in his belt, pulled out a bundle, and unwrapped it, "eat this."

"What is it?"

"My sister made bread this morning. It is quite good. It will help settle your stomach."

"I will not… able… keep it down," Zephath muttered.

"Try."

Zephath took the bread and bit into it. "Mmmmm…."

"See? Good, right? What did I tell you? Now, eat the whole thing—every last crumb. Then get up and wash your face with water—clean water. And no more drinking!"

"Yes, yes…. I will do as you say." Only then did Zephath's eyes land on the skinny figure of a lad near the doorway. "Who is that?" he asked, slurring his words. "I thought he was my servant, but…."

"I have no idea, actually," Luke responded. "I found him outside."

"I am Darash," Darash said. "I have come from Yerushaláyim with a message from your brother, Obed."

"Obed?" Zephath's voice perked up. "How is he doing?"

"Not well, I fear."

"Business is bad?"

"No. Their business thrives. The problem is with his son, Nimrah. He has disappeared. He left two nights ago, and they have no idea where he is. Obed has been ill, so since I was traveling this way they asked me to visit you and ask if he might be here, since you are a relative."

"No… no…. I have not seen Nimrah since the last time I was in Yerushaláyim—over a month ago. If he had passed this way, surely I would have heard of it."

"Thank you," Darash said, preparing to take his leave, "that is all I came to ask."

"Say," Zephath said, propping himself up on one elbow, seeming to come awake, "when I was in the city, I heard of a young Greek woman who had been killed. Do you happen to know what came of it? Did they ever find her killer?"

"Yes, …I, uh, do. Her killer was a young Sadducee named Ratash. I believe his execution has been scheduled for this week."

The thought of having cost a man his life—even an evil man—gave Darash a sour feeling in his gut. He swallowed hard and took a step back from the men. They failed to notice.

"I heard of that, too," Luke said. "Quite a story! The people of Gophna are still talking about it. They will be glad to know it has been settled. Tell me… is it true that a mere youth helped find the killer?"

Darash fidgeted. "Uh, yes… it is true."

"And that he was stabbed in the process?"

The wound on Darash's chest smarted. "Yes. That is also true," he said, feeling uncomfortable with the turn of the conversation.

"Who was the young lad?" Zephath asked. "Do you know him?"

"Uh… well…."

The men waited for Darash to continue until the silence grew uncomfortable.

"Actually… it was I."

The men looked at him in stunned silence for a moment, and then both began talking at once.

"You?" Zephath asked. "You are the boy?"

"How are you able to travel so soon after such an injury?" Luke wanted to know.

"The wound was not very severe," Darash answered. "That is, it could have been much worse."

"Does it still trouble you?" Luke asked.

"Yes, but only sometimes."

"When?"

"Mostly at night and when I think back on what happened."

"Hmmm… odd…. Here, let me see it," the physician rose and approached Darash.

Darash complied, pulling open his robe and untying the strings of his tunic at the neck. He pulled his tunic down over his left shoulder to expose the dark pink scar on his chest.

Luke held the oil lamp higher, letting the light spill onto Darash's skin. He put his hands on the pink line, and Darash sucked in a breath.

"Does that hurt?" the physician asked.

"No. Your fingers are cold."

The man pressed around the wound and on the wound itself. "How about that?"

"A little… but not much."

"From what I can see," Luke said, "your wound is practically healed. No sign of infection, no angry-looking, red wound, no bruising at all. You should not be experiencing pain any longer."

Darash slipped the tunic and robe back over his shoulder and tied the knot at his neck again. "I usually do not. Just sometimes."

Luke opened his mouth to ask Darash another question, but was interrupted.

"Tell us more about the murder and how you found the killer," Zephath said.

סֶ לָ ה

Two hours later, Darash rose to leave. Zephath had rallied, apparently no longer believing himself to be at death's door, and they had moved into the family room. Darash tried to steer the conversation away from the murder, for he did not like discussing his involvement in it. The memories were still fresh and his wound ached as he relived them. And though Darash knew justice was being served, he felt an odd sense of misery at the fact that Ratash would soon be executed.

The drunkard, Zephath was indeed the famed winemaker Darash had come to find and, though the last thing a drunkard should be was a winemaker, Darash was glad to know he would be acquiring wine that he could resell at top price. He managed to purchase four *baths* of wine to take back with him to Jerusalem. He told Zephath he would return for the wine with Nekoda just prior to leaving Gophna.

"Perhaps you should go to Shechem first," Zephath said as he opened the door for his guests to take their leave.

"Why is that?" Darash asked.

"Because that is most likely where Nimrah has gone," Zephath said.

Darash had almost forgotten about Nimrah. He figured his business regarding the young man had come to an end, now that he had done what he had agreed to do.

"Why do you say so?"

"Because I remember that the last time I was at Obed's home, I overheard a conversation between two of their customers about a brothel in Shechem."

"But what has that to do with Nimrah?"

"He was very interested."

"In a brothel? There are brothels in Yerushaláyim… at least, from what I understand."

"Indeed there are, but this one is special. The customers spoke of a woman there who could not only find a young man a woman, but a wife—a wife who would be in love with the man forever—no matter how backward the young man might be."

"But surely Obed will find a wife for Nimrah," Darash said.

"He has tried, but very few fathers want a simpleton for a son-in-law."

IV

Strange Things

As Darash left Zephath's gate, his mind returned to the missing child and the brief conversation he had with Ira that morning. Though Hazaiah and Eliana still held out hope their son would be found, Ira had seemed certain no good news would come.

"That child who went missing… he is not dead. But he will be. And soon," Ira had said.

"How do you know?" Darash had asked.

"I do not know. I only suspect."

Though Darash had pressed for more, Ira did not offer any reason for his suspicions. He only muttered, "There are strange things going on in these parts of late… very strange things."

Perhaps tonight Darash might persuade the man to talk—if they could find a place where they would not be overheard. No need to cause Hazaiah and Eliana additional worry.

Darash passed the small shuk of Gophna and returned to the inn. The dinner hour was nearing, so he decided to check on Nekoda. He found her corralled amongst the other beasts of burden. They had been moved out of doors to a small stable yard at the back of the house so the servant could clean the lower level. Nekoda raised her head and nuzzled him when he approached.

"Are you happy to see me, girl?" Darash asked.

As if in response, Nekoda pushed harder into his chest as he rubbed her neck. He chuckled and gave her a good long scratch behind the ears. He noticed, as he did so, that the pressure of Nekoda's head caused him no pain.

Perhaps the physician was right and I am finally healed, Darash mused.

Darash grabbed a fistful of hay from a nearby feedbag, careful to select the softer pieces. He fed them to her by hand, letting her thick, moist lips move across his palm.

"I will take you for a walk tomorrow, I promise. We will go to the shuk and try to sell what we brought from home." He dropped his voice to a whisper, "I need to earn a little more," he confided in her. "Otherwise, I will not be able to afford the jewelry and wine I promised to buy."

Darash gave Nekoda one last pat on the neck before turning back to the inn. After a short search, he found Ira out front waiting for dinner.

Dusk had settled over the city. The man sat on a stool beneath the apricot tree by the road, watching for any sign of new guests. The street was empty, and the women who had occupied that spot earlier had gone home.

"Who were those women who were sitting here earlier?" Darash asked. "I know one of them has a sister who sells clothing in the shuk."

"Ha! If you can call her rags clothing," Ira joked. "The woman you speak of is my aunt. The other—the seller—is her friend who lives with her. They are widows and their children provide little for them to live on. I told them I would give them two prutot for any customer they can convince to stay at my inn."

Odd, Darash thought. *They said nothing when I arrived. Normally women in their situation would be calling out to passersby.* But then he had another thought. *Of course, I was with a Roman at the time— Magistrate Quintus Arrius. No Jew would want to draw a Roman's attention unnecessarily—especially a Roman soldier.*

"I wondered if you might tell me more about what you think happened to Hazaiah and Eliana's child."

"Oh, son," Ira said, shaking his head and letting his gaze travel beyond the road to the hills beyond. "The wicked things that happen in these parts are not for your ears. You are young. You should be thinking of happy times—of your work... of getting married—not dwelling on that which you cannot change." Ira paused and turned his eyes upon Darash. "But, then again, perhaps you can do something. After all, you have caught a killer already, have you not?"

Darash's eyes widened. He swept his bangs to the side and looked Ira in the eyes. "How do you know about that?"

"This is Gophna and I am the innkeeper!" Ira said and chuckled. "I know everything the townspeople know." He smiled and leaned back against the tree, still watching Darash with interest and amusement. "So tell me... is it true?"

Darash sighed.

סֶ לָ ה

Ira's wife called them in to supper before Darash had been able to draw Ira back to the conversation about the strange things he claimed to have witnessed.

Entering the inn, Darash spotted Luke, the physician, kneeling next to Hazaiah. Luke cleaned the wound again, smeared fresh honey on it to stave off infection, and replaced the bandages.

After checking Hazaiah's forehead with the back of his hand, Luke pulled a small, cloth bag from his belt and handed it to Eliana. "Here," he said. "Make some tea from these herbs and get your husband to drink some every two hours. It will help with his fever. It is quite bitter, though, so add some honey to it."

Ira's wife drew Darash's attention away from Hazaiah by announcing that the meal had been served. Darash joined the other guests on some pillows that had been positioned around a table mat on the floor. The simple meal consisted of coarse bread, dill-seasoned cheese curds, and a dish consisting of boiled eggs that had been chopped, mixed with leeks and roasted fava beans, and served with a pine nut sauce. A servant carried a clay jug of wine from person to person, filling their wooden cups. Despite the simplicity of the meal, Darash ate with gusto.

Darash still hoped to get Ira alone to ask him about the odd occurrences he had mentioned. Now, however, Ira sat with two other guests in the courtyard next to the front wall of the house. One was a tall shepherd with a graying beard who had come to town looking to hire another man. The other, a middle-aged man with an expensive robe, had arrived while Darash was out. A fire crackled before them, casting dancing rays of light into the growing shadows.

Darash sat nearby to see if he might be included in the conversation. He hoped to outwait the other two and, eventually, have Ira all to himself.

"…all the way from Beersheba," the shepherd was saying. His voice sounded much less weathered than his hands and face looked.

"That is a long way to travel to visit a rabbi," Ira responded. "But I can understand why you did it. He was a fascinating man. Too bad the Romans crucified him."

"We crucified him," the third man countered. He spoke with a Galilean accent. He was slight of build and had a patchy beard. He wore a thick, blue outer cloak with a turban-style head covering of the same material. "The Romans just did what we asked them to do."

"True, true…." Ira stroked scratched his chin behind the flowing beard. "They lost no love on him—that is for certain. But the fool seemed to welcome their derision. He brought it on himself."

"I remember one of the stories he told," the shepherd said. "The attack on the road the other day recalled it to mind. He told a story of a young man who was traveling along the road from Yerushaláyim to Jericho. He was attacked by bandits, stripped, beaten, and left for dead. A priest came along, saw the man, but continued on. He did not stop to help. A little while later, a Levite happened by. But he, too, did not stop. Then a Samaritan passed that way. He took pity on the man and bandaged his wounds. Then he placed the man on his own donkey and took him to an inn." He looked at Ira. "Once there the Samaritan paid the innkeeper to look out for the injured man and let him stay there until he recovered from his wounds—just as you are doing for poor Hazaiah in there. The Samaritan even promised to return and pay for any additional charges the man incurred during his stay."

The men were silent for a moment, absorbing the shepherd's story.

"I find it hard to believe a Samaritan would do such a thing," Ira said, voice tinged with scorn.

"I think that is why the teacher told the story," the skinny Galilean said, "to show us that it is not our heritage that defines us, but who we choose to be… for good or for bad."

"But a priest and a Levite would know that to touch such a man would make them unclean," Ira argued. "The injured man would have been covered in blood. And, if he happened to die along the way, the priest or Levite would be unclean for a full seven days for contact with a dead body."

"Indeed," the Galilean said. "But I think Yeshua's intended question was: what makes a man holier in Adonai's sight? His state of ceremonial cleanliness? Or his compassion for others?"

A moment of silence followed. Ira shifted his feet in the dirt. The shepherd kept his eyes on the Galilean, but said nothing, simply contemplating as he nodded his head slightly.

Darash's mind went to the times his father, Tuwr, would sneak him off to listen to Yeshua speak. It had been their little secret, for Revayah would have vehemently disapproved. The story the Galilean now told sounded like something the teacher would have said—even down to the accent with which it was delivered.

"Tell me," the shepherd said, after a while, to the man who had just spoken. "What is your name and where are you from?"

"I am Jehiel of Capernaum in Galilee."

"Yeshua was a Galilean, as well. Did you know him?"

"I did."

"Tell us, brother," the shepherd pressed. "How did you come to know that man? What was he like? Was he really the heretic, as the chief priests claim?"

"Peace, peace!" Ira raised a hand and interrupted, before Jehiel could answer. Ira looked in Darash's direction. "You might want to guard your tongues. I like this boy, but he is a servant to none other than a Roman magistrate of Yerushaláyim—Magistrate Quintus Arrius. Perhaps you would not like the details of your conversation getting back to him."

All three men stared at Darash, eyes hard.

"No!" Darash sputtered. "No, I do not work for that man. I am not his servant. I work for myself as a merchant." Seeing that the men said nothing, still unconvinced, Darash continued. "I helped him once," he admitted, "with a crime that happened in Yerushaláyim. I helped find the murderer of a Greek girl." Darash hated telling the story. Each time he forced the words from his lips, his chest ached. The darkened image of Raphad holding a knife flashed through his memory. "Now the magistrate seems to think I can help again." He paused and swallowed. Still the men said nothing, waiting for him to continue and watching him with expressionless faces. Darash moistened his lips. "He wants me to help with two cases of missing people—Jewish people. The small boy who was taken on the road and a grown man named Nimrah who disappeared from Yerushaláyim in the night. He is Zephath's nephew. But I am no servant to the Romans!"

With this last statement, Darash looked the men in the eyes. They glanced one to the other. Finally, Jehiel nodded.

"I believe you, boy," Jehiel said. "I will let you hear my story. Indeed, even if I knew you were a spy for the Romans, I would not be able to keep from telling it. I feel Elohim would not be pleased with me if I refused to speak to any who might want to hear." He glanced at Ira. "However, I warn you. My story of meeting Yeshua is a strange one. You good men might decide you do not want to share a roof with me once I tell it."

"We receive people of all kinds here," Ira said, no longer staring at Darash. "Go on and tell your story, Jehiel. We will listen."

Jehiel, sitting on a three-legged stool, looked down at his feet for a moment before beginning.

"Yeshua once lived in Nazareth but, when they tried to kill him by throwing him off a cliff, he escaped and traveled to Capernaum where I lived. Though I had heard of an unusual teacher from Nazareth, I had never seen him before, so I did not know who he was until he got up to speak at the synagogue. …And here I must back up in my story and tell you more about my life at that time, or you will not understand. …You see, though I attended synagogue faithfully every Shabbat and followed the law in the presence of my neighbors, I did not follow Adonai in my heart. Many years before Yeshua came to us, though I had a good wife, I had fallen in love with a prostitute. My only thought was of her. She was a woman of Gennesaret. She told me she was also a priestess of a powerful god… the god Molech."

Jehiel glanced up to gauge the expressions on his listener's faces. Ira, the shepherd, and Darash all stared at the man, eyes wide and mouths slightly parted in shock.

"M-Mol—!" The shepherd began with a stutter, but then stopped abruptly and clapped a hand over his mouth. Many believed it was dangerous even to say the name of such a detestable god out loud, for just saying his name might be enough to summon him. Shepherds were known for being particularly superstitious in this way. "That ancient beast! The detestable god of the Ammonites! How can this be? Did good King Josiah not chase the old religions out during his reign?"

"He did indeed," Ira, the innkeeper, answered. "But, like Rachel who stole Laban's household gods and took them with her into her new life with Jacob, there are those who have not let go of the ancient gods. Some strongholds are not so easily broken." Ira shook his head. "I have seen the sign of Molech around the necks of some of my visitors from time to time in the past, but never so frequently as I have in these recent months. And I have begun to suspect that there are those—right here in Gophna—who have begun to follow this new revival of the ancient religion." He turned to Jehiel. "But go on. Tell us the rest of your story."

"Well, I doubted the woman at first. Like you," Jehiel looked at the shepherd, "I did not believe such things were possible in Judea. I thought she was simply using that story to intrigue me so I would keep visiting her. Over time I realized there was much more going on, but I was too much the fool to care!" He spat, overcome for a moment with anger at his own guilt. He paused and rubbed the back of his neck before continuing. "She began with simple things—charms she said would deepen our love for one another—simple spells and incantations. Once she had me drink a potion that made me sick for a week. Still, I found it all so exciting that I began to believe the spells were actually working. The further she drew me into her religion, the more fascinated I became. I began to look forward to the next trance—the next vision—as much as I did to seeing her."

Jehiel stopped to take a drink of wine from a skin tied to his belt. He swooshed the liquid around in his mouth before swallowing.

"In time she bore me a daughter. Only then did I realize how dangerous my association with her had become. You see, she became very ill shortly after giving birth. When she suggested we sacrifice our infant daughter to Molech in exchange for a cure, I finally realized how far I had gone."

"Child sacrifice!" the shepherd breathed. "Not here in Israel!"

"Yes, indeed! Believe it," Jehiel said. "But, I refused to sacrifice our child! No matter how much she pleaded, I did not give in. My wife was barren and this little girl might be the only child I would ever have. I could not give her up. …The sorceress of Gennesaret died a few months later. She suffered greatly in her illness and cursed me again and again as she lay there dying. But when she was gone, I took my daughter home and gave her to my wife. I lied and said she had been abandoned and needed a home. My wife was overjoyed to finally have a child." Jehiel paused again, remembering. "Though I believe she knew I was lying, she never said a word to me. …I decided to try to become a better man… to be worthy of both my wife and my daughter. …I did not realize it was already too late for that."

"What do you mean?" Ira asked.

"I began acting erratically. I experienced terrible nightmares. The visions I had sought while in Gennesaret would now not leave me alone. I became angry over the smallest infractions. Strange rashes broke out on my skin from time to time. They were not infectious, but I lived in constant fear. Sometimes I would slip into a trance and walk about as if asleep. Do things without realizing it. Once I came to my senses in the middle of the shuk with my hand holding tightly to a woman's hair… but had no idea how I had gotten there or what I was doing. Another time I nearly set our house on fire by taking coals out of the fire and setting them about the floor in an odd pattern. I only awakened from my trance when my wife started yelling and kicking the coals away from our cushions."

"You had contracted a demon," the shepherd guessed, "a filthy spirit of the deep!"

Jehiel nodded. "Yes. It is true. I did not even know it until the day I went to the synagogue and met the teacher, Yeshua." Jehiel swallowed and continued. "I had gone to the synagogue often, but as this man spoke, the strangest sensation came over me. The rest of the men listening that day were in awe of his words and the authority with which he spoke. But I experienced a kind of… of panic. My chest burned. I did not understand what was happening to me, but the demon within me writhed. A great hatred rose up in me against Yeshua, but I found my lips sealed until he had stopped speaking. Then I jumped to my feet and cried out at the top of my lungs, 'Ha! What do you want with us, Yeshua of Nazareth? Have you come to destroy us? I know who you are—the Holy One of God!'

"'Be quiet!' he commanded me—only he was not really speaking to me. He spoke to the creature within me. 'Come out of him!' Yeshua said. I felt a great power throw me down to the ground. The men gasped and jumped to their feet, overturning benches in their attempt to get away from me. But Yeshua did not back away. He came closer. And the closer he came, the more the demon's grip on me loosened. When he touched me on the shoulder, and the demon fled."

"Incredible!" the shepherd breathed, eyes wide. "I have heard of such things. I have even known those plagued by evil spirits… but I have never seen a man who once was their captive but is now free."

V

Change of Plans

Darash lay on his mat listening to the sound of moaning in the darkness. Not a speck of light penetrated the space. The darkness felt heavy and thick upon him, like a heavy blanket of sand.

Where is that moaning coming from?

He could not pinpoint the source. He lay there in frustration for many moments trying without success to push the noise away.

Who is making that noise? I wish he would stop!

Darash turned his head one way and then the other, trying to locate the direction of the moans with his ears, for his eyes could not penetrate the black of night.

Wait.... I think it is coming from... from....

He moved a hand to his chest. He felt a rumble beneath his fingers through his thin tunic. He opened his tunic and moved his hand to his bare skin, covering his stab wound. Horror filled Darash as he realized his wound was no longer sealed with flesh—but open, like a window into his body.

The moaning is coming from... within me! But I am not doing it. Something is inside me!

As the realization hit, Darash felt something moving inside his chest and abdomen. It was large and had sharp claws.

"Ah!" he cried out in pain and terror. He felt a ripping sensation near his heart and lungs.

The creature moaned again, but this time the moan turned to deep laughter.

In a panic, Darash sat up and clawed at the wound in his chest, trying to make it big enough for the beast within to get out. But no matter how hard he tried, he could not release the demon. It lodged itself inside his chest and laughed at him.

"Help! Help!" Darash cried and he clawed at himself in vain, tears of panic streaming down his cheeks. "Adonai, please!"

The form of a man appeared before him. The man's body created light in the dark of the room. Finally, Darash could see again. The man approached, looking directly at Darash's chest. He pointed a finger at the beast and said in a loud, unwavering voice, "Come out!"

With a cry of anger and despair, the beast pushed itself out of Darash's chest through the stab wound and disappeared into the shadows.

Suddenly, Darash's wound was once again healed. He felt his chest and scar. The pain was gone. And, to his great relief, nothing moved inside his chest except his own heart, beating rapidly but steadily. He was himself again.

Darash looked up to thank the man, but the man had disappeared.

סֶלָה

The sound of moaning met Darash's ears, and he woke with a start, fearing the demon had returned. He sat up on his mat in the lower room of the inn. The deep darkness was gone. Light pushed through the small windows on the second level and through the cracks in the front door.

"Shh, my husband," Eliana whispered from the other side of the room. She sat next to Hazaiah, rubbing his arm. "You have kept people up all night with your moaning. You must try to rest now. I will fetch you some tea, and the physician will be here soon."

It was a dream. The whole thing was a dream….

Darash's hand moved to the wound in his chest. The ache had subsided and, to his relief, he found only a scar.

It took Darash several moments to shake off the feelings of fear and confusion. He sat on his mat, his robe across his lap, staring toward the door. Glowing specs of dust danced in the morning light. Light streamed through the cracks between the wooden planks, making the planks look black by comparison. He got the feeling that the light very much wanted to get in.

סֶלָה

Though he still felt disoriented and unusually anxious, Darash joined the others for breakfast. The food he had brought with him had run out. He always had the best of intentions of rationing, but he could not keep himself from eating if food was available.

"Where is Jehiel?" he asked Ira. The man from Capernaum was not at the table.

"He left early this morning," Ira answered. "He is headed to Samaria."

"Not to Capernaum?"

"No. After his wife died earlier this year, he and his daughter moved to Samaria. Then he became very ill—near death, he claims. So he traveled to Yerushaláyim to visit the physicians there. He claims the

Roman physicians are quite good. Of course, I have not found the Romans to be much use for anything except frightening my guests and taking my money! Hmph!"

"Jehiel did not look ill to me," Darash observed, "of course, it was pretty dark last night when I was with him."

"Yes, I thought the same thing and said as much. He said he had gotten better, but it was not from anything the Roman physicians did for him. I could have told him that! The illness cleared up on its own." Ira gave Darash a curious look and then added, "Speaking of Samaria… if you are going there to help your Roman friend find the men who took Hazaiah and Eliana's son, you could stop by Shechem to ask about Nimrah."

"I was not thinking of doing that at all, and the magistrate is not a friend," Darash reminded him. "I am going to the shuk here in Gophna this morning to sell my wares. Once I have concluded my business here, I am returning to Yerushaláyim. My family is only expecting me to be gone for a week or so. Besides, neither I nor my donkey are up for such a long walk."

"Ah, well," Ira said, looking a bit disappointed, "then I will be sure to send some business your way."

Darash nodded in appreciation. "Thank you. That would be helpful."

It did not take long for Darash to rope Nekoda and load her with supplies. The animals had stayed in the corral outdoors last night, since the night had been a warmer one.

Despite trying to think of other things, memories of last night's dream overtook Darash's mind as he walked toward the shuk of Gophna. The darkness, the beast, the pain, the terror…. And then the man who made it all go away. His dream had undoubtedly been caused by Jehiel's story. One should never listen to such frightening tales right before going to bed, as his mother, Revayah, had often warned. He must have simply dreamed he was Jehiel.

Except I was not Jehiel in my dream… I was myself. I had the same stab wound in my chest… and the beast was within me.

The man who had appeared—the man of light—had to have been Yeshua. Darash recalled Jehiel's story of how Yeshua had cleansed him of the evil spirit from the inside out… with only a few words.

Imah would find this story too fantastic to be believed. She would spit and claim it to be a pack of lies. But Nib'haz… what would he say?

Darash missed his mentor. He tried to imagine what insights the blind basket-weaver might share, but Darash had trouble thinking of how Nib'haz might react to such a strange dream. For when it came to Yeshua, Nib'haz preferred to listen rather than to comment.

Darash led Nekoda past a dormant vineyard and turned down a gravel-strewn path to the left. The road dipped slightly and then leveled out again. The shuk lay just ahead. Ira's aunt had already set up her booth with clothing to sell, but the surly youth had yet to arrive.

Darash wished he could sit down with Nib'haz and discuss the thoughts swirling in his mind. Even Valad might have something of value to add, despite his often ill-timed sense of humor. But he was glad his mother, who he called Imah, was not there to make a comment. Any talk of Yeshua aroused her anger.

Ima believes Yeshua killed my father… or had one of his followers do it.

Darash's father, Tuwr, worked as a merchant and part-time moneychanger at the Temple during Passover and certain Jewish religious festivals. Last year at Passover, Yeshua had flown into a rage and cast the moneychangers out of the Temple grounds with a whip. He overturned their tables, scattered the money in all directions, and kicked holes in the birdcages so that the doves—intended to be sold as sacrifices—escaped into the sky. Darash's father had been among those men.

The night following Yeshua's outburst at the Temple, Tuwr had left home, taking a scroll with him. His body was found the next morning. He had been stabbed to death in an alley. Because of the altercation the day before, the Roman guards and Revayah suspected Yeshua. But Yeshua was already on trial for his life for something the Jewish council considered far more dangerous than murder. Yeshua claimed to be the Messiah—the very Son of the Most High God.

Jehiel's demon said as much…. Odd that demons would agree with Yeshua when man denied his word.

Darash nodded and smiled at Ira's aunt, but spread his blanket on the other side of the shuk from her. He did not feel like getting pulled into a conversation.

Yeshua told the demon to be quiet… as if Yeshua did not want his identity known.

Darash untied a bundle from Nekoda's pack saddle and unpacked a series of painted bowls of various sizes, sacks of exotic spices, and intricate jewelry made by a Jerusalem artisan. He arranged them in an eye-catching manner across the blanket.

Did Yeshua have anything to do with my father's death? If Yeshua can command demons, surely he can command men. His followers, even now, continue to disobey the chief priests, insisting on preaching Yeshua as the Messiah. They would do anything for him. They would die for him. …Would they kill for him? Darash shook his head. *If Yeshua cared so little for life… why would he bother to free Jehiel—a hostile Galilean—from the grip of a demon? The law says men who practice sorcery are to be put to death. But Yeshua healed them instead. Surely only Elohim can cast out demons!*

Even as Darash had this last thought, his mother's words returned to him. She would say the devil, too, could command demons.

Darash's mind returned to his dream. The man of light had come to save Darash's life, not take it. And, though Darash realized it had only been a dream, he could not so easily explain away Jehiel's story—nor the fact that Yeshua had freed Jehiel even before he agreed to follow him… even as he hurled accusations….

What if Jehiel's demon was right? What if Yeshua truly was our Messiah? …And we put Him to death?

סֶ לָ ה

The people of Gophna did not disappoint—possibly due to Ira's encouragements. Though Gophna was not known for its wealth, they were happy to save themselves a trip to Jerusalem by buying up a good quantity of Darash's stock. The spices went the fastest—which elicited a scowl from the youth at the booth next to Ira's aunts clothing booth. Darash tried hard not to smile when the young man shot Darash an angry look past the heads of Darash's customers.

By early afternoon, Darash had made enough to cover his promised purchases to both the metalworker and Zephath, the winemaker. By the end of the day, he had made enough to pay Ira the amount owed for his lodgings and have a little extra to take home with him.

I may not need to stay all week, after all. I could even go home tomorrow and spend Shabbat there.

"Young Darash," Zephath said, approaching from between two booths about an hour before dusk. "I have come with a proposition for you."

"Oh?"

"Yes. I have decided to go to Shechem in the morning, and I want you to come with me. In exchange for your help locating my wife, Phoebe, I will give you the wine you want. We will also inquire there about my nephew."

"You have been speaking to Ira."

"Of course, I have. Everyone speaks to Ira."

Darash could not help but laugh, but he had no interest in extending his journey. "I am sorry," he said, as he secured a bag of unsold pottery to Nekoda's back. "Your offer is a good one. I could use the extra income, but I could not make such a long journey on foot right now, and my donkey cannot carry both me and my supplies."

"That is no trouble at all! I have a strong horse and good cart. You can ride with me and your donkey can remain in Ira's care. I will take you to Shechem and bring you back. And, if you are too tired from the journey when we return, I will even give you a ride to Yerushaláyim."

VI

Shechem

Despite Darash's initial reluctance to travel so far from Jerusalem without alerting his family, he could not pass up the opportunity to earn free wine. He might even get a chance to sell the remainder of his stock in Shechem. Tsarah needed new sandals, and Amah would need a bed, blankets, and new clothing. With all the additional expenses of bringing her into his home, he needed to earn all he could.

Darash climbed onto the cart and plopped down next to Zephath.

Zephath made a sound with his lips and lightly slapped the reins against his mare's flanks. She started pulling the cart loaded with their supplies, though Darash had left the wine and metal purchases behind.

Ira waved as they passed the inn. "Be sure to stop back by here when you return! I will want news of your trip!"

Zephath drove the cart beyond the stone and clay homes of Gophna, past the orchard of gnarled olive trees, and the outcropping of boulders. As they passed the many vineyards toward the road to Samaria, Zephath reached into a bundle at his feet and pulled out a wineskin. After taking a long swig, he handed it to Darash.

Zephath's mare pulled them up an incline and around a wide bend where they met the main road and took the route leading north. The road was largely empty of travelers, except for a contingent of Roman soldiers in the far distance heading in the same direction as Zephath and Darash and moving at a much faster pace. Soon they could no longer be seen at all.

Once Zephath had started drinking, he did not stop. An hour into their journey, he began to sing.

"Oh, sing me a song of Dinah! Tell me of Shechem, her prince! Woe that he e-ever saw her! Their names intertwined ever since!" He raised his wineskin in the air and launched into the second verse. "Shechem was only a man... who fell in love with a maid! But he should have asked her father... before he went and got l—"

"How long will it take us to get there?" Darash asked, interrupting.

"Let me see... We should be there by dinnertime, I suspect. ...Now... where was I?" Zephath took another swig of wine and went back to his song, inflecting his voice to match the words. "Oh, Jacob and his sons were angry! How could Shechem be so bold? But Levi and Simeon were tricksters... and double-crossed Hamor's household!" Zephath looked at Darash and shouted, "Sing with me! Oh—"

"Forgive me. I do not know this one."

Zephath shrugged, looked back at the road, and bellowed, "'We cannot give you our sister... until you agree to this deal! Go and circumcise your sons! Trust us, you will soon heal!'" Zephath laughed heartily and continued, "Old Hamor went back to his city. His news gave his men a great shock! But out of respect for their master... they all had their foreskins lopped off!'"

Darash colored a deep red. Though he had heard the story of Dinah and the Shechemites many times, his rabbinic instructors would not sing such a song. Zephath, however, laughed at Darash's discomfort and kept going, swinging his wineskin in rhythm.

"Now, while all the men of the city... were still in a great deal of pain... Levi and Simeon took their swords... and by morning the city lay slain! ...When Old Jacob heard of the massacre... he flew into a rage in his tent. 'How could you, my sons, be so wicked? You made our whole family a stench!'" Zephath lowered his wineskin for the last verse and draped a heavy arm around Darash's shoulders. With a low, soulful voice he sang, "Poor Dinah was now a widow... her future looked bleak, yes, 'tis true. And all because Levi and Simeon... her lover and husband they slew."

Zephath sighed deeply and said in a voice thick with wine, "Such a sad story. ...Too many lovers have been kept from one another by a world they cannot control. My own wife has left me... my dearest Phoebe... and there is nothing I can do about it."

Zephath's shoulders slumped and his grip on the reins loosened. The man's mood, which had so quickly become joyous with drink and song, just as quickly descended into depression. The mare noticed the slack and slowed her pace.

"Do you expect to find her in Shechem?"

"I know not... perhaps," he slurred. "I thought she had gone to Yerushaláyim to visit family, but when I went to fetch her a few days later, her family told me she never arrived. ...I assumed the worst. That she had been killed or taken by bandits. When Ira told me she had been seen, I knew she had simply tired of me and left." Zephath's face contorted with pain. "She was too good for me, anyway."

The further Zephath descended into his alcohol-induced sorrow, the slower the cart moved. No longer focusing on keeping his mare moving at a steady clip, the animal began to meander.

"I am not even sure what I will say to her when I find her," Zephath continued. "...If I find her."

Zephath's shoulders dropped, and the reins slipped even lower along the mare's sides. The mare lowered her head, and the cart ground to a crawl.

"Zephath," Darash said. "Perhaps you would like to lie down in the bed of the cart and rest. I can drive the cart for a while."

Zephath turned bloodshot eyes on Darash and tried to focus. "Very well," he slurred. "But I have to relieve myself."

Ten minutes later, Zephath lay snoring in the bed of the cart, his head on a sack of grain, and a line of spittle running down his cheek. Darash took up the reins and snapped the mare back to attention. He had no intention of being caught on this road after dark.

סֶ לָ ה

They passed a number of travelers along the road, and Zephath even roused long enough to share a meal with a caravan of merchants who were traveling from Tyre to Beersheba. The larger group, many of whom were armed, provided safety, and Darash managed to make some good trades with the head merchant. He exchanged a set of Egyptian onyx ibex figurines for a sack of abalone shells. The jewelers of Jerusalem would pay well for such a find.

Despite his fortunate trades, Darash was relieved to see the city of Shechem come into view several hours before darkness claimed the valley between Mount Gerizim and Mount Ebal. Dusk signaled the start of Shabbat when it would be forbidden to travel.

Darash pulled the cart up to the railing in front of one of the larger inns of Shechem, having been directed there by some men at the city gate. He jumped down and tied Zephath's mare to a post before going inside to inquire about a place to stay for the night.

"Shalom," he greeted the innkeeper—an elderly man with a long beard and spindly fingers. "Do you have space for two guests tonight?"

"Indeed I do, young one," he answered. Darash detected a hint of a Sidonian accent. "You can choose whether you want the upper or the lower level."

The lower level of an inn was always less expensive, since it was often shared with the animals. Darash hoped Zephath might be willing to splurge for the better arrangement, but he did not want to presume.

"Let me ask my companion. May we put our horse in your stable?"

"Certainly." He led Darash back toward the front door of the inn and, from the threshold, gestured toward a corral where a servant boy slumped near the gate, leaning, half asleep, on a rake made of thick reeds. "That boy there will assist you." Then to the boy, the innkeeper yelled, "Boy! Wake up and help these men, or so help me, I will be giving you a thrashing you will not soon forget!"

The boy jumped to attention and started raking before realizing he was supposed to be helping someone with their animals. He dropped the rake and sprinted toward the front of the inn where Zephath's cart waited.

After dinner, Zephath spread his sleeping mat against the wall on the upper level and invited Darash to sleep up there as well.

"Do not worry about the extra expense. I will cover it," he said. "I will cover all your expenses on this trip, since I made you come."

Darash thanked him and helped bring their bags and supplies from downstairs, plopping them in the corner nearby. One of the sacks made a clack as it hit the ground.

"Oh, careful with that," Zephath said and retrieved a gourd of wine from the sack. "This is my traveling wine."

"I thought you drank your traveling wine on the way," Darash said.

Zephath laughed. "Oh, no. That was my horse cart wine. I always keep it in my horse cart. And in that bag over there," he indicated a second sack with a tilt of his chin, "is my destination wine. For when we reach our destination." He unscrewed the stopper from the gourd and sniffed deeply. "Ah, yes! This is quite a good batch. Would you like to try some?"

"Very well." Darash took a swig of the offered drink. Indeed, it was quite rich. "You are a very good wine-maker," he admitted. "Perhaps you should sell it instead of drinking it."

Zephath laughed again. "Why should I limit myself to one activity when I do both so well?"

After settling in, Zephath and Darash sat down with the innkeeper of the inn of Shechem to ask if Phoebe or Nimrah had been there. Though it was unusual for a woman to be traveling alone, the innkeeper did not recall Phoebe.

"Well, I expected as much," Zephath responded. "If she had come here that would have been three months ago, and she might have joined another family for the journey. But perhaps you have seen my nephew. He would have come through here… oh, about four days ago. His name is Nimrah. He is taller than I, but not so tall as that man over there." He indicated a fellow traveler standing near the front door. "His shoulders droop a bit and he has no beard."

"Ah, yes! I remember him well," the innkeeper said. "An awkward lad with a pockmarked face. He did not look people in the eye properly when spoken to." He stopped, thinking better of his words and quickly added, "Nice enough, though, in his way. He paid his bill, anyhow."

"Do not worry," Zephath said. "We all know he has strange manners. We fear he has gone off and gotten himself into some kind of trouble. Perhaps you saw or heard something that would help us locate him."

"I did hear something…" the innkeeper said and paused. "You know, I understand you are a winemaker, and a quite good one. …It has been a long time since I have had a truly good wine."

"There is a *hin* of my best wine among my belongings upstairs. Tell us what you have heard, and I will fetch it for you."

The innkeeper smiled, revealing a blackened tooth. "Your nephew was here asking about the brothel of Shechem. Many men do, of course, but your nephew—uh, Nimrah—had a particular interest. He asked me to set up a meeting for him with the *shadchan*, the matchmaker."

"See?" Zephath nearly shouted, looking at Darash and clenching his fist in triumph. "What did I tell you? I knew he was looking for a wife!" He turned back to the innkeeper. "Did you arrange this meeting?"

"I did, but he was afraid to go to the brothel to meet her."

"Of course, he was." Zephath shook his head. "My brother's wife has always babied him. Go on."

I would be afraid to go there, too, Darash thought, but said nothing.

"She came here and sat with him on those cushions right over there." He gestured to a low couch against the far wall where some of the guests still lounged, finishing their dinner. "They talked for an hour or so, and then she left."

"Is that all you know? Did she find him a woman? Did he pay her? Did she send him to meet someone?"

"He did not discuss any of that with me," the innkeeper responded, leaning back. "….But I know the woman, and I can ask her, if you wish."

"Yes, please do," Zephath said, rising. "Any information would be very valuable to me."

"Oh? …How valuable?"

"There would be a second hin of wine in it for you—if the information is good." Zephath paused and glanced around. "Excuse me. Where is your latrine?"

Darash lingered after Zephath had left. "Excuse me, but I have some questions for you, as well, if you do not mind."

"Of course, young one," the man answered, still smiling about Zephath's second hin of expensive wine. "I will help you if I can. What is it?"

"Perhaps you have already heard about the attack along the road two days ago. A couple and their servants were set upon by bandits. The servants were killed, and their child was taken."

"Oh, dear." The innkeeper's smile faded. "I have heard from people who saw the burning wreckage, but they could only guess at what happened."

"The owner of the cart's name is Hazaiah and his wife is Eliana. I believe they may have stayed here the night before the attack."

The innkeeper scratched behind his ear before responding. "Hmm… Yes… I seem to recall a Jewish couple with a young child—about yea high," he indicated the child's height with his hand "and they had three servants with them. The man said they were from Dothan."

"Yes, that is them! Did you happen to notice if they met anyone here? Did they talk with any of your guests?"

The innkeeper nodded. "One man took an interest in them. He sat with them at dinner and struck up a conversation with Hazaiah. Later, he even took the child on his lap and played with him."

"Was his name, perhaps, Bagad?"

"Hmm…. That may be right. I am not certain. He only stayed one night, and I get so many guests."

"Perhaps you could describe him for me."

The innkeeper shifted uncomfortably. "Forgive me, but why do you want to know all this? It is not in my habit to speak so openly about my guests. Many of them come here looking for just a place to sleep for the night and a good meal. They want to be left alone, so I give them as much privacy as I can."

Darash nodded, but said, "I understand, but not all of your guests are viciously attacked shortly after they leave here, are they?"

The man sighed and looked toward the front door. "I suppose you have a point."

Darash waited.

"He was bit strange," the innkeeper began. "When he first came he acted cross. He barked at my servant boy and argued with one of the other guests over a place near the fire. I could not wait to be rid of him. But when the young family came with their son, his mood changed. He smiled and treated them kindly, even giving up his spot to Eliana and the child so they would not be cold at night. I was just glad the man was no longer abusing my servant and guests."

"Can you describe him?"

"Tall," he said, "and skinny."

"Anything else?" Darash prompted. "Eliana, the mother of the child, said he smelled sweet."

The innkeeper furrowed his brow. "Sweet? I think not." He paused, considering. "He smelled mostly of goats to me…. But she may have been thinking of the other smell that was strong on his clothing… the smell of spices or, perhaps, incense."

"Has this man, by any chance, returned since that night?"

"No, no…. I have not seen him since, nor do I have any desire to."

VII

Claiming Territory

The following morning, Darash strolled along a Shechem street lined with whitewashed houses. He looked toward the sun creeping into the sky and tried to shake the darkness from his mind. Again he had dreamed of the demon, the clawing pain, and the man who could command spirits.

It was the morning of Shabbat, the seventh day—a day of rest; however, the people of Shechem did not seem to be doing much resting. The narrow road emptied into an open patch of dirt where the well stood. A group of shepherds had come to the city, likely to sell the flock of about sixty sheep and a dozen or so goats, which they now watered. The sound of bleating met Darash's ears long before he saw them. Some of the animals meandered about the shepherds' legs. Others pushed forward to the trough running perpendicular to the well, where they could help themselves to a drink. A broad-shouldered, weather-beaten man, his shepherd's staff propped against the wall of the well, lifted pitcher after pitcher and splashed the water into the trough.

Darash moved on and soon others joined him along the road, but they were not out for a casual, Shabbat stroll. They bustled by—women with bundles or baskets balanced on their heads, men leading pack mules, children herding sheep with sticks and dogs toward the sheep pens. Unfortunately, even in Jerusalem Shabbat was often a busy day. But there the activity was mostly that of Romans or Greeks or other foreigners who did not observe Jewish religious custom. Here in Shechem, though, the Jews were just as busy as the Samaritans, Arabs, and Greeks.

Darash passed beyond a Roman arch built over the road. People bustled past him into a wide market area. The shuk of Shechem was at least ten times larger than the one in Gophna—about the same size as the lower shuk of Jerusalem where Darash usually sold. However, unlike Jerusalem, which had three main shuks, Shechem had only one. Booths of various kinds dotted an open patch of dirt just a couple of blocks past the well. As it was still early, many of the booths sat empty, waiting for their masters to return and fill them with good things. Men and women worked hard in others to set up their displays quickly to catch the eyes of the early shoppers.

Darash stopped beneath a dormant olive tree to scrape encrusted dirt from his sandals. A woman sat behind a fruit stand to his right, and at his left stood a wooden booth that had yet to open.

"Shalom, young man," the fruit seller said to him, smiling. She was middle-aged and spoke with a distinctly Samaritan accent. "Have you had your breakfast this morning? I have dried figs, dates, and apricots." She held up a bowl containing the mix. "Roasted almonds, too." She picked an almond out of the bowl with her thumb and forefinger and held it up for him to see.

Darash smiled. "It looks delicious, but I have already eaten."

"Oh, but you will need a snack soon—a growing young man like yourself." She moved closer and pushed the bowl to within a hand's breadth of his face. "Here, try one of my dates. I removed the pits and steeped them in honey-water before drying them. They are the best that can be had."

Darash had not wanted to point out the obvious to the woman— seeing that she was a Jewess—but, finally, he said, "Forgive me. I am sure it is delicious. But I will have to wait until tomorrow before I can make any purchases."

A look of confusion crossed her brow but soon realization opened her eyes. "Ah! Of course! Today is Shabbat." She paused, eyeing him for a moment. "You must be from Yerushaláyim. Your mother must be very proud to have such an honorable son."

Darash could not be certain, but he detected a bit of sarcasm in her voice. She plopped her bowl of mixed fruits and nuts back on the counter of her booth and turned her back on him.

Darash decided it was time to move on but, as he stepped back into the road, the owner of the empty booth arrived. Darash watched as a heavyset man with a broad forehead and clean-shaven jaw emptied his baskets of goods. One by one, with delicate precision, the man filled his booth with stone, clay, and wooden idols of all varieties and sizes.

Darash moved on, strolling along the booths. He came upon more than one idol-seller. He soon had his fill of listening to them describe the healing powers of the Egyptian goddess, Sekhmet, the vengeance one could have by sacrificing to the Amorite god, Hadad, and how the Canaanite goddess, Anat, could increase one's enjoyment of the carnal pleasures. But beyond all of this, what truly made Darash feel sick was an interaction he witnessed as he passed back by the first idol booth he had seen.

"Of course… if you are in search of real power, you will need to consult someone else," the heavyset idol-seller told a dark-skinned, young man before leading him to the back of his booth where he uncovered a basket and dug around in it. "This is a figure of the most powerful god in this entire region… Molech."

The young man gasped and took a step back.

"Do not be afraid," the seller hissed, grabbing the man's elbow to pull him back. "He is only dangerous to those who do not serve him."

"But I thought he had no power here… at least, he has not for a very long time."

"True, true…. They tried to expel him, but once a god claims a land for his own, he does not willingly leave it. He will always seek a way to come back." The seller pushed a metal idol of a seated man with a bull's head toward his potential customer. "And Molech is back."

סֶ לָ ה

"Did the innkeeper talk to that woman from the brothel for you yet?" Darash asked Zephath, joining him on a wooden bench in the lower room of the inn.

"Shh! Shh!" Zephath shushed him, and glanced around for possible eavesdroppers.

"Forgive me," Darash whispered.

"He did," Zephath answered with another furtive glance. "She says she sent Nimrah to Samaria." Zephath growled. "What a fool! Does he really think he can bring a Samaritan woman back to Yerushaláyim with him? Millah and Obed would never accept her! Does he not realize that a Jew and a Samaritan can never—"

"Get out of my spot!"

Darash and Zephath were jolted from their conversation by a cry from one of the other guests. A stocky Samaritan man who smelled of beer towered over a man who had recently arrived from Damascus and had unwittingly placed his bedroll in the already spoken for spot near the fire. However, when the man from Damascus stood to face his rival, he proved himself to be more than a match. He stood at least two handbreadths taller. Rather than a paunch at his middle, he boasted a heavily muscled frame and Goliath-like hands.

"What did you say to me?"

Unfortunately, the beer-soaked Samaritan did not recognize the danger. "I said, 'Get out of my spot!'"

The Damascene curled his hands into fists and took step closer to the Samaritan, his chest now in the man's face. "If you had intended to claim that spot, you should have left your belongings there!"

"Please, please!" the spindly innkeeper broke in, trying to step between them. "Do not fight! There is a perfectly good spot right here!" He gestured to an empty patch of hard-packed dirt on the other side of the fire. "No one has claimed it. One of you could sleep there."

"I was here first!" the drunken man insisted. "Let him move!"

"Just try to make me!"

Darash did not know who laid hands on whom first, as the innkeeper was blocking his view, but the first punch was thrown by the Damascene. The Samaritan reeled from the blow. He stumbled back two paces before falling hard on his right side, barely missing the fire.

A woman gasped and pulled her child out of the way of the men, but several others drew closer to watch.

"Men of Judea, men of Judea, please!" the innkeeper cried, trying desperately to intercede. The Damascene shoved him out of the way and reached for the Samaritan's neck, but the Samaritan fought back, punching the larger man in the nose with his right and then following with a left to the ribs.

The Damascene retaliated, sending the Samaritan headlong into a bench, where Darash and Zephath had been seated only moments earlier. The Samaritan's body broke the bench in half down the middle. Blood flowed from the man's nose and a new cut ran the length of his brow.

Zephath said, "Come! Grab your belongings! It is time we find different accommodations!"

The men still fought with brazen gusto as Darash and Zephath left, along with two families with small children. Zephath paid the servant boy what they owed. Darash loaded their belongings into the cart while Zephath hitched up the mare. The sounds of shouts, blows being exchanged, and furniture breaking followed them from the inn.

"Fools!" Zephath said, shaking his head. "Fighting over nothing! Like children!"

"Where will we go now?"

"Oh, Shechem has many inns. We will come upon one soon enough." He slapped the reins lightly against his mare's back as they made it onto a flat, straight road. "Besides, the innkeeper there knew nothing about my wife. I think I will have better luck elsewhere."

"How far will we have to go?" Darash asked.

"Do not worry. We will not break any Shabbat laws."

We already have, by loading the cart.

"You did not stay in town as long as I thought you would," Zephath added. "It is not even dinner time yet."

"The owner of the booth next to where I was sitting was selling idols," Darash said. He paused, unsure how Zephath would respond. Though Zephath was Jewish, Darash had begun to realize that one's heritage alone did not necessarily dictate one's religious beliefs.

"I see… and you found this… disturbing?"

Darash nodded.

"Well, it may not be such a common thing in Yerushaláyim—although I guarantee it still happens. But out here, away from the teachers of the law, the chief priests, and the Sanhedrin, it happens much more openly. After all, the Romans and the Greeks like to be able to find representations of their many gods within the territories they control. I assume you saw some images of Athena and Zeus among the man's wares."

"I did. It seemed he had an idol for every god man has ever dreamed up. He even had some metal ones of Molech."

"Molech!" Zephath leaned to the side and spat in disgust. "I knew it!" He shook his head with vigor before continuing. "I knew something strange has been going on! And do not think people have dreamed up these gods—these evil spirits. They are quite real. And very dangerous."

"But surely Adonai will protect us from them if we follow Him as the Torah commands."

"Of course, of course, He will… but lately, I…." Zephath adjusted himself on the seat of the cart. "Lately, I have begun to wonder…."

"About what?" Darash looked at his new friend, earnestness in his voice and eyes. Images of his nightmare threatened to resurface.

"About whether more may be required." Zephath paused again and then shrugged his shoulders in defeat. "I do not know. I am no rabbi. I do not even attend the synagogue regularly. When my wife left me I stopped going and turned to drink instead. None of it seemed to matter anymore… and the rabbis were unable to answer my questions, anyway. But I get the feeling that our old ways of defeating evil—by following the law—no longer works."

"What do you mean?"

"I do not know how to explain it, young one." Zephath sighed. "With all that has been happening in Nazareth and Yerushaláyim… I just feel something has changed."

"Are you speaking of Yeshua?"

Zephath paused. "I suppose I am." He looked at Darash and hurriedly added, "I am not a follower of His, by any means… but His teachings are still changing the way people think. Even though He is gone."

They lapsed into silence for a few moments. They passed an ancient vineyard that withered behind a crumbling stone wall.

Darash asked, "How long has your wife been gone?"

"Three months." Zephath allowed his mare to slow as he scanned the rows of buildings coming into view. They drove along a row of homes that, like the inn they had just left, lay outside the remains of the old city walls. He caught the eye of an old man standing by a rickety gate. "Is there an inn nearby?" he asked.

The old man pointed with his chin in the direction they were headed. "A block and a half that way if you want something cheap," he said. "Three blocks if you want a half-way decent meal and fewer bugs."

"Thank you, Uncle," Zephath said, dipping his head in respect. He slapped the reins again and turned to Darash. "I think I prefer a decent meal and not having to fight bugs during the night. How about you?"

Darash smiled and nodded. It was Zephath's money, after all.

Zephath gave the reins a slight slap to hasten his mare again. He sighed before returning to the subject of his wife. "She had been receiving messages," he said, "which she hid from me. I caught her throwing a scrap of leather into the fire. I caught the sight of words written on it before the flames consumed it. I asked her about it, but she said it was nothing—just a message from a friend. But why burn it? She kept asking for permission to visit her family in Yerushaláyim. But I was angry and did not trust her, so I told her no. Then one day she received a visit. I believe it was just a messenger boy. I asked her about it. She said he had simply come to try to sell sweetbreads and she had turned him down. …But afterward she appeared very distraught. She hardly ate, and she tossed and turned all night. Again, she refused to tell me the truth. I grew very angry. I yelled at her, and then I got very drunk. The next morning, she was gone."

"And you have not heard from her since?"

Zephath shook his head.

"Do you think she is simply visiting a friend here in Shechem?"

Zephath made an odd noise—something between a groan and growl—as he considered the question. "No, I do not. She has no friends in Shechem. …I think she has found a lover and has finally left me." He sighed. "I almost do not blame her. I have not been a very good husband. I am sloppy and I drink too much. I have few manners. I am not even a very good Jew."

Zephath grew silent as they approached the first inn. A snaggle-toothed old woman stood outside and beckoned to them.

"Come to my inn!" she cried, speaking louder than the distance between them required. "The best place in Shechem! Cheapest lodgings in town! You can sleep right next to your beasts! Come! Come! I will give you a good price!"

Zephath waved her off and put another home between himself and her before saying more.

"And we have had no children. I have complained too much on that count. But there is nothing she can do about it. Perhaps she has finally tired of me."

"But what of the messenger? What kind of lover would send a message that would make her so upset just before leaving?"

"I have thought on that for a long time. I think, perhaps, she was putting him off—waiting for me to get better—to become a better husband. He finally gave her an ultimatum. Then, instead of showing her I loved her, I simply got angry and drunk. That is why she was so upset... and why she left."

Hmm... maybe.... But there are any number of reasons why a message might cause distress. Darash's mother, Revayah, often received distressing messages from her friend, Sapphira—a woman who offered no end of crises. Revayah also regularly received summons from other members of the Jewish community for help with a wedding or to assist a midwife in delivering a baby. Darash said nothing to Zephath, though, as they now approached the second inn. *Of course, Imah never stays away for more than a few days at a time....*

VIII

Samaria

Two hours later, Zephath and Darash sat down to eat with the other guests at a different inn. Dusk had fallen and Shabbat had ended, leaving Darash feeling relieved. Normally, he regretted the end of Shabbat as the pressures of earning a living descended on him once again. But this Shabbat had been anything but restful… and he missed his family.

How do these people manage to go through life without ever taking the time to be still? Never seeking God's help in their constant struggle to put food on the table? It must be exhausting.

Darash surveyed his new surroundings as he ate his lentil stew, which had been flavored with bits of dried lamb and garlic. Though this inn was considerably smaller than the one they had stayed at last night, it proved more hospitable. A woman and her two grown daughters ran the place alone, though it was rumored the owner of the inn was simply away.

"Did a man named Jehiel stop here recently, by any chance?" Darash asked one of the daughters. She was several years his senior, but she smiled at him in a way that made him uncomfortable. "He was not much taller than I," he continued, "and slight of build. He wore a blue cloak."

"Yes, I remember a guest by that name. He stayed here two nights ago and left early the next morning."

"Did he seem to be in good health?"

"He did."

"Thank you." Darash took a bite of stew.

"Why do you ask?"

"Oh, it is not important." Darash kept his eyes down, letting his bangs drop. "I met him in Gophna and heard he had been ill. I knew he was traveling this way. I am glad to hear he is well."

The woman set a plate of bread before him spread with a generous amount of fish paste. "Well," she said, as she moved behind him, "if you want to know anything else, do not hesitate to ask."

Darash was about to accept her offer. But, as the question formed on his lips, the woman drew her fingertips across the back of his neck and leaned down to whisper in his ear. "We innkeepers know everything that happens around here. And I am particularly generous with information on all subjects. I am sure I could teach a young man like you a thing or two. You need but to ask."

סֶ֫לָה

"My wife is not in Shechem," Zephath said later that evening as they prepared for bed.

"How do you know?"

"The woman innkeeper told me if Phoebe had stayed in Shechem she would know it by now. I believe her." Zephath pulled a clay jug from his bag of destination wine. The traveling wine had already been consumed.

"Are you certain she came this way?"

"Yes. I heard it from a reliable source. My brother was traveling to Jerusalem from Beth Shan. He stopped in here and saw my wife. He even spoke to her. She told him she was going to visit a friend."

"Perhaps she was."

"No. She has no friends here. She found herself another man."

"But perhaps she only stopped in Shechem for the night and...." Darash stopped.

Zephath tipped the clay jug up and chugged, head back, eyes closed. He drank for several seconds. When he stopped, he wiped his wine-stained chin on the sleeve of his robe and burped loudly.

"If she has left this place," Zephath said, no longer looking at Darash, staring instead at his wine jug, "then I have no idea where she might have gone. My search is over."

"Well," Darash spoke tentatively, sensing Zephath's shifting mood, "we know she did not go to Beth Shan to visit your family there, or she would have told your brother. And we know she did not head south, or she would not have come north to Shechem to begin with. So... it only makes sense that she was headed to—"

"She would not go to Samaria!" Zephath cried, causing wine to slosh from the top of the jug. "She knows I would never allow it!" Zephath took another long draught of wine, laid down on his bed, and turned his back to Darash.

Which might explain why she did not tell you where she was going.

סֶ֫לָה

Darash lay awake, afraid to sleep lest his nightmare return. He thought of home, of Nib'haz blindly weaving baskets, of his mother holding Amah as she cried.

I should be there. Not in Shechem chasing Millah's foolish son, not sleeping next to a drunken man in an inn run by harlots, and not in a town taken over by idolatry!

As the night wore on, Darash's thoughts wandered to the untimely death of his father, Tuwr—murdered in an alley the evening after Yeshua expelled him and the other merchants and moneychangers from the Temple. There had to be some connection there. But what?

He sighed.

If Abba was still alive, he would be making this trip, and I would be at home taking care of Imah, Tsarah, and Amah.

Amah.

Darash did not even know her age for certain. She was not much bigger than Tsarah, his eight-year-old little sister. But Tsarah was tall for her age and plump around the middle. Amah had lived a life of such poverty, she may not have grown correctly. He suspected she was closer to twelve or thirteen. Her eyes, though… her eyes were much older….

I wonder what her real name is….

Darash resolved to find out Amah's real name as soon as he returned home. She had not spoken a single word to him during the short time she had been in his home, but perhaps his mother, Revayah, would have more success.

Imah is good with her, he admitted to himself.

Though Revayah could be harsh and demanding, she had sensed the hurt in Amah and recognized the child's need to simply be held. At the same time, he knew Revayah would have expectations. Amah would have to make herself useful before too long.

Maybe that is not such a bad thing….

Darash shifted on his mat. A lump in the clay floor of the upper room made it hard for him to find a comfortable position. Zephath had begun to snore—deep, steady, wine-thickened rumbles.

Darash did not mind so much. His father had been a terrible snorer. Tuwr used to snore so loudly Darash could put his hand on the wall and feel the vibrations. Though Revayah often complained, Darash drew comfort from knowing, if he ever awoke from a troublesome dream but could hear Abba snoring, all was well. Now the nights at home were horribly silent.

סֶלָה

"We must go to Samaria, after all." Zephath sat on his sleeping mat in the light of morning, his shoulders slumped. He looked up at Darash with unblinking, bloodshot eyes.

"What?" Darash, who had stood to shake out and roll up his mat, stopped what he was doing to look at Zephath, eyes wide. "But I thought we would head back to Gophna today. I expected to be home by tomorrow."

"We have not succeeded in our quests. Nimrah is still missing, and my wife is not here. She has gone to Samaria."

"You said there is no way she went there."

"I was wrong. You were right," Zephath shrugged. "Besides, we know for certain Nimrah went there."

Zephath stood but was unsteady on his feet. Darash grabbed Zephath's arm to stabilize him.

"Thank you, my son," Zephath said. "You are a good boy. Forgive me for being so obstinate last night. I am glad you are with me. Besides… Samaria will have more merchandise for you to acquire and sell when you get home."

True…. As long as I do not tell anyone in Yerushaláyim where it came from.

סֶלָה

Zephath and Darash wasted no time getting back on the road. Though Darash looked longingly southward, Zephath turned right and headed north toward Samaria.

If Imah finds out I went to Samaria, she will take me to the Temple and make the priests scrub me with hyssop until I have no skin left!

Jews, at least faithful Jews, avoided Samaria at all costs, often traveling an extra day or two to avoid going through the city. Though the city of Samaria had once been the capital city of the united nation of Israel, it later became a center of idol-worship. When the people of Israel split into two warring factions after the death of King Solomon, with Israel to the north and Judah to the south, Israel rejected the true God and followed the ba'als. Over seven hundred years ago, God finally gave them over to their enemies, the Assyrians. The Assyrians carried off most of the Jews from Israel and resettled their own people in the region of Samaria. The Assyrians intermarried with the Jews who had remained and produced the Samaritan half-breeds—products of forbidden unions between Jews and foreign idolaters.

"You know, I heard Bar'abbas is back living in these hills somewhere," Zephath mused as they left Shechem's valley and headed toward a steep curve through a mountain pass.

"The man Pilate pardoned instead of Yeshua?"

"The same."

"I thought he would stay in Yerushaláyim and make a new life for himself," Darash said.

"Indeed, so did we all." Lines crossed Zephath's face, and he drew his mare to a stop. "The road is too steep here," he said. "The horse cannot pull us. We must get out and walk until it levels out."

They disembarked and Zephath retrieved a flask of wine from the cart. He took a long swig and then tucked it in his belt. Only then did he take hold of the reins. He pulled them ahead of his mare's head and encouraged her to move again.

"Do you think he is a member of the Sicarii?" Darash asked, resuming the conversation.

"I think, if the rumors are true and he really has returned to live in the hills, that would pretty well confirm it."

Darash had heard that the murders Bar'abbas had committed were actually acts of calculated attacks on key Roman figures—likely masterminded by someone other than Bar'abbas himself. But no proof had arisen and neither the Roman government nor the Jewish chief priests had confirmed the rumors.

However, the stories intrigued Darash. The men of Jerusalem often sat together around fires or at the dinner table and told tales of a new group of extreme rebels called Sicarii for the sicae daggers they carried concealed in their cloaks. These men had begun slipping into Roman political and sporting events, religious festivals—even private weddings—blending with the crowd. They got close to their chosen victim—sometimes luring him into a private chamber or corridor—and stabbed him. The assassin would then slip out before the body was discovered.

Darash surveyed the stone mountain walls they now passed and swallowed hard. Huge boulders rested precariously against hillsides—a perfect place for a bandit to hide. And now, at a walking pace, Darash and his fat friend undoubtedly made very easy targets.

Zephath looked at Darash and laughed. "Do not worry, my young friend! It is still early morning! Everyone knows bandits like to sleep in." He laughed again and slapped the youth on his back.

Somehow, Darash found Zephath's words less than reassuring.

Zephath took another draught of wine.

"Ah, it is a beautiful morning, is it not?" Zephath said as they crested the hill, swinging an arm wide to indicate the landscape. The road stretched before them, meandering along a rocky embankment on one side with a grassy valley on the other. Despite the winter weather, the valley looked green.

"But why," Darash asked, ignoring the scene, "would a man—who had so recently escaped death—return to the life that had brought him to such danger?"

"Oh, I do not know…." Zephath took another drink from his flask. "I suppose some people simply feel more comfortable with what they know, even if it seems uncivilized to people like you and—" he burped loudly, "me."

IX

Simon the Sorcerer

Samaria bustled with activity. Zephath drove to a large inn at the outskirts of town and instructed one of the servants to unload the cart and care for the mare.

The innkeeper, a friendly young man with a round belly and patchy beard approached them as they entered the courtyard.

"Greetings!" he said cheerily. "Welcome! It is not often I get Jewish visitors."

"Then perhaps you will recall a young Jew by the name of Nimrah?" Zephath responded. "He came to Samaria sometime within this past week. He is my nephew."

"Oh, no! I have had no Jewish visitors of late. I could ask my father, though. He knows more than I about the comings and goings of the people here." The young man led the way through the courtyard toward he building.

"I would appreciate that," Zephath said. "Is he inside?"

"No, he is in Sidonia."

"What?" Zephath stopped in his tracks. "When do you expect him back?

"Oh, any day now. Perhaps even tomorrow." The man smiled again.

"How long has he been gone?" Darash asked.

The young man paused. He looked at his right hand and touched his thumb to his pointer finger, then his middle finger, and so on until he had to move to the next hand. Finally he stopped counting and said, "Seven years."

"Seven years!" Zephath blurted. "How long since you have heard from him?"

The young man lifted his hand and started counting again.

"Never mind," Zephath stopped him. "Just show us the accommodations."

"Very well," the innkeeper said without losing any of his joviality. He pushed open the inn door and stepped inside.

Zephath gave Darash a look of incredulity before following.

The man is touched, Darash thought.

"Greetings!" A voice greeted them again from near the hearth. An older woman approached, smiling. "I see you have met my son. He is a simpleton, but friendly." She turned to her son. "Go out and help the servants care for the animals."

The young innkeeper smiled and gave a little hop before running off toward the back door. "He greatly enjoys working with animals," she explained to Zephath and Darash. "How long will you be staying with us?"

"That depends on how successful we are in our search," Zephath said.

"I see. And what do you search for?"

"Not what—who," Zephath corrected her. "We are searching for my nephew—a young Jew named Nimrah. And also for my… uh… a woman named Phoebe."

"Phoebe…" she mused, thinking. "I am sorry. No. I do not know her. Perhaps you should walk over to the city gate, though, and speak to the elders there. One of them might know something."

"Thank you," Zephath said. "That is an excellent idea."

"You have about two hours until dinner," she said, as she turned away from them to head back to the hearth where a pot had begun to boil.

Ten minutes later, Zephath and Darash arrived at the wide, arched West Gate and sat down with an old man there. He had a skinny frame and a beard that reached to the middle of his chest. He wore a robe too thin to effectively stave off the chill in the air.

"I have not heard of this young man you mentioned," he said in response to their questions, "this Nimrah. But I might have heard of the woman, Phoebe… from Gophna, you say?"

"Yes. She is my wife." Zephath's words came quickly. "Do you know where she is staying?"

"No, no… I know nothing so specific as that. But, I might have overheard one of the leatherworkers mention that they had a visitor by that name."

"A leatherworker?" Zephath's voice changed. His brow drew together and the eagerness left him.

"Yes… maybe… I am not certain."

Zephath, lost in his own thoughts, turned away.

Darash stepped forward and said, "Thank you, Grandfather, for your help."

"My pleasure, Son," he said, but his eyes followed Zephath.

Zephath walked away from Darash and the old man as if he had forgotten them entirely.

Darash doubled his steps to catch up. "Zephath," he said, "what is the matter?"

"Oh… it is… it is nothing."

"The old man said something to upset you."

"No… no…." Zephath waved Darash's questions away. "It is nothing. I do not believe the Phoebe he heard of could be the same woman as my wife. Let us continue our search. We will find someone else to ask in the shuk."

Darash and Zephath followed a newly constructed Roman colonnaded street until they arrived at the Roman Acropolis. The shuk lined the road in that section, spreading along its borders with several rows of booths on either side. Though it was too late in the day for Darash to set up shop, he looked for a good area for tomorrow. Zephath questioned a few of the shoppers and store owners about his wife's possible whereabouts. None had heard of her.

"Come!" A voice met them from the far side of a wide, booth-littered courtyard. "Come discover the mysteries that await you! I will guide you to peace, to security, to love!"

Curious, Zephath and Darash came upon a small gathering of people crowded around a seated figure on the ground—a middle-aged man with a turban wound tightly around his head. Thick earrings of gold hung from unnaturally distended earlobes, and a charcoal tattoo crossed his left temple and spanned above his left eye—lines and curves and dots—ending in a star positioned in the middle of his forehead.

"Consult the spirits and discover your destiny," the man cried. He held up a terracotta talisman—an object chiseled roughly into the shape of a fat-bodied man with a bird-like head. "Find healing and wisdom! Wealth and long life! Peace and security!"

"Who is that man?" Darash asked.

Zephath shrugged his shoulders, but a middle-aged woman standing nearby answered, "That is Simon the Sorcerer. For a shekel he will divine your future or consult the dead. He is quite powerful."

"Can he find lost things?" Zephath asked her. "Or missing people?"

"Oh, I have no doubt! He once allowed me to speak to my mother for over an hour. She died when I was a mere babe."

"Zephath," Darash said, pulling on the man's sleeve, "I think we should move on."

"Oh… yes. Yes, of course," he responded, and together they moved away from the spectacle. But as they passed out of the crowd, Zephath caught Simon the Sorcerer's eye.

"I can help you find what you seek," Simon called, looking directly at Zephath. "I can find what has been lost."

"Come on," Darash said, pulling on Zephath's sleeve to get him moving. "We must have no part with divination."

"Of course," Zephath said. "Of course."

סֶ לָ ה

Despite Darash's wish to be home instead of in this cursed city, he enjoyed the dinner served at the inn of Samaria. Gentiles were undoubtedly among the guests, but Darash reasoned that, since he was traveling and conducting business, the social infraction of eating with Gentiles could be overlooked. Besides, the food served did not violate any Jewish restrictions, and it smelled delicious.

With the help of her son, the innkeeper served a stew of leeks and lentils, a side of roasted beets with coriander-flavored curds, and warm bread with honey. Knowing Zephath would be paying, Darash found it all especially tasty. He helped himself to seconds and then thirds.

Zephath also enjoyed generous portions. And, though he complained the wine was cheap, he drank three glasses. After dinner, Zephath made certain the innkeeper's servant had cared for his belongings properly. Satisfied, he told Darash he would be going out and would be back later.

"Where are you going?" Darash asked.

"I, uh… I am going to inquire about my wife."

"Would you like me to join you?"

"No, no. You relax. It has been a long day. I will not be long."

Zephath tightened his cloak about his thick frame and ducked out the front door. Darash thought of Nib'haz. What would his blind friend say about Zephath's behavior? "He is hiding something. He does not want you to know where he is going," Nib'haz would say. Darash sighed.

Zephath is going to see the sorcerer.

סֶ לָ ה

Darash pulled his cloak over his shoulders and headed out into the early dusk. Making conversation with strangers at the inn exhausted him. Though he had not planned on looking for Zephath, he found himself back at the shuk where the sorcerer had been conducting his heathen business. Simon the Sorcerer's spot was empty, and Zephath was nowhere to be seen.

Darash walked between the rows of shops and booths, most of them closed or in the process of closing. A well-lighted store caught Darash's eye. The small store occupied the bottom floor of a two-story building. Undoubtedly, the owners conducted business from the lower floor but lived in the quarters above.

As Darash passed near the wide open doors, he spotted a girl about Tsarah's age playing with a rag doll in the corner. A man and woman sat together, laughing and talking. The sparkle in the man's eyes as he listened to his wife and the woman's laughter sparked a memory in Darash. His own parents used to sit together in the evenings, talking over their day and joking about the silly things that had occurred. His mother had been happier then.

The woman spotted Darash and beckoned him inside.

"Please, come in, and shalom," she said, nodding in his direction. "We are still open." She wore a heavy cloak, but no head covering. Her straight, black hair shone in the light of multiple oil lamps.

Her husband, a tall, bearded man with smooth features, also noticed him and rose. "Yes, please, enter." He smiled broadly and swept one arm wide in welcome. He, too, wore a warm cloak over a long-sleeved, winter tunic, tied together at the middle with a rope belt.

Darash gazed in appreciation at the myriad of items lining multiple shelves, small tables, and built-in, stone ledges. Skillfully painted pottery, soft fabrics of all colors, beaded and hammered metal jewelry, baskets woven with reeds stained with various colors. Darash realized that everything here—even the practical items—had been carefully selected for their aesthetic appeal as much as for their usefulness.

"Do you make all of these things yourselves?" Darash asked as he fingered an ivory comb that had a line of flowers etched into it.

"Oh, no!" The man laughed. "My wife, Photina, paints the pottery, which she receives from a potter we know. I make those stools over there." He indicated a collection of three-legged stools of various heights. They had been sanded and painted with images of birds, pomegranates, and flowers. "She painted those, too," he explained. Then he smiled, "My name is Ethan. What is yours?"

"I am Darash, from Yerushaláyim. I am impressed with the variety of items you have to sell."

"We have a wonderful community of friends here," Photina explained. "Many of them are skilled craftsmen and women. They bring us items to sell and we share the proceeds equally with everyone."

"You might not believe me," Ethan said, "but the comb you are holding was carved by a blind man."

Darash looked again at the delicate patterns—flowers with fat petals, perfectly-shaped leaves, flowing lines that made them look like they were being blown about in the wind.

"Oh, I believe you," Darash said. "I sit with a blind man every day in the market of Yerushaláyim. He makes the best baskets in town." Darash paused and then added, "He has become like a father to me… since my own father was taken from us."

He did not know why he said it. Darash normally would never mention something so personal to strangers. But this young family, in a span of moments, had put him at ease. He had simply forgotten, for a moment, that they were Gentiles.

"Then that must explain why you are here alone," Ethan ventured.

Darash nodded. "I only intended to go as far as Gophna… but other circumstances brought me here." He held up the comb. "How much are you asking for this? I would like to take a gift back home for my mother."

"Two shekels."

Darash paid him without bothering to haggle. The price was not inexpensive, but it was fair.

"You have a beautiful shop," Darash said, looking around. "My father once had a shop like this. Well… his items were mostly practical things—not so beautiful as these—but he had a great many of them and a wide variety of choices. Someday I would like to have a place like this." He paused. "You say you do not purchase everything outright? That the artisans get paid when their items sell?"

"That is correct. Only, we have a rather large community we serve, and we split the money between all of them—not just the artisans."

Darash looked Ethan in surprise. "But, then… how…?"

Ethan smiled. "Everyone serves in some way and everyone gives freely. For example, a certain older man in our group has no skill for painting or carving, but he owns a flock of goats. He milks them, makes leben and cheese, and, from time to time, butchers one for its meat and skin. He contributes nothing to my store for me to sell, but he provides food for the group, of which my family receives a share. No one among us—not the widow, the blind, the orphan—goes hungry. Everyone has warm clothes and a place to sleep at night." He glanced at the little girl still sitting in the corner of their home, playing with the doll. "This child was an orphan," he said.

The child's hair was combed and plaited on the sides. She wore a thick, blue tunic beneath a long smock that covered her shoulders and reached to her feet. She was not plump, but she was healthy-looking, with ruddy skin and a clear complexion. Bright brown eyes caught his. She held up her doll to show him.

"Oh, yes," Darash told her. "That is a very nice doll."

She grinned and returned to her game.

"One of our members found her living on the streets," Ethan said, voice lowered, "stealing food from the vendors and sleeping in the garbage heap. The woman brought her to one of our meetings and asked if anyone could take her in. We had no children, so she is our daughter now." He smirked and glanced at his wife. "It was Photina's idea."

Photina smiled back at him with one raised eyebrow, as if daring him to complain.

"It was a wonderful idea," Ethan added, still smiling at Photina. "You know," Ethan said slowly, turning back to Darash, as if something had just occurred to him, "my wife and daughter and I are about to close up shop and go to a meeting with the members of this group I have been telling you about. Please join us. We will be sharing a meal together and there is always plenty of food for guests."

Darash found the offer tempting, but anxiety filled him. These people were all strangers to him and, apparently, had a very tight connection to one another. They also behaved strangely—even if a second dinner sounded appealing.

"I should tell you," Ethan continued, noting Darash's hesitation, "our community is an unusual one. We are a community of Jews, Gentiles, Samaritans, and others. We do not reject people based on where they are from, what language they speak, or what they look like on the outside. All are welcome. We come together out of mutual respect and shared belief." He paused and glanced at his wife. "In fact, my wife started this group... after she met an unusual man at the well. His name was Yeshua."

X

The Woman of Sychar

Darash's hands trembled—not from the cold, but from nervousness.

Way Followers! This is a meeting of the followers of Yeshua, and I am going with Gentiles! If Imah ever finds out I have been to one of these meetings, she will drag me before the chief priests so they can excommunicate me!

As he followed Ethan's family along a narrow road, Darash imagined himself living on the fringes of society, barefooted and begging for food, shunned by all his former friends.

No. Imah would not do such a thing. I am the only one supporting the family, after all.

And... she does love me.

Despite Revayah's complaints and demands, she had shown her love for him as she nursed him back to health. He had never felt more secure in it... at least, not since before his father had passed. Still, he could not help fearing her moods and stalwart opinions—especially when it came to pleasing the Pharisees... at least outwardly.

Soon the small party arrived at a well-lit home. The doors and windows stood open, allowing the sound of voices to spill into the outer courtyard and the street beyond. As a servant girl opened the outer gate for Ethan's family, the people inside launched into an impromptu and rather boisterous rendition of the Song of Miriam, sung in Hebrew.

> *"The LORD is my strength and my defense*
> *he has become my salvation.*
> *He is my God, and I will praise him,*
> *my father's God, and I will exalt him."*

The sound brought a smile to Darash's lips. He knew the tune well, though he had never heard it sung with such gusto by both men and women alike. Even some children's voices could be heard trilling above the others.

Darash stepped into the room and was immediately drawn into a circle of new faces.

"Ah! Ethan, Photina, you have brought a young guest! Welcome, young man, and shalom!" The speaker, a Samaritan man with a thick white beard, embraced Darash and kissed him on both cheeks—as if he had been a long-lost grandson finally come home.

A group of older women surrounded him, stealing him away from the man. One grabbed his right hand. Another took his left arm. A third put a hand on his shoulder. They led him to a long table spread with a grand feast.

"Come, sit! Enjoy!" the one on his left said, speaking Greek.

"Yes, there is plenty of food," said another.

Though it was not a festival day—at least, not any Darash recognized—the meal consisted of copious amounts of vegetable dishes, sweet breads, delicacies, and several varieties of meat dishes. Darash spotted quail, lamb shanks, and even a whole roasted duck. Though he had eaten a mere hour or so earlier, Darash intended to sample everything.

"Shalom," a young man said, smiling at him from the other side of the table. "My name is Melchi."

Darash paused, aware that the young man who spoke to him was also a Gentile, though he had used the familiar Hebrew greeting. "Shalom," Darash finally managed. "I am Darash, son of Tuwr, of Yerushaláyim."

"Nice to see someone of my age here," Melchi said. "There are some girls, of course, but they mostly keep to themselves."

Naturally, Darash thought, but followed Melchi's gaze to the far end of the table. Three girls chatted and laughed together, but a fourth sat quietly, her hands in her lap. She was quite beautiful, with hair of a lighter hue than the other girls, and fair skin.

"The quiet one is Jada," Melchi said, catching Darash gaze. "My stepfather is trying to arrange a betrothal between us, but her adopted father, Jehiel, is ill. That is why she is here alone… and why she seems so sad."

"Jehiel?" Darash perked up at the name. "Do you mean Jehiel of Capernaum?"

"Indeed. Do you know him?"

"I met him a few days ago in Gophna. You say he is ill? When I saw him, he was returning from Yerushaláyim and had regained his health."

Melchi nodded but sighed. "Yes, he returned in much better health, but he had a relapse. He can barely get out of bed now. I am going to visit him tomorrow. You can come along, if you like."

Ethan moved to the head of the table and clapped loudly. The buzz of voices and private conversations died away.

"Shalom and good health, my brothers and sisters in Yeshua the Messiah," he said, speaking loudly. "Thank you for coming again on this, the evening of Yom Reeshone, the first day, on which we meet together to celebrate the resurrection of Our Lord and Savior. Let us give thanks together for the meal He has provided."

סֶלָה

Approximately fifty people had crowded into the family room, eaten together, and now sat in huddled family groups to listen. Ethan stood before them next to the dying embers of the hearth where much of the meal had been prepared.

"Photina and I will be speaking to you again this week, although it was supposed to be Jehiel's turn. As you know, he is quite ill. I was with him this morning. He asks us to pray for him."

Photina rose and joined Ethan. Together, they kneeled and bowed their heads to pray. Taking turns, Ethan asked God for healing for Jehiel, Photina prayed for a woman who had lost her husband to a venomous snake bite and a feverish child. Ethan ended with a request for peace and resolution for a man involved in a dispute with a hostile neighbor. Darash did not recognize the names. Afterwards, Ethan took a seat on the hearth, facing the group. Photina sat beside him.

"Since there are many new faces in the room this evening," Photina said, glancing in Darash's direction, "Perhaps it is best that we give our testimony… to explain why we are here tonight and how we found a new reason to live."

Photina glanced at Ethan. He nodded and cleared his throat.

"I have always lived here," Ethan began. "My parents grew up here worshipping the ba'als, the gods of our ancestors. Indeed, not long ago, I was a familiar face in the brothels and high places of Samaria. I had no desire for a family or anyone to care for other than myself. I took a woman—Photina—into my house, but refused to marry her. I justified myself, saying she had been treated worse by the men she had married."

"Yes," Photina said. "Though I do not speak of it often, many of you know, at least, part of my story. My first husband beat me so badly I miscarried the child in my womb and became barren. After he died, I served my second husband like a slave, but he found another woman and gave me a certificate of divorce. My third husband, who was also unkind and violent toward me, finally divorced me because I could not give him children. My fourth was very old and died soon after we married. My fifth husband already had a wife. The woman abused me. Eventually, I ran away."

Photina paused. A woman in the front row in a yellow headdress, whose back was to Darash, put out a hand and touched Photina's knee. Photina smiled at her friend, took the offered hand in hers, and squeezed it.

"Though I was mistreated for much of my life, starting with my own father," Photina said, "I cannot blame the condition of my heart on my abusers. I chose to worship false gods, I told lies, I allowed my heart to fill with hatred, bitterness, and finally, despair."

"And I was certainly no better," Ethan said. "Despite all the suffering she endured, I failed to make her life any better. I found her by the side of the river, hungry and alone. But she was beautiful. So, I deceived myself into thinking that, by giving her a home, I was helping her. I even believed I had the right to use her. ...For two years, I treated her abominably."

Ethan rubbed the back of his neck. He glanced at Photina. A flicker of a smile passed from her lips to him before she picked up the story.

"Then one day the most unusual man passed through Sychar, where we were living at the time. Most God-fearing Jews avoid going through the region of Samaria, but this Jewish man came to Jacob's well at the noon hour and saw me there. I had come alone during the hottest part of the day merely so I could avoid the other women... to avoid the stares, the laughter, and the cruel remarks."

Photina chuckled. "This man actually spoke to me! He asked me to draw him some water to drink. I was surprised. A Jewish man speaking to a woman—a Samaritan woman—in public? It simply is not done! But this man was like no one else!"

"Indeed," Ethan agreed, laughing. "I met him myself. She came running back to the house in such a state of excitement, claiming the Messiah had come and that I had to go see for myself. 'Come,' she told me in a commanding tone she had never used before, 'Come see! A prophet has come to Samaria!'"

Ethan folded his hands before him and took a deep breath, as if contemplating the mystery of it all.

"As we walked to the well," Photina continued, "I tried to explain what had happened. This man, Yeshua, had asked me for some water but then he spoke of God and offered me something he called 'living water.' I did not understand. I even mocked him, believing him arrogant. I accused him of claiming to be greater than Jacob himself, who gave us the well. But then Yeshua looked into my eyes and told me everything about my life. Though I had never met him before, somehow he knew me." She paused, remembering. "Yeshua then told me that he, indeed, was the long-awaited Messiah and that one need not be a Jew nor live in Jerusalem to worship the true God. One need simply receive him and the eternal life he offers."

"From that moment on," Ethan said, no longer looking at the crowd, but gazing into Photina's eyes, "our lives changed. And, thanks to Yeshua, we never have to return to our old way of living again."

סֶ לָ ה

Night had fallen by the time Darash followed Ethan, Photina, and their daughter back to the shuk. He munched on a piece of sweetbread left over from the feast, his mind churning with all he had heard.

Yeshua... the Messiah. I know many believe it, but is simply declaring it enough proof?

Yeshua had done more than simply declare it, Darash realized. Yeshua had intimate knowledge about a woman he had never met from a region rarely visited by Jews. He spoke with unusual authority and grace.

But Simon the Sorcerer performed such tricks, as well. Yeshua could be a mere charlatan and trickster—or worse, a sorcerer in league with dark forces.

Darash chewed, unsatisfied with where his thoughts were taking him. *A great many Torah-trained Jews in Yerushaláyim believe that, though the Romans crucified Yeshua, he conquered the grave itself. ...Indeed, his tomb still lay empty—the massive stone cast aside to reveal the silent interior of the cave where he once lay.*

"Here we are, dear one," Ethan said to his daughter, as they approached the front door of their shop and home.

She yawned and stretched, sleepy from the long night and happy to be home.

"I must return to the inn," Darash said. "Thank you very much for your hospitality and for inviting me to come with you to the meeting. It was very… uh…." Darash searched for the right word.

"Oh, please stay with us," Photina said. "We would love to have you as our guest, for as long as you are in Samaria."

"Yes, by all means," Ethan added. "I can help fetch your belongings from the inn and bring them back here."

"Oh, thank you for the offer," Darash said, "but I do not travel alone. My traveling companion is still at the inn, and I cannot abandon him."

"Well, in that case," Ethan said, "if you would both like to stay with us tomorrow night, we would be happy to have you."

"Thank you, again. I will ask him." Darash was about to bid them goodnight, but the thought of Zephath brought something to mind. "Oh, I meant to ask if you happen to know of a woman from Gophna named

Phoebe. We believe she might be here… possibly staying with a leatherworker?"

"I know Phoebe," Photina said. "She is a close friend. She was at the meeting this evening, in fact."

"Really? Which one was she?"

"She was sitting next to me, holding my hand as Ethan spoke."

Darash tried to remember what the woman looked like. An image of a woman a bit older than Photina with a few strands of white hair escaping from beneath a yellow headdress came to mind. But he did not remember having seen her face.

"That was Phoebe of Gophna?"

"Yes. And she is staying with the leatherworker's family. I will tell you where they live, if you like."

XI

The Leatherworker

By the time Darash arrived back at the inn, Zephath was already snoring loudly and exuding the distinct smell of fermented grapes with each breath.

He would not have missed me after all.

Darash sighed and shook out his sleeping mat before moving it off the lump in the floor. He lay down and stared at the ceiling. A series of beams ran parallel to one another above his head, packed in between with mud-caked thatch. From time to time, as people moved above, a chunk fell off and landed on his bed mat and cloak, but as long as it did not land on his face it bothered him little. Once a spider had landed on his sister's face in the wee hours of the morning. She almost stopped his heart by sitting up in her bed screaming.

It was just a little spider.

As Darash lay there, waiting for sleep to claim him, his mind returned to Jehiel.

Strange that he is ill again so soon after returning home. I wonder what could be making him sick.

He thought of Jada, recalling the look on her face as she sat amongst the other girls ...as she ate ...as she listened to Ethan speak. Melchi said she was sad because her father was sick. So why was she at the meeting and not home with him?

Jada must be Jehiel's daughter by the shrine prostitute who died— the priestess of Molech. But Jehiel said he passed her off as an orphan. I wonder... does she know? Do Melchi or the others know?

Darash then remembered that Melchi had referred to Jada as Jehiel's adopted daughter. Evidently, Melchi, at least, was unaware she was, in fact, Jehiel's natural daughter.

That might cause issues with Jehiel when it came to betrothing her to someone like Melchi—a Gentile and, from the look of his clothing, not a very wealthy one. Furthermore, Melchi had said his stepfather was the one trying to arrange it. That meant Melchi's own father had either died or abandoned him. If they believed Jada was an abandoned child, as well, perhaps that gave them hope of a betrothal.

But Jehiel might not be so comfortable with the idea, since she is his own.

Darash reflected on Melchi's offer to let Darash join him on his visit to Jehiel. He decided to take the young man up on it. Darash liked Jehiel and wanted to wish him well, but he was also curious.

However, Darash intended to visit Phoebe first—without letting Zephath know where he was going. He wanted to find out what kind of situation she was in before alerting Zephath to her whereabouts. With Zephath's constant drinking and mood swings, Darash wanted the chance to gently break any bad news to him when they were alone.

"The leatherworker's house is the fifth house along the street just opposite the northern city well," Photina had said. "The street is lined with olive trees, and his house is the one with all the drying-racks in the yard. It should be easy to find."

סֶ לָ ה

The next morning, Darash rose early but let Zephath sleep. He took his breakfast of cheese, olives, and warm bread with him and asked the innkeeper to let Zephath know he would be back in an hour or so.

"The street just opposite the northern city well...." Darash said to himself as he moved north through the city. The inn where they were staying was at the south. After about a quarter of an hour of walking, he located the northern well. "A street lined with olive trees." He looked around. "They are all lined with olive trees." He frowned.

But those look bigger.

Darash headed west and entered an older section of town where the olive trees had grown fat, gnarled, and heavy with thick branches.

"The fifth house. On the left or right?" Darash tried to think back and realized Photina had not specified. However, as she had claimed, he had no trouble spotting it.

Indeed, the fifth house on the left could belong to none other than a leatherworker. Large wooden frames dotted the yard, stretched with hides in various stages of drying. Awnings had been erected over most of them to keep off the winter rains, and the rich, musty smell of cow and goat hides filled the air. In the middle of the yard sat two large bronze vats of water used for soaking large pieces of leather to soften them so they could be molded or cut. Herbs floated on the water to help with the softening process.

Though the morning was yet young, Darash spotted movement in the yard over the low outer wall. A man sat by the house, his back to Darash, bent over something at his feet.

"Shalom!" Darash called.

The leatherworker looked up and turned toward the sound of Darash's voice.

"Shalom," he said, setting down his tools. He had been working at a table with wooden legs and a stone surface. He was a large man with heavily muscled arms, broad shoulders, and a thick neck. He unlatched the outer gate from the inside and opened it. "What can I do for you, young man?"

"My name is Darash. I am from Yerushaláyim, but I stopped in Gophna. I gained a traveling companion there. Perhaps you know him. His name is Zephath."

"Zephath!" The man spit in disgust at the name. "Yes, I know him!"

Darash did not know what to say. He took a step back, worried the man might grab him and cast him back into the street. Perhaps Zephath was right after all, and this man had stolen his wife.

"You did well not to bring him here," the leatherworker said, brow pulled together in anger. "That man is a fool! But...." His voice softened and his brow relaxed. "I owe him a great deal."

Darash's brow rose in surprise.

"You do?"

"Indeed, I do. Come." He beckoned Darash to follow. "My name is Zuar." He led Darash toward the front door of the house. "Zephath and I grew up together. We were like brothers. We both lived in Gophna at that time. His house was right next to mine, and our mothers were close friends. We spent most of our days together—whether at home or at the House of the Book where we studied the Torah and our sums."

For a moment, the ridiculous image flicked through Darash's mind. A young Zephath sat at the feet of a rabbi, a book of sums in one hand and a large flask of wine in the other.

They passed a sack of white, powdered lime next to a workbench under one of the awnings. Next to it sat a stinking pile of dog dung in a clay bowl. The smell brought Darash back to reality. Both lime and dog feces were used to treat the hides before they could be hammered smooth. Darash held his breath as they passed.

Zuar led Darash passed a smoking fire pit, as well, which, from the smell and the singed hair around it, had recently been used to burn up the hair and flesh Zuar scraped from the hides. At the front door, Darash spotted a bench filled with various iron tools next to the stone-topped table. Upon it lay the items Zuar had been working on—a pair of leather soles for sandals, which he had been cutting out with a sharp, iron knife following a cloth pattern. They looked like they were a woman's size.

Once inside, Zuar indicated a place for Darash to sit on a low couch next to the northern wall. The home was a comfortable one, with soft pillows on the couch, wooden shelving on the walls, and a wide piece of leather on the floor used as a rug. A bundle of folded, freshly cured hides sat in one corner, making his home, like the street, smell of animal hides. Thankfully, most of the smell from the clay bowl and the fire pit remained outdoors.

Darash sat and accepted the glass of goat milk Zuar poured him from a leather pouch. After pouring himself a glass and taking a swig, Zuar joined Darash on the couch.

"When Zephath and I were young men, we quarreled."

"What about?"

"My father worked for his as a vineyard laborer. One year the land experienced a very bad drought, and his father had to let my father go, along with several other good workers. My father told my mother, sisters, and I that we had to move to Samaria where he knew he could find employment. I was angry, not really understanding why we had to leave Gophna. I hated the idea of living among heathens—as I then thought of them. It turned out alright, though. My father found work, and he secured an apprenticeship for me with a prominent leatherworker in town. But, before I left Gophna, I foolishly told Zephath his father had betrayed us." Zuar, who had been looking straight ahead as he told his story, now glanced at Darash. "You can imagine how he took that. He said some things. I said some things. I left his home upset, but I decided to return the next day and apologize. After all, Zephath was my closest friend. I tried to smooth things over before I left. But Zephath refused to forgive me."

"That is because my husband does not know when to quit."

Darash looked up to see Phoebe. He recognized they yellow headdress of the woman who had been sitting next to Photina last night at the meeting. She now stood in an arched bedroom doorway, one hand on the frame looking at them.

"The next day," she continued, "Zephath taunted Zuar mercilessly in front of the other boys and young men of the city. They came to blows and, like children, neither one of them apologized for their foolish behavior." She shot Zuar a look. "Zuar moved away shortly thereafter, and they have not spoken a word to one another since. I know, because I was there. But why are we talking of such things on such a beautiful morning? And you look familiar. Do I know you?"

Darash, though a little taken back by her abruptness of manner, stood and took a step toward her. "You must be Phoebe," he said. "It is good to meet you." He dipped his head in respect. "I am Darash ben Tuwr, of Yerushaláyim. You might have seen me at the meeting last night. I was there alone, but I am traveling with your husband, Zephath."

"Zephath…. He is here?" Her eyes opened wide. "Now?"

"He is at the inn at the southern end of the city."

"He came here for me?"

Darash nodded. "Yes."

"Oh, dear." Phoebe's right hand moved to her chest and she took a seat on a small bench opposite them, her composure gone. "This is not good. I am not ready."

"Worry not, Phoebe," Zuar told her. "We knew this day would come eventually."

"But what must he think of me? Whatever will I say to him?" Phoebe's face contorted with fear. Her breath came in short gasps.

Darash, feeling uncomfortable, sat down again.

Zuar moved toward Phoebe. He patted her left shoulder.

"We will deal with him. He cannot hurt you as long as you are in my home."

"Hurt me? I do not think he will hurt me," she said, "but he might…." She looked toward the front yard.

Darash heard it, too. The sound of the front gate opening, something crashing, and heavy footsteps.

"Zuar," a loud, demanding voice met them from the front yard. "Zuar, come out! I know you are in there! I know you have my wife!"

"It is Zephath," Darash said, recognizing the drunken cry and jumping to his feet. "Let me go out and—."

"No, no," Zuar said, waving Darash back and stepping between him and the front door. "He sounds drunk. He could be dangerous!"

The door swung open, banging loudly against the wall. Zephath stepped inside, his face painted with rage. His eyes landed on Zuar, crossed to where Phoebe sat, and then back to Zuar.

Zephath hauled back and punched Zuar as hard as he could across the jaw.

XII

Straying

Zuar stumbled back from the blow and lifted his left arm to block further attacks. Zephath moved forward and swung again. This time, his punch was blocked. Zuar, in much better physical shape, blocked the second blow with his left forearm and pulled back to level Zephath with a punch of his own.

"No! Stop!" Phoebe cried, moving to step between them. "Please stop!" She forced herself between the two men, like a lamb caught between two warring bighorn sheep.

Darash ran forward, fearing one of the men would inadvertently strike her in their mad struggle. But Zuar held back his fist, and Zephath took his eyes off his opponent to look at his wife.

"Stop now," she commanded again. "No fighting!"

Zephath and Zuar's eyes returned to the other. Though anger still marred their countenances, they shoved each other away to glare at one another over her head.

"That is enough!" She stood between them, arms extended with a hand on each of their chests as if to keep them at a distance. Only when she felt satisfied they would obey did she lower her hands.

"What is going on?"

All four of them turned toward the new voice. During the ruckus a woman had emerged unnoticed from the same bedroom doorway where Phoebe had been.

"You have another woman?" Zephath said, his rage still close to the surface.

"Yes," Zuar responded, matching his temper. "She is Mithcah, my wife!"

"Your wife! Then why have you stolen mine?" Zephath cried.

"What?" Phoebe and Zuar responded in unison.

"I have not stolen your wife," Zuar yelled, glancing between Zephath and Mithcah. "She came to be with my wife during her illness! Mithcah was very near death and...." Zuar stopped, eyes locked on his wife. Indeed she looked pale and thin. "And your wife... saved her." Zuar's voice lost its fervor, melting into relief and gratitude. "I will never be able to repay her for what she has done for me."

Zephath, dumbstruck, stared at Phoebe, saying nothing.

Phoebe moved to Mithcah's side, and Mithcah slipped a hand into Phoebe's but kept her eyes on Zephath.

"Thank you," she said, smiling, her eyes glossy. "Thank you so much for sending her to me. She was a gift from Adonai!"

"I... I...." Zephath muttered then paused. "You are welcome."

Zuar took a small step forward. He extended a hand to his old friend. Zephath stared at it for a moment, but then took it.

"I thank you, as well," Zuar said. "I heard you had married a woman renown for her medical skill and knowledge of the healing herbs. No one in Samaria could help my wife, so I sent you a message asking for her to come." He glanced at Phoebe. "And, to my great surprise, she came." He looked back to Zephath. "Can you forgive me for causing so much trouble? And for all the foolishness of our youth?"

For the first time since he burst into the room, a smile crossed Zephath's face. "Yes, my old friend! Indeed, I can—but only if you forgive me, as well. I have been such a fool! ...And, it seems, jealous for nothing."

The two men embraced and kissed one another on both cheeks, laughing.

"Come! Sit," Zuar invited everyone to sit together on the couch. "I will pour you some milk."

"No wine?" Zephath said.

"I think you have had enough of that already," Phoebe said, taking his arm. He laughed, nodding, and she smiled up at him. "It is good to see you again, my husband. I have missed you terribly."

"And I you."

"So you forgive me?"

"I am just glad to be wrong about why you left," Zephath told her as they sat together. "I understand why you did not tell me. ...I have been very difficult."

She smiled and took his right hand in both of hers. She gazed in his eyes for a moment, but then her countenance shifted as a new sadness spread across her face. "I know I have not been the ideal wife, either," she said. "If I had been able to give you sons...."

"What?" Zephath said, looking at her.

"You have every right to divorce me," Phoebe said. "I thought, perhaps, that was what you were planning. My leaving only made that possibility more real. That is why I stayed away so long." She glanced at Mithcah. "I could have left earlier, as Mithcah is almost fully recovered. But I was afraid of what I might find when I returned."

"You would have found a husband who was very, very glad to have his wife back," Zephath said, tearing up. He grabbed her and pulled her to his chest. "Sons or no sons."

Zuar, still standing awkwardly by with the pouch of milk and a cup in his hand, said, "Well, you may take her home whenever you like. But know you both have friends in Samaria."

"Let us go home at once," Zephath said, smiling with sudden excitement and releasing her but keeping a hand on each of her arms, "right now! This very morning!"

"Uh," Darash said. "We still have to find Nimrah."

Zephath's smile faded. "Oh… I almost forgot… Nimrah."

סֶלָה

Darash walked back toward the inn alone. Zuar had invited them to stay at their home instead, but Darash decided to take Ethan and Photina up on their previous invitation. He headed to the inn to collect his belongings, arrange for Zephath's cart to be loaded and driven to Zuar's home, and pay for their accommodations with money Zephath had supplied. He also wore new sandals and carried three additional new pair, one for each of his family, including Amah—gifts from Zuar for Darash's help, though Darash did not feel he had done much. After all, Zephath did end up finding Zuar's home on his own.

I wonder how he did that?

Darash had not asked, but he feared Simon the Sorcerer had something to do with it.

The morning's business at the shuk had blossomed into a bustle of activity during Darash's time at Zuar's home. Darash used his skinny frame to his advantage, expertly slipping between shoppers, dodging merchant-led donkeys, and side-stepping hand carts. As he circled a pottery stand he caught sight of Jada, Jehiel's daughter, on the far side of a row of merchants' tables. She was speaking to a tall man with hunched shoulders. They turned to head down a side street and, as they did so, Darash caught sight of the man's face.

Nimrah!

Darash intended to follow but, before he could get through the crowd, they disappeared down an alley between a row of two-story buildings. By the time Darash arrived at the last place he had seen them, they had vanished completely. He walked down the narrow street, looking for possible signs of them to no avail. They were gone.

Darash gave up and headed toward the inn.

Whatever would Nimrah be doing with Jehiel's daughter? Is she the one the shadchan, the matchmaker from the brothel in Shechem, set him up with? But she is soon to be promised to Melchi! What is going on?

סֶלָה

Darash tied Nekoda to a post outside Ethan and Photina's shop. Photina saw him from inside and came out to greet him.

"Ah, young Darash!" She smiled broadly. "I am so glad you decided to take us up on our offer."

"Thank you for inviting me to stay," Darash said. "I am not certain how long it will be, but I expect to return home soon."

"Oh, well, you are welcome to stay as long as you like." Photina led the way inside. "In expectation of your arrival, my husband will be butchering a lamb for supper, but I am afraid it will not be ready until this evening. In the meantime, my daughter is enjoying some bread and cheese inside. She would be happy to share some with you, if you are feeling hungry."

"That sounds wonderful!" Darash smiled. He followed Photina inside, but paused. "Oh, how might I get a message to Melchi? He invited me to join him on a visit to Jehiel today."

"Oh, that is no trouble. I expect my errand boy to arrive soon. I will send him to Melchi's home asking him to stop by here on his way."

"Thank you."

סֶלָה

Melchi arrived to find Darash being led around the shop by Ethan and Photina's daughter. She held his hand in one of hers and, with the other, pointed out all of her favorite items.

"This is my favorite of all," she said, pointing to a rag doll with blue braided cords for hair and a blue dress. "Blue is my favorite color."

"Mine, too," Darash said, as Melchi caught his eye from the front door. "Thank you for showing me around," he told her. "I have to go now, but I will be back later."

"Will you play a game with me when you get back?" she asked.

"Certainly." Darash smiled, and she released his hand.

"I am glad you decided to join me," Melchi confessed as the two young men walked away from the shuk toward a section of middle-class living quarters. "I get nervous around sick people. I never know what to say."

"I feel the same sometimes," Darash said. "My mother always knows what to do, though. She is often called when a woman goes into labor or when one of our friends falls ill. She says the best thing to do is to pray for them so they can hear you."

"I am not very good at praying out loud."

"Neither am I," Darash laughed.

Despite Melchi's obvious Gentile heritage, Darash liked him. Melchi's ready smile and open manner put Darash at ease, even as Darash's Jewish convictions pricked his conscience. *He is helping me, in a round-about way, to find Nimrah. Surely Millah will reward me for finding him and bringing him home. So, this is business.*

Darash noticed a small bag in Melchi's left hand.

"Are you bringing them a gift?"

"Yes. Just some food and their weekly allotment of silver from the other believers. My stepfather told me to bring it. He helps with the collections and distributions."

Darash smiled. Melchi's stepfather was undoubtedly an honest man, given the worn look of Melchi's cloak.

"So, tell me about Jehiel's illness," Darash said. "Have you visited him before?"

"Yes, with my stepfather. It is not proper that I go alone, given my relationship with Jada." Melchi led Darash to a side street on the right. "This way," he said, then resumed. "He fell ill about a week and a half ago. The physicians thought he might die. Not wanting to believe it, Jehiel hired someone to take him to Jerusalem to seek medical help there. Jerusalem has more to offer than we do. From what I heard, he began to feel better, even as he traveled, and by the time he arrived, three days later, he was nearly healed."

"Yes, that is what I heard, as well. I met him in Gophna a few days ago. He appeared perfectly well. When did he fall sick again?"

"The same day he returned."

סֶ לָ ה

Jada opened the door to Melchi's knock. Unlike the homes of the wealthier inhabitants of the city, their front door opened directly into the street. After Melchi greeted her and introduced Darash, she led them inside their one-room home. They had to step down into the room, which rested at a lower level than the street. A single oil lamp burned on a table in the far corner, but sufficient light filtered through the small window in the wall above the kitchen side of the room.

Indeed, if there had been any doubt, Darash now felt certain it was Jada whom he had seen with Nimrah earlier. Same hair, same stature, same clothing. He wanted to ask her about it, but decided to wait.

Jehiel lay on a sleeping pallet on the floor against the far wall under several blankets. A three-legged stool—closely resembling Ethan's creations—sat nearby topped with a cup and a bowl with remnants of some sort of stew in it.

"Here you go," Melchi said, handing Jada the sack.

"Thank you," she said, taking the bag and looking him in the eye with familiarity. She turned to Darash, "Who are you?"

"A new friend," Melchi answered for him. "His name is Darash. He was at the meeting last night, remember? He claims to know your father."

Jada's eyebrows narrowed a bit. "How do you know him?"

"I do not know him well," Darash said. "I met him in Gophna a week ago. Is it alright if I sit with him for a few moments?"

She glanced at her father then back at Darash. She nodded. "You may if you like. But I am afraid he is not very alert today. He has become delirious. You must not pay too much attention to what he says."

Darash moved to kneel next to Jehiel. As he did so he overheard Jada, in a lowered voice, ask Melchi, "Has your father said anything more?"

"No." Then Melchi said something Darash did not overhear.

Darash turned his attention to Jehiel and was amazed at the difference. The man who had told such a lively story only last week now lay with eyes partly open, breathing erratically. His face looked flushed.

How could he have deteriorated so quickly? Unless....

"Jehiel," Darash said. "I am Darash. I have come to visit you. We met in Gophna several days ago. Do you remember?"

Jehiel moaned at the sound of Darash's voice. He fought to focus on the source of the voice.

"Yeshua," he muttered. "Yeshua, is that you?"

"No," Darash said. "It is Darash of Yerushaláyim. We met in Gophna. I heard you were ill, so I have come to see you."

"Yeshua… Yeshua…."

Darash glanced up helplessly at the others.

"I cannot stand it when he begins to talk that way," Jada said. "Forgive me."

She opened the front door and stepped outside.

Melchi moved to follow her, but glanced over his shoulder and said, "She is upset. I will be right back." He followed Jada out and closed the door behind him.

Darash sighed. He hoped Jada would return soon so he could ask her about Nimrah. He had little hope of getting any information out of Jehiel. Looking at the man before him, his heart grew heavy.

What can I do for this man? I am no physician. And the physicians of Samaria have not been able to do much for him.

Suddenly, an idea occurred.

Phoebe! She brought Mithcah back from the brink of death. Perhaps she can help Jehiel, as well.

Darash moved to stand up, intending to fetch her from Zuar's home, but felt a tug at his arm. Jehiel had managed to grab hold of his sleeve.

"I remember you," he breathed, finally focusing on Darash's face.

"Shalom, Jehiel," Darash said. "I am sorry you are so ill. I am going to see if I can get you some help."

"No... no. There is no help for me."

"But there might be. I know a woman who—"

"It is... too late," Jehiel said between breaths. "Adonai has judged me... and found me guilty."

"What? What are you talking about?"

"The sins of my youth. I will soon pay... the price."

Jehiel's eyes closed and his fingers lost their grip on Darash's sleeve. He breathed out a long sigh. Just before Jehiel lost consciousness again, Darash thought he heard two words escape his lips.

"She knows."

XIII

The Mandrake

Darash ran through Samaria, dodging people and objects as best he could. He tore through the shuk, leapt over a hand cart, and accidentally toppled a pile of winter gourds as he slid past a fruit stand.

"Hey!" The shopkeeper shook his fist at Darash's back.

"Sorry," Darash cried as he spun but did not slow.

Before long the northern well came into view, and he raced toward the street lined with large olive trees where Zuar lived. He tried the front gate and found it still unlocked. He barely noticed the foul smells of the yard as he pounded on the front door.

"Darash!" Zuar said, opening it. "Come in, come in! Whatever is the matter?"

"Please," Darash said, barely able to get the word out between gasps and ignoring Zuar's invitation to enter. "I need Phoebe to come with me. Now!"

סֶלָה

"You were right," Phoebe told Darash as she knelt next to Jehiel, holding open one eye and looking at his oddly dilated pupil in light of the oil lamp Zephath held for her. "He has been poisoned. Probably with dried mandrake root, ground to a powder and added to his food or drink. I have seen the same symptoms in a child who had accidentally eaten some. His mother, who had been barren for six years—since the birth of her son—was using the root, thinking it would help her conceive again. Instead, it killed the child she did have." She turned to Zephath. "Hand me my satchel please, husband."

"Will this man die?" Zephath asked, handing her the satchel.

"He is in Yeshua's hands now," she said, retrieving a small clay vial from the bag. "But I intend to do all I can for him."

"Yeshua?" Zephath asked, receiving no further comment from his wife.

She handed the vial to Darash, along with a bowl. "This is mustard seed powder. Add enough clean water to make it into a paste in this bowl. But do not get water from any container in the house. Go next door to one of the neighbors. And ask if you can have some goat's milk, too."

Darash hurried to do as she asked and returned in short order, having been successful on both counts.

"The bowl first, please," she asked, and took the bowl from Darash's extended hand.

With her finger, Phoebe scooped out some paste and placed it on Jehiel's tongue.

"The milk now."

Darash handed her the skin of goat's milk he had received from the neighbor woman. Phoebe gently lifted Jehiel's head and induced him to drink enough milk to wash the mustard paste down. She repeated the process three more times until he started to rebel at the strong taste.

"Now we wait," she said, seeming satisfied with her progress. "The mustard powder will do its work before long."

"And what is that?" Zephath asked.

"It will make him vomit."

Zephath made a face, but said nothing.

"We need to purge his body of the toxins any way we can." Phoebe put a hand on Jehiel's brow as she spoke. "Once we are certain there is nothing left in his stomach, we will need to boil some mint in water. There are some dried mint leaves in my bag. That will help with the stomach cramps."

Jehiel groaned and rolled to his side.

"Husband, grab that rag," she motioned toward a scrap of cloth in the kitchen. "If he vomits, we will catch it in that." She turned to Darash. "My son, you have already done a great deal to help this man… but I need you to do me another favor."

"Anything."

"You know Ethan and Photina, correct? You came with them to the meeting."

"Yes. I am staying with them."

"Good. I need you to fetch Photina for me. She will help me care for Jehiel. Ask her to bring a pot of clean water and cooking utensils. We cannot trust anything in this house. Tell her to also bring more goat's milk, some barley porridge, and juniper oil—perhaps she can purchase the oil from one of the physicians. Three to five drops a day will aid his body in purging the poison over the next couple of weeks." Phoebe looked back and Jehiel and sighed. "I only hope we discovered the truth in time."

Darash moved to the door to obey.

"Oh, and Darash. One more thing," Phoebe said. "Ask Ethan to look for Jada. Whomever is with her might be in danger."

"Melchi is with her now," Darash said.

"Then you should hurry."

סֶ לָ ה

Photina wasted no time following Darash's directions. She gathered the items she had on hand, left her daughter with the neighbor, and left to visit the home of a physician to inquire about the juniper oil.

Ethan and Darash went the opposite direction toward the home of Melchi, with Ethan leading the way.

"He does not live far," Ethan said. "Just a couple of streets this way."

They passed out of the market area into a narrow alley lined with homes and businesses. Rounding a corner onto another narrow road, Ethan pointed ahead.

"Just there," he said. "Left down that street and his is the third door down on the right."

Ethan's knock was answered by Melchi himself.

"Oh, you are home!" Ethan said, trying to mask his concern.

"Yes," Melchi glanced one to the other and opened the door wider. "Would you like to come in?"

"No, we just came by to thank you for delivering the food and silver."

"Certainly." Melchi turned to Darash. "What happened? I went back to find you at Jehiel's home, but you had left."

"Oh, yes. Forgive me," Darash said. "Jehiel looked so bad that I ran to find Phoebe. She is with him now."

Understanding lit Melchi's eyes. "Oh, I am sorry to hear that. I knocked on the door and when no one answered, I knew you had gone. I was afraid you had gotten lost." He glanced down and bit his lower lip. "I had no idea Jehiel's condition had gotten so bad, though. I thought he might be resting. Now I realize I should have gone inside and stayed with him."

"No, no," Darash said. "Do not concern yourself on that account. He was unconscious and there was nothing you could have done. Besides, Phoebe is with him now and doing what she can for him."

"Does she know what is the matter with him? Does she think he will recover?"

Darash glanced at Ethan, and Ethan hurried to respond, "Time will tell. We must be vigilant in our prayers for him."

Melchi nodded. "Of course. Certainly."

"And, in the meantime," Ethan added, "do you happen to know where Jada went? We would like to speak to her, as well… about her father's condition."

"She is not at home?" Melchi asked.

"No. I have not seen her since she left with you," Darash said, aware that his words sounded a bit like an accusation of impropriety.

"We spoke briefly around the corner from her home and then she said she needed to run an errand—I assumed she needed to make some purchases. I returned to Jehiel's and found you gone, so I came home. I have not seen her since then." Melchi paused. "Are you sure you do not want to come inside?"

"No, no," Ethan said. "We must be going. Perhaps we will find Jada still in the shuk making her purchases. She should know about her father's worsening condition."

"Of course," Melchi said. "Would you like me to help you find her?" He reached for his cloak on a peg near the door.

"No need," Ethan said. "I will let you know what happens."

"I will pray for you to find her soon," Melchi said as they left.

"We need to find Jada," Darash told Ethan as they walked back toward Ethan's shop. A quick search of the shuk had revealed nothing. "I hardly know her. Do you know where she might have gone?"

"Sorry, no. I have no idea." Ethan scratched the back of his neck. "She and Jehiel have been a part of our community of believers for less than a year. I have gotten to know Jehiel quite well, but my familiarity with Jada is considerably less. She is a quiet sort." Ethan paused, then took another approach. "Melchi said he followed her out of the house, they took a short walk and spoke for a while, and then she left. Melchi returned to Jehiel's home, but you were gone by then as well."

"I doubt she returned to the house. She was not there when I arrived with Phoebe and Zephath."

"Perhaps she saw you returning with them and became frightened."

"Perhaps. …Do you know a man named Nimrah?" Darash asked. "He is not from here. He is from Yerushaláyim and one of the reasons Zephath and I came to Samaria. He is Zephath's nephew, and we are trying to find him. I saw him with Jada this morning."

"I have not heard of him. Why did he come to Samaria?"

"He went to Shechem to speak to a shadchan who works out of a brothel there. She sent him here to meet a woman. That is all we know."

Ethan let out a deep groan and crossed his arms across his chest. He stopped walking and leaned against a wall. Darash stopped as well.

"I think I know where he might be," Ethan said.

"Really? Where?"

"There is a two-story building at the edge of town," Ethan said. "It is an inn, but also a brothel."

Darash's eyes widened, but he said nothing.

"I know," Ethan said. "That is bad enough, but this brothel is also controlled by a local cult. They use it as a place to lodge foreign, foolish young men, charging exorbitant prices, charming them with wine, women, and false promises until their guest no longer have any money. Once a man's purse is drained, he is driven out of the city in a horse cart, beaten, and abandoned… or worse."

"How do we get Nimrah out of there?" Darash asked.

"That, my young friend, will not be easy."

סֶ לָ ה

The following morning, Ethan again dropped his daughter off at the neighbor's house, and he and Darash went to visit Jehiel. Photina opened the door at their knock and let them in. Entering, they saw Phoebe asleep in a seated position, her head resting on her arms across the three-legged stool.

"Phoebe and I were here all night," Photina said, shaking her head with worry. "Jada never returned. I hope she is alright."

"If she is mixed up with the people I think she is, she is likely not alright," Ethan responded, his tone serious. "Has Jehiel said anything more?"

"No—at least nothing we could make out. Phoebe says he was hallucinating. …He has had a very difficult night. Now he sleeps. But what is this about Jada?"

"She may be in a great deal of trouble," Ethan said "but there is nothing we can do for her right now. I will tell you everything I know later, but it looks like you have had a difficult night, as well," Ethan put a hand to her cheek and tucked stray hairs behind her ear. "You and Phoebe should go home now and try to get some rest. Darash and I can stay with Jehiel."

"He already looks much better," Darash said, noting the lighter hue of Jehiel's skin and placid breathing.

"Yes, thanks to Phoebe's skill. I knew she had come to stay with a sick friend, but I had no idea how good a physician she is."

"Yeshua was gracious to send her to us for a time such as this," Ethan observed, and Photina nodded her agreement.

They keep talking about Yeshua as if he is synonymous with Adonai.

The realization made Darash uncomfortable, but he said nothing.

Photina moved to Phoebe and grasped her shoulder, waking her. "Ethan and young Darash are here," she said.

Phoebe roused and moved to Jehiel's side again. She opened his tunic at the neck and slipped her hand onto his bare chest.

"His heart is beating steadily," she said and sighed with relief. "He seems much improved."

"Indeed, he does," Ethan agreed. "Darash and I will care for him now. Go home and get some rest."

Phoebe, satisfied with Jehiel's progress, agreed but stayed long enough to give the men specific directions as to Jehiel's care and treatment.

"Let him sleep for now," she said. "He has had a restless night. When he wakes, try to get him to drink some of this goat's milk. We have added juniper oil to it, so he might not like the taste, but make him drink it anyway. Then, if you are able, get him to eat some of the porridge your wife brought. Have him to drink as much clean water as you can, and be sure not to use any food, containers, or cooking utensils that you find in the house."

When the women left, Ethan and Darash found places to sit on some old pillows next to the wall. They spoke little, not wanting to disturb Jehiel's sleep. As noon approached, Jehiel began to rouse.

"Jehiel," Ethan said, moving to Jehiel's side, "how are you feeling?"

Jehiel groaned but focused on Ethan's face. "You should have let me die."

Ethan's brow furrowed. "How can you say such a thing? Phoebe says you will likely recover. We have much to be thankful for."

Jehiel lifted a hand, covered his face, and wept.

"Jehiel… Jehiel," Ethan said, putting a hand on his friend's chest. He looked at Darash, a helpless look on his face.

Darash scooted to Ethan's side. "You discovered the source of your illness when you immediately become ill again after returning from your trip."

A nod.

"But you told no one, because you believe you deserve to die."

Jehiel wept louder, but nodded, still covering his face.

"And you are afraid for your daughter… because you believe she is the one who has been poisoning you."

Jehiel's weeping turned to sobs.

"She found out," Darash said softly, "about you and the woman who was her mother."

"She was innocent! Innocent!" Jehiel's chest shook with the force of his weeping. Great rivers of tears streamed from his face toward the rolled blanket beneath his head. "And my guilt destroyed her!"

סֶ לָ ה

"I have tried to get close to Jada over the past months," Photina said over dinner later that evening.

Phoebe and Zephath had relieved Ethan and Darash an hour earlier, intending to stay the night with Jehiel. Zephath had promised to come alert Ethan if Jada returned.

"She is not an easy person to get close to," Photina continued. "She keeps to herself, does not participate in the singing or discussions, and has made no real friends among the other girls—though they, too, have tried to draw her into their circle."

Darash took a bite of lamb. With all the excitement of the previous evening, Ethan had postponed the preparation of the special meal. But the wait had been worth it. The meat had been slowly roasted on a spit in the back yard. They would eat as much as they wanted this evening, Photina would dry some of it for later, and the rest would be given to other members of their group of fellow followers of Yeshua.

"Jada seems to know Melchi rather well," Darash observed, recalling how the two had slipped out to talk a walk together—something a traditional Jewess would never do.

Photina frowned. "Yes."

Ethan spoke up. "Melchi is a nice young man, but he has only recently come to the faith. Until the recent marriage of his mother to his stepfather, he was her sole support. He often engaged in… less than honorable means to bring money into the home. I believe he has tried to put away those old ties, but the past has a way of… of…."

"Staking a claim," Darash said.

Ethan looked at him and nodded.

"I have been wondering where the mandrake root came from," Darash said. "Would either Melchi or Jada know where to find it?"

"Hmm…. I know not. Perhaps," Ethan mused, as he took a piece of bread and dipped it in the leek and fava bean soup Photina had made to accompany the lamb. "It grows wild not far from town, but in the winter it would be much easier to simply purchase it."

"Who would sell it?"

"Since it is so poisonous, normal physicians and herbalists are careful about giving it out. And, as the plant is most often used to enhance fertility, it is unlikely an unmarried person would seek it from any of them. Doing so would open them up to suspicion of promiscuity or even adultery. I doubt either Melchi or Jada would risk such a thing."

"So it must have come from a different source. Would someone like Simon the Sorcerer possess it?"

"Certainly, but I doubt Jada would be able to afford his prices." Ethan paused, chewing thoughtfully. "Tomorrow I can take you to the part of town where we might find the young man you search for and, possibly, Jada as well."

"Ethan," Photina said, looking at him with concern crossing her brow, "you know that place is dangerous—especially for you. You said you would never return."

He sighed and looked at his wife. "I know… but I will not be going there for the reasons I used to go. And, if we are to help our friends, I do not see what choice we have."

XIV

Whispers of the Past

Ethan and Darash waited until the next morning before heading to the inn Ethan had described.

"It is best to catch them in the morning," he explained. "They are much less… lively."

They left the main part of the city of Samaria, crossed through the Roman Acropolis, and passed the theatre until they reached a narrow, sloping street into a valley populated with older buildings. The homes in this section of the old city had crumbled on the edges. Wide cracks in the stucco revealed mud brick underneath. A woman wearing a tattered goatshair robe spotted them from across the street and approached.

"A prutah for your fortune," she offered. "A prutah for your fortune."

"No," Ethan told her, holding up one hand against her without slowing, his voice firm. "If you are hungry, go see Photina. She will give you something to eat."

At the sound of Photina's name, the woman's placid supplications disappeared, and her brow pinched together in the middle.

"Feh!" She spat and called to their backs, "I would starve first!"

"As I suspected," Ethan breathed, speaking too quietly for her to now hear him, as the distance between them widened.

Darash could not help but looking back over his shoulder at her.

"Why does she react so?" he asked.

Ethan sighed. "Like many in town, she believes people like Photina and I have betrayed them. When we chose to follow Yeshua as the true Messiah, we turned our backs on the lives we once lived. They resent us for it."

"She knew your wife's name, but she did not know you."

"She does know me, and I remember her well. She simply did not recognize me." He chuckled. "It is incredible how different my wife and I are now—though only a few years have passed since the day she met Him."

Ethan pointed Darash to a side street—more of an alley—and they headed in that direction.

"There," Ethan said, indicating the only two-story building on this road. "That is the inn—the brothel—where your friend might be staying."

He is no friend of mine, Darash though, but said nothing.

The house—a larger structure than the ones around it, yet in no better condition—sat silently watching the street. No activity moved within, no sounds of the morning meal being prepared or eaten met their ears as Ethan and Darash arrived at the outer gate, despite that the sun had risen well over an hour ago.

A large dog with brown, matted hair, looked up at them from a patch of weeds where he lay and snarled. Darash took a step back. Ethan ignored it. As Darash watched it, the dog vomited without standing up, dropped his head into his own vomit, and closed his eyes.

"What is wrong with it?" Darash asked.

"He is drunk."

"The dog?" Darash had never heard of such a thing.

Ethan nodded. "The people here are nothing like your friends in Yerushaláyim."

Ethan moved to a place in the outer door where a piece of the wood was missing. The break had created a hole large enough for a man's fist to pass through. He leaned over and peered into the inner courtyard.

"Hey, you!" he cried, causing Darash to jump. "Wake up! Come open this door! I have come to speak to one of your guests." Ethan paused a moment. "Come over here," he yelled at whoever he saw lying in the yard, "before I tell Bagad what a worthless, lazy slave you are!"

Bagad! Could it be?

A groan of frustration and the sound of movement—sandals shuffling in the dirt—met them.

"He already knows," the servant mumbled but obeyed, removing the locking post from the inside of the outer gate and opening the door. "Oh." He perked up when he saw the source of the voice and smiled. "Hello, Ethan. You have finally returned." Bloodshot eyes slid to Darash. He looked him up and down. "And you have brought us a new friend."

"Nothing of the sort! Get out of my way!"

Ethan pushed him aside and headed toward the front door. Darash followed, stepping wide around the slave, not liking the way man's eyes followed. Ethan flung the front door open, not bothering to knock.

"You may want to avert your eyes," he told Darash, but then changed his mind. "Actually, you should wait out here."

Darash moved away from the entrance, but not before catching a glimpse of the darkened interior and a floor covered with bodies of sleeping people—men and women together—in various stages of dress. Darash moved to stand with his back against the front wall of the inn, trying not to make eye-contact with the servant, who stood staring at him brazenly, a half-smile playing at his lips.

The sounds of moans and slurred complaints emanated from inside as Ethan searched for Nimrah, rolling sleepers onto their backs with his foot and calling Nimrah's name. At one point Darash colored deeply at the sound of a woman's voice.

"Ethan, my love! You have come back to me! Come, come! Let me remind you of what you are missing!"

"Let go of me, woman," came Ethan's harsh reply. "Where is the one called Nimrah?"

Ethan received an answer and a moment later emerged, leading a sleepy-eyed Nimrah before him.

"Is this he?" Ethan asked Darash.

"It is," Darash smiled for the first time since they had arrived.

"Who are you and where are you taking me?" Nimrah rebelled, squinting against the bright morning sun.

"I am Darash ben Tuwr of Yerushaláyim," Darash told him, taking him by the arm to lead him away from the brothel. "Your mother and father asked me to look for you and to bring you home. Your father has been ill and your mother is worried. You must come with us."

"No!" Nimrah wrenched free from his grip and stumbled a few paces away. "I am not going back! Not without my wife!"

"Your wife?" Darash and Ethan asked simultaneously.

"Yes. My beautiful wife-to-be, Jada. She will be mine very soon!"

"You say you are betrothed?" Ethan asked, facing him. "To a girl named Jada?"

"Yes, and without my mother or father's help, too! And she is beautiful! Wait till you see her."

"Yes, yes…. They are all beautiful." Ethan shot a sideways glance at Darash.

"Nimrah," Darash said, "Where is Jada? Is she here with you?"

"No, no." Nimrah frowned and shook his head. "She will not stay with me. She is not mine… all the way, yet."

"Then why not come with us for now? We can take you to—"

"What are you doing here?" The voice boomed from the front door. A man hung in the threshold, a hand on each side of the frame, staring with loathing at Ethan. Darash noticed several thin scars on the man's forearms.

Ethan turned to face the man. His eyes and jaw hardened in thinly veiled contempt.

"Hello, Bagad."

The man staring at Ethan with glossy-eyed hatred was tall and thin. A hooked nose angled toward his chin where a sparse beard grew. From the description Hazaiah and Eliana had given the magistrate, this man must be the same one who befriended the couple and their child the day before he was stolen from them.

"What are you doing disturbing my honored guest?"

Darash did not like the sarcasm with which Bagad pronounced the word 'honored.' But Nimrah, not seeming to notice, moved closer to Bagad and readjusted his robe, which had become dislodged from one of his shoulders.

"Yes," Ethan responded. "I know how you honor your guests, Bagad. But this man has a friend here, sent from Yerushaláyim by his family to fetch him. Let us take him back with us. Surely you have no further use for him. We will take him off your hands, and you can keep whatever he has paid you."

To Darash's surprise, Bagad seemed to be seriously considering Ethan's offer. His eyes dropped to the ground for a moment, then he hacked up a wad of phlegm left over from the night's revelry, and spit into the dirt.

"Very well... But he still owes me five denarii."

"What? I do not," Nimrah cried, taking a step back.

"How much do you have left, Nimrah?" Ethan asked.

"But I do not owe him anything! Not until I get my wife."

"How much do you have?"

Nimrah felt in his belt. "Two denarii and a half. …And some prutot."

"Give it to me."

Nimrah handed it to Ethan, and Ethan added enough coins from his own belt to make up the difference. He approached Bagad, who extended his hand to receive the money, but Ethan hesitated.

"The girl, Jada," Ethan said. "Where is she?"

"I have been cooperative enough for one day," Bagad sneered.

סֶ לָ ה

Ethan and Darash let Nimrah away from the brothel toward Zuar's home, where they hoped to reunite him with his uncle, Zephath. Nimrah kept looking back and asking why he had to go.

"Where are you taking me?"

"We told you already," Darash said, unable to hide the annoyance in his voice. "We are going to Ethan's home. When you are feeling better, your uncle, Zephath, and I will take you back to Yerushaláyim."

"But what about my wife? When will she come?"

"Jada will not be going with you," Ethan said. "She is not legally betrothed to you, as her father knew nothing about it."

"But Bagad is her father!"

"No, he is not. Bagad lied to you. He is a trickster and a very dangerous man. You should be glad we got you out of there when we did."

"But I gave him my money!" Nimrah swung around to head back.

Ethan grabbed him by one arm and Darash grabbed hold of the other.

"Oh, no! You cannot go back! Your money is gone," Ethan said, as they pulled him back around and got him moving toward town again. "You must accept that and come with us."

Despite Nimrah's complaints and his seeming inability to comprehend what had happened, Ethan and Darash managed to get him safely to the leatherworker's home.

"Ugh! What is that smell?" Nimrah cried upon approaching the front gate.

"Shh," Ethan said with force. "Surely it can smell no worse here than the brothel where you just were."

"That was no brothel! That was a the most reputable inn in Samaria!"

Ethan just shook his head, and knocked on the gate.

An hour later, Darash stopped by Jehiel's house to see if Zephath was still there with Phoebe, as they had not found him at Zuar's house. He was.

"Nimrah has been found," Darash announced with a moderate smile. "He is not happy about it, but he is at Zuar's home with Ethan. They sent me to fetch you."

"Good, good!" Zephath said. "Then we can finally start making plans to return to Gophna."

"Yes… almost."

"Eh?"

"There is one more thing I must do here first," Darash said.

"Very well. I suppose we can stay another day or two." Zephath glanced at Phoebe who nodded her consent. "After all, Jehiel might still need my wife's help a bit longer."

"Yes, thank you, husband," Phoebe said, "but he is improving rapidly."

Indeed, Jehiel was no longer lying on his pallet, but sitting, propped up on pillows and steadily eating a bowl of barley porridge.

"I will fetch the neighbor woman to sit with him," Phoebe told her husband, "so we can go greet your nephew."

"I will do it. I can stop and ask her on my way out," Darash offered. "She will remember me. I will ask her to come."

"Thank you," Phoebe smiled.

סֶ֫לָה

Moments later Darash retraced his steps and returned to the section of town they had just left. He was not sure what he hoped to discover. All he knew was that he needed to find out more about Bagad… the only link Hazaiah and Eliana had to their missing son.

Darash turned left one street early, hoping to find a way to angle around to the brothel from a different direction and avoid being waylaid by the old fortune-telling woman or being spotted by those who might have seen him there earlier. The streets had come alive with people leaving their homes and walking along the street toward the shuk or toward one of the city gates and the surrounding pasturelands to check on herds and flocks. He found it easier to blend into the background.

Darash located a patch of earth under an ancient olive tree where he could sit and watch the brothel without being conspicuous. He dropped to the ground, leaned against the tree, and focused on the wooden gate with a hole in the door. He waited a long time.

Each time the door opened, Darash perked up and watched with interest. The servant came and went, men stumbled out holding their heads, women with rumpled clothing filtered out in pairs. The noon hour approached, and no Bagad.

He may have left while I was helping Ethan get Nimrah to Zuar's home.

Darash frowned. His stomach growled with hunger. Photina would be serving that delicious lamb again right about now—possibly holding the meal for him. He shifted, uncertain what to do.

It sure would taste good with some olives, cheese, and warm bread…. She might even give me some warm milk with honey if I asked for it.

Darash moved to stand up. At that moment, the brothel's outer door opened again. Bagad stepped out.

He had changed clothes, washed his face, and combed his hair. He walked briskly, moving toward Darash but not seeing him. He kept his eyes straight ahead. After he passed, Darash followed.

Darash kept about half a stone's throw behind, so as not to be detected. Bagad led him to the end of the row of crumbled homes, then left, back toward the heart of the city. They came to a section of nicer homes. These had gardens, well-kept trees, flat stucco, and newer rooves. Finally, Bagad arrived at a house with a low fence surrounding a large front yard. As he opened the outer gate, the front door of the home opened. A woman came out of the house. A child was with her, holding her hand—a little boy who looked to be about four years old.

XV

The Sign of Molech

"He has been waiting to play with you all morning," the woman said, a hint of reproach in her voice.

"You know I have business to conduct," Bagad growled. "Besides, after tonight it will all be over. We will be able to leave this place."

Darash stood at the edge of Bagad's yard, just behind a higher outer wall of the neighbor's property. Though he kept out of sight, their voices reached him.

"I am here now," Bagad said. The tone of his voice changed and he asked, "What game would you like to play?"

The child said something unintelligible, but Bagad seemed to understand.

"No, no, Abba has a headache this morning. Let us play a quiet game."

From down the street came the noise of a man calling to his mules. Darash spotted them coming around a corner and heading his way. When they passed in front of Bagad's home, Darash took his opportunity. He moved along with the team of mules, using them as a cover so he could get a better view of the house with less likelihood of being spotted.

As he passed, Darash noticed that the woman had gone back inside, but Bagad sat on a bench with the child. The boy had a reed hoop in his hands. He was playing with it, but putting it over Bagad's head like an odd-shaped necklace, and Bagad patiently let the child do so. But what Darash found most interesting was that, as the boy lifted his arms to reach Bagad's neck, his sleeves slipped down on his arms.

Nothing. No marks at all.

סֶ֫לָה

A great clatter of hooves against stone and the jingle of horse bridles emanated from the new, colonnaded Roman road. A group of four Roman soldiers approached Darash from a distance as he walked back toward Ethan and Photina's home. Leading the group, on a black steed, sat Magistrate Quintus Arrius.

Quintus caught sight of Darash and pulled up his horse to a sharp stop in front of the youth.

"Darash!" he cried, sounding gruff but smiling. "Whatever are you doing in Samaria? The last time I saw you I dropped you off in Gophna."

"Yes, my search for Nimrah took me farther than I thought."

"Who?"

"Nimrah."

The magistrate's face remained blank.

"Millah and Obed's son," Darash prompted. "The dyers' of Yerushaláyim. Their son went missing and asked you to find him, so—"

"Oh! Right, right, Nimrah," Quintus said, the light of recollection dawning in his eyes.

"I found him," Darash said, "in case you still…." He trailed off.

The magistrate was no longer paying attention. One of his men had said something in Latin about whoever they were supposed to meet.

He glanced back at Darash before continuing on his way, and said, "Come ask for me at the acropolis if you are in need of work. My errand boy fell ill. But I cannot speak now. The cult of Molech has been very busy of late."

Darash watched in stunned silence as Quintus and his men resumed their course and disappeared beyond a bend in the road.

סֶ֥לָה

Zuar's wife, Mithcah, welcomed Darash into the house. The noontime meal had already passed, so he was pleasantly surprised when she offered him something to eat. She placed a large bowl of mixed olives and almonds before him. He ate them all.

"How is Jehiel doing?" Darash asked Zephath, chewing.

"Still very weak, but much better. Phoebe believes he will make a complete recovery. She is there with him now." Zephath sat across from Darash and watched in dismay as the youth ate by the handful.

"Oh, before I forget, I must tell let you know that Ethan paid nearly three denarii for Nimrah's safe release from the man who was holding him."

Zephath groaned in frustration and drew a hand over his face. "How could my brother have such a fool for a son?" He sighed. "I will repay Ethan. It was good of him to do so. Few others would consider my nephew worthy of such an expense!"

Darash cringed and glanced toward the back bedroom. Nimrah was likely in the house somewhere.

"Fear not. He will not overhear," Zephath said. "We fed him and then he passed out on my bed. A moment ago I accidentally dropped a clay jar and it shattered. He did not even flinch."

"Well, then, uh… I also have a question to ask you."

"What is it?"

"Can you tell me about the cult of Molech? I just spoke to a Roman magistrate. He said the followers of this cult have been making trouble. He came all the way from Yerushaláyim to deal with them. But why would the Romans care about what a bunch of Canaanite heathens do in the Judean wilderness? After all, they follow false gods, as well."

"Ah, yes, but the Romans—particularly the Roman soldiers and magistrates—have been entrusted with keeping order in the provinces. So, if a crime is committed—no matter whether it was done in the name of religion or not—they will respond." Zephath lifted a cup of wine from the low table before them and took a drink.

"Why do you think they have gained interest in this particular cult?"

"The cult of… of Molech," Zephath shuddered at the mention of the name, "is particularly brutal and ruthless. Molech is the old Ammonite god of the netherworld, you know—the god of the realm of death and chaos and destruction. He requires human sacrifices—more particularly, child sacrifices. Though, as you say, the Romans also serve wayward gods, I have never heard of a Roman offering a human sacrifice—not in my lifetime, at least. They offer wine, grain, and animal sacrifices… and, from what I have seen, they only offer animals when they want to feast on it later. Their priests are little more than paid meat butchers."

Darash paused, considering what Zephath had said.

"Where might such a cult meet to conduct their rituals and perform these sacrifices?" Darash asked. "Surely, if the Romans do not allow human sacrifices, they would have to find a discreet place."

"Certainly, they would. They would have to find a place out in the wilderness, likely on some hilltop—but not one that was too high, lest the lights of their fires be spotted." Zephath ran a hand through his beard and looked toward the door, thinking. "There are likely many places like that in the hills surrounding Samaria… a place where they could make a fire large enough to heat their bronze statue of Molech."

"What bronze statue?"

Zephath turned back to Darash, an apologetic look in his eyes. "It is quite a horrible thing, young one." He paused. "If these people are truly following the ancient ways of that despicable Ammonite god, they will have a large, bronze image of Molech that is hollow on the inside and has hands extending before it. They build a fire beneath it so that the entire thing is red hot. Then, if the child is an infant, they lay it on the hands, or, if the child is older, they open a door in the belly of the idol and throw the child inside."

A look of horror crossed Darash's face. His chest felt tight. His heart rate and breathing increased.

"Yes," Zephath said, seeing Darash's revulsion, "it is quite terrible. Though I have never witnessed such a ceremony, I have heard that the priests beat drums during this time so as to block out the sounds of the children's cries." Zephath paused. "You see, it is their own children they offer in this way. One must offer his or her own child in order to receive from Molech what they ask."

Darash sat in stunned silence for a while. The olives and almonds he had just consumed no longer sat well in his middle. He found it difficult to swallow.

"Forgive me, son," Zephath said. "I should not have told you this."

"No… no, it is alright," Darash responded, rubbing his chest to still the burning sensation there from the poorly digested olives. "I needed to know. The Roman magistrate offered me employment as a replacement errand boy. If he is on the trail of these cult members, I should know what I am getting into."

"Well, no doubt these heathens will keep the magistrate very busy tonight."

Darash looked up.

"Why do you say that?"

"Because tonight we will have a new moon."

סֶלָה

"Faster, you beast!" Darash said, his frustration plain.

Ethan rode a mare borrowed from another member of the community of believers but, as most of the members were not wealthy, he only managed to get one horse and one small mule. Darash rode the mule.

"I can make no promises as to what we will find there," Ethan said. "When Bagad and I were friends we used the ruins of the ancient high place for certain Canaanite rituals—but nothing so grotesque as this new cult revival."

They left the city by North-East Gate and traveled down a sloping road through a rocky mountain pass. Then the road split, one path going northwest and the other heading east. Ethan turned east. Darash followed.

Sometime later Ethan turned onto a smaller path—one so obscured by brush and boulders Darash would have missed it.

"How does anyone ever find this trail?" Darash asked.

"Look." Ethan pointed to a large stone at the crossroads.

"It is just a stone."

"Look closely," Ethan said. "What image do you see on the face of it?"

Darash dropped from the mule's back and knelt next to the rock. Sun, age, and various elements and textures on the stone surface created what looked like a serpent's head in lighter relief. On closer inspection, one could make out the body, extending from the head and even the tip of a tail coming back toward the head from the other side, as if a serpent had wound itself completely around the rock.

"A serpent," Darash said. "It has wound itself around the stone. Now that you pointed it out to me, it seems so obvious."

"Yes. But one must know what to look for to find it."

Darash climbed back atop the mule, and they continued on. The second path wound up the back side of a brush-covered hill overlooking a narrow valley, but well out of sight of the city of Samaria.

"The path has been widened here," Ethan observed, "and not long ago."

They approached an outcropping of trees in a hidden grove ahead, just at the ridge of the crest of the hill. Next to a spreading terebinth tree, Darash noticed what looked like the remains of a stone pillar. As they pulled up next to the crumbling structure, he saw that the ground here had been leveled, and a floor of stone—recently swept—stretched before them, wide enough to hold fifty or more people comfortably. The mountainside's rocky embankment created the back wall of the old high place, and the only wall still standing. But a great pile of branches lay against it.

"Those were not there before," Ethan said, dropping to the ground. He tied his mare to the old stone post.

Darash, too, climbed down. He slipped the lead rope forward and drew the mule up next to Ethan's borrowed mare. As he looped the rope around the post, Ethan began to pull branches away from the pile. Both men gasped as the afternoon sun caught the shine of the object beneath.

The massive idol of a man with a head of a bull gleamed in brazen grandeur. It stood over ten feet tall and was wider than Zephath's horse cart. Molech's hollow eyes defied them as he waited, hands outstretched, for his next meal.

XVI

The Acropolis

Darash meandered through the streets of the Roman acropolis past a myriad of buildings, wondering where he might locate Quintus Arrius. Great temples to heathen gods and goddesses lined the road he traveled. Passing them, he felt the hair on the back of his neck stand up. He felt as if he was being watched by unseen eyes from the growing shadows of dusk. Soon it would be dark. He hurried, feeling uncomfortable and knowing he had little time to find the magistrate. He had to point him and his men in the right direction.

No doubt he is staying at the governor's home... but he may not be there now. Perhaps he is at one of the municipal buildings. Or at a military meeting place of some kind, conferring with the Roman soldiers stationed here.

Darash groaned in frustration. He decided to stop to ask at an official looking building with wide stairs and tall arched columns. Inside the massive, arched doorway he approached a group of men who had ceased their conversation to look at the Jewish youth with interest.

"Are you lost, young man?" one of them asked in Greek. He was old but clean-shaven and balding on top.

"Perhaps," Darash answered, also speaking Greek. "I am looking for the magistrate who arrived today from Jerusalem. He offered me employment as an errand boy, but I am not sure which building he is in. His name is Quintus Arrius."

"I know the man," one of the other men spoke up. He had a thick gray beard and large ears protruding from beneath a cap of sorts. He, too, spoke Greek. "I saw him and his men being let into the courtyard at the home of the governor not more than a half hour ago. You will likely find him there."

Darash nodded and thanked the men, who smiled at him in return, before he turned to retrace his steps back to the street. It did not take Darash long to locate the governor's home, as it resembled Pilate's home in Jerusalem in design, only smaller. Four Roman guards armed with both sword and lance guarded the front gate, watching all who approached with suspicion. Darash swallowed hard as they caught sight of him.

"Shalom," he said, but then corrected himself. "I mean, pax," he stated in Latin. "I have come by the request of Magistrate Quintus Arrius of Jerusalem, who is a guest here."

The head solder glanced at one of the others before turning to Darash. "What is your name, Boy?"

"D-Darash."

The soldier made a motion with his chin to one of the other guards, who ducked inside the gate to check the truthfulness of Darash's claim.

Why do Roman soldiers always look so angry? Darash wondered. *Are they this grim with their own families?*

Of course, these men were unmarried, for they could not marry until their term of service of twenty-five years was complete. That might be enough to make them angry all the time, Darash supposed. Still, the restrictions against marriage did not prevent many of them from having families.

Darash took a few steps back while he waited for the fourth guard to return. He did not like the way the head guard stared at him in unblinking silence.

Sometime later, the fourth guard reappeared, mumbled something to the head guard, who turned to Darash and said, "Come with me."

The man headed down a tiled, pillar lined pathway, through an outer courtyard decorated with statues of nude Roman gods and goddesses, and through a series of rooms—some with floors covered in colorful mosaics, others with intricate images painted on the walls of nymphs and satyrs drinking and enjoying the music of the flute. Whitewashed urns of out-of-season foliage dotted the hallways, undoubtedly carefully tended by servants. As they passed a hall that led to the kitchens, Darash caught the scent of something delicious being prepared, and he felt a knot grow in his middle.

They came to the arched threshold of a room at the end of a long hallway. The soldier stopped at the threshold, looked inside, and said, "The errand boy you requested has arrived. Shall I send him to the stables with the others?"

No, no! I must speak to the magistrate!

Someone muttered something from inside the room. Since Darash still stood in the hall, out of sight of the quarter's occupants, he could not make out the words. The soldier nodded and turned back to Darash.

"I will take you to the stables."

"No, please, I must speak to the magistrate. I have vital information that I must—"

"To the stables with you, boy! The magistrate cannot be bothered right now." The soldier grabbed hold of Darash's arm to lead him away.

As they moved down the hallway, Darash felt his chances of helping the magistrate slipping away. Night would fall soon. Nearly every religion he had heard of, including Judaism, celebrated a New Moon festival. No doubt the cult of Molech would do the same. And, though it did not yet make sense, Darash could not help but suspect that Ikaiah—Hazaiah's and Eliana's young son—might be sacrificed this very evening.

If I do not get the magistrate to listen, all might be lost!

As they moved back down the hallway, Darash felt the soldier's grasp loosen just slightly on his upper arm. He took a deep breath and wrenched free, dodging the man's thick arms as the soldier tried to grab him again.

"Hey!" the soldier called, but Darash was now out of reach, racing back toward the room they had just left.

"Please!" he said, racing to the threshold and catching sight of Magistrate Quintus Arrius. "I have important information you must here!"

As he got the words out of his mouth, great hands grabbed him again from behind, pulling him away from the doorway.

"Forgive me, your eminence," the soldier said, gripping Darash so hard he cried out in pain. "I will flog this one and then throw him out in the street for his impertinence. I will find a new errand boy for you myself."

"Wait, wait!" The voice belonged to Quintus. "I know that boy. Let him enter. I will hear what he has to say."

Great relief washed over Darash as the soldier reluctantly released his painful grip. Darash entered the room. Three men and two women lounged on couches in a narrow but richly decorated chamber. A colorful Greek tapestry hung on one wall, opposite a wall painted with a scene of a great feast. Magistrate Quintus Arrius stood in the center of the room next to a table spread with the remnants of a meal, having risen from where he had been seated only moments ago.

"Forgive me," Darash managed, now suddenly timid at the prospect of speaking to these people. Undoubtedly, one of them was the Roman governor of Samaria, and one of the women was probably his wife. Darash swallowed, took a breath, and continued. "I have come with information you might find of use." He tried to keep his eyes on the magistrate, but found it difficult to avoid the stares of the others, knowing any one of them could order him flogged, thrown in prison, or worse, simply for being an annoyance. "If you are still looking for the cult of Molech, I know where you can find their idol."

The magistrate blinked and then glanced at one of the other men, an older gentleman with a round belly and graying hair. Surely this man was the governor.

"Well, Quintus," the man said, amusement playing about his upper lip. "You are full of surprises. Even your errand boys are of use."

סֶ֖לָה

"This is what we will do," Quintus said, after hearing Darash's description of the old high place, the new idol of Molech, and the serpent-stone. He sat across from Darash, looking at him over a large plate of stewed quail breasts in a pine nut sauce. A plate of soft bread and a bowl of garlic lentils had been placed nearby.

Darash's stomach had been growling so much during Quintus's interrogation that the magistrate finally ordered some more food brought in, "if only to allow me to hear our conversation."

"My men and I will leave town around two hours past sundown," Quintus continued. "That will put us at the high place you described approximately one hour later. Surely their ceremony will still be in progress at that time, and we will catch them in the act. If human sacrifices are being made, we will discover it."

"But that may be too late to save the victims," Darash said. "We have no idea when the sacrifices will begin. If they begin at sundown, all their victims might be dead by the time you arrive."

"I am afraid that cannot be helped," Quintus said. "It is too late for us to travel there now. They will already have someone watching the pass. And we cannot risk running into them too early, lest we miss the opportunity to find the proof we need."

Darash considered this for a moment. He took another bite of quail, savoring its flavor. Food always helped clear his mind.

"What do you plan on doing to the followers of this cult if you catch them?" he asked.

"I will arrest them and bring them in to stand trial," Quintus said, but added, "if I can."

"What do you mean?"

"If they are armed—which they undoubtedly will be—and they resist—which, given that the penalty for murder is death by crucifixion, they surely will—my men and I will respond with whatever force necessary."

Darash swallowed a bite of bread, and it stuck in his throat. He had to take a drink of wine to get it clear.

"I see."

"I suggest you stay as far away from that place as possible," Quintus added, noting the strained look on Darash's face. "In fact, I do not want to see you anywhere near there. You could easily be mistaken for one of the cult members—and that is a fate I would not recommend."

סֶ לָ ה

Darash left the governor's home, passed the four glaring guards at the entrance, and headed down the main road of the acropolis. He could not help going over and over a certain possibility in his mind—that if there were to be human sacrifices this evening, Hazaiah and Eliana's son, Ikaiah, might be among them.

It makes no sense, though, not if what Zephath told me is correct. The cult members must offer their own children to their god, not the children of others.

His mind returned to Bagad, the only connection he had to the child's disappearance, but a connection that seemed to have run its course. He no longer had any reason to suspect that Bagad had taken Ikaiah. The child he had seen with him was definitely Bagad's own son. And there was nothing to directly connect him to the cult of Molech, other than Ethan's suspicions. Running a brothel—even being capable of robbing, beating, or murdering foreigners—did not make him a cult follower. Still, Darash could not stop thinking about him and what he had overheard.

He said something about tonight, Darash recalled, *and how their lives would change... as if he is planning on taking his family away from Samaria after tonight. Something big is happening for him, and soon... but what?*

Darash considered going back and speaking to Ethan and asking what more he knew of Bagad. Did the man have ties to the cult activity in the region? Had he been known to kidnap children? But if Ethan knew more, he would likely have already said something.

Jada....

The girl was still missing. And though they had not yet proven she had been the one to poison her father, Jehiel, she clearly had ties to Bagad—given the charade she had been playing with Nimrah. And Bagad, given his nefarious activities and connections, would be someone who could have easily acquired the poison for her.

Perhaps she made a trade with him. She would trick Nimrah into thinking she would marry him, so Bagad could continue to extort money from him, in exchange for the poison.

A neat and tidy arrangement. No money needed to exchange hands, which would be convenient for Jada, since she had none.

But where is she now?

Darash passed a Roman public house. He had to avoid a stream of laughing men heading inside to the baths, dressed in togas, followed by their errand boys.

I wonder how Melchi fits into all of this? Does he know of Jada's association with Bagad?

Somehow Darash doubted it, but he could not rule out the possibility. At the moment, though, he saw no reason to suspect the young man. Melchi had seemed hopeful that the betrothal would eventually be settled and he had seemed genuinely concerned for Jehiel, indicating he had no reason to dislike the man. Jada, though, did.

I should speak to Jehiel again. Perhaps he will be well enough to speak to me now.

Darash left the acropolis and cut back through the city and the shuk toward Jehiel's home. Phoebe opened the door to Darash's knock.

"Oh, good," she said at seeing his face. "I was hoping someone might stop by. Would you be willing to run back to my house and fetch some more goat's milk and the ingredients I need to make more barley porridge? Jehiel has eaten all that Photina brought."

Lines of exhaustion lined Phoebe's brow, and her eyes looked red and puffy from lack of sleep.

"Actually, why not go yourself? You could ask Mithcah to make the porridge and then send it over with Zephath. And then you could finally get some rest and a good meal. I can stay with Jehiel for now."

"Please," Jehiel's voice reached them where they stood at the threshold, "do not trouble yourselves any longer on my account. I can care for myself."

Phoebe opened the door wider and let Darash inside all the way. The small quarters had been transformed. The kitchen area and all the dishes had been scoured. The dirt floor had been swept and the rug shaken out. The few items of furniture had been wiped down, and most of the clothing and blankets had either been taken to be washed or folded and put away out of sight. The place was spotless.

"Hello, Jehiel," Darash said, smiling. "It is good to see you looking so well."

Jehiel sat on a pile of cushions before a tablemat and the remains of a bowl of barley porridge. He looked stronger and more relaxed than he had the last time Darash was here. Darash took a few steps closer and knelt opposite the man.

"Now, Jehiel," Phoebe said, "I know you are feeling better, but you are still weak. I will not be satisfied until you are walking on your own without stumbling." She turned to Darash. "Thank you, Darash," she said. "I will take you up on your offer. Zephath will be along shortly with more food for him. He can sit up with Jehiel tonight, if necessary."

Darash nodded his agreement. When the door had closed behind her, he turned back to Jehiel.

"I hoped we could talk," he said but paused before adding, "about your daughter, Jada."

XVII

The Power of Guilt

At the sound of his daughter's name, Jehiel closed his eyes and put his head in his hand, leaning his forehead on his palm. He took a deep breath that rattled through his thin frame.

"I cannot speak of her," he said in a near whisper. "It is too painful."

Darash sat in silence, recalling something Nib'haz had once told him. "People need to tell their stories. We need to be seen and heard—especially when we are in pain. The best thing you can do, when someone is resistant to your questions, is to wait. Just wait."

As the silence settled around them, Jehiel raised his head again and looked Darash in the eyes. "I love my daughter," he said. "You must understand this."

"I do," Darash said. "I see it plainly."

"And I do not want any harm to come to her—no matter what!" He sucked in a ragged breath. "Whatever she has done to me, I deserve ten times over!"

Darash nodded in understanding. Jehiel took a breath, took a moment to collect his thoughts and then said, "My wife and I spoiled her too much, as she was our only child, but I never thought she could... she could...." He trailed off.

Darash paused.

"When I was last here you said you realized your food was being poisoned, since your mysterious illness went away once you left your home but it came back again as soon as you returned." When Jehiel did not respond, Darash continued. "How did she find out about her real mother, Jehiel? Did you tell her?"

Jehiel shook his head. "No, I did not. No one here knows of it, and I would not have spoken of it in Gophna had I thought any of you would turn up here and recognize me."

"She had to have known long before you shared your story with us," Darash observed. "And your friends here seem unaware of it."

"Indeed."

"Then who around here would have had that information and then told her?"

"I know not," Jehiel said. "The woman—Jada's real mother—claimed to be a priestess of Molech. She was also a consort of a priest of Molech. I only saw the man once—he was not from Gennesaret—but I am certain he knew about my association with her and, in particular, about the child. It was he who suggested sacrificing Jada to save her mother. When I refused, he was not happy, but there was little he could do. Neither he nor she knew my real name nor where I lived, and the woman was already dying."

"Do you remember his name—this priest of Molech?"

"No, I do not. His followers simply called him Esh'Molech—man of Molech. ...I suppose it is possible he found me somehow and told her the truth, but I do not know how that would be possible."

"What about Melchi?" Darash asked.

"What of him?"

"He wants to marry Jada. Did you oppose the match?"

Jehiel sighed. "I did."

"Why?"

"I know his family thinks I am simply proud and stubborn. Melchi is a fine young man, and I have a great deal of respect for his stepfather and mother. Indeed, they are valued members of our family of believers... but Jada is my only daughter—my only child. I wanted something... different for her."

"Forgive me, but I do not understand."

Jehiel's shoulders dropped and he looked down for a moment before returning his eyes to Darash. "The fact is, Darash," he said in a quiet voice, "Melchi does not know who his real father is."

Normally such a fact would be plenty of grounds for a prospective father-in-law to reject a match but, by Jehiel's own admission, Jada herself was the daughter of a prostitute. Darash was not sure what to think of Jehiel's hesitation regarding Melchi's suspect parentage.

When Darash said nothing, Jehiel struggled to explain.

"Melchi's mother is from Capernaum."

Still, Darash stared blankly at Jehiel.

"His mother—though a very respectable woman now—was once a... a prostitute." He paused. "I was a frequenter of the brothels at that time." He paused again. "And I knew her."

Only then did the light of realization come to Darash's eyes. Jehiel was not sitting in judgment on Melchi nor his mother. He was not rejecting the young man based on religious or cultural biases. He feared Melchi might be his own son.

סֶלָה

When Zephath knocked on Jehiel's door with the food Phoebe had prepared for Jehiel, Darash answered and stepped outside to speak with him. The sun had set and the shadows blended together to form a graying dusk.

"Shalom, Zephath," Darash said. "You will find Jehiel doing much better, thanks to your wife's treatments."

"She is a miracle-worker, is she not?" Zephath smiled a little too broadly, giddy at his recent reunion with his wife. "I am glad he is doing better. Perhaps we can finally go home. Do you think you are about ready?"

"I am not sure," Darash said.

"Well, I cannot wait too long, or I will lose control over Nimrah. The fool keeps threatening to leave in search of Jada. I have to get him out of here."

"I understand." Darash paused, then asked, "Zephath… perhaps you will find it impertinent of me to ask… but how did you find Phoebe that day? I did not tell you where I was going. Did you follow me?"

Zephath shook his head. "No… actually, I am ashamed to admit it, but I paid Simon the Sorcerer for the information. As it turned out, it was a waste of money. I could have asked just about anyone, and they would have told me."

"This man—Simon the Sorcerer—does he, by any chance, go by any other names?"

Zephath shrugged. "I have no idea. I only spoke to him for a brief while."

"Do you think he might have any connection to the cult of Molech that is active in this area?"

Zephath shook his head vigorously at that question. "Oh, no! That I do know. He kept going on and on about how they are interfering with his business. He has found them very annoying of late—so I am certain he has no affiliation with them."

"Is there anything else you can tell me? Did he, by any chance, mention any names in connection with this cult?"

"No names," Zephath said, then stopped. "But… he did say something about the man he despises most of all. He said this particular man owns a brothel in the older section of the city. I believe he referred to him as Esh'Molech."

סֶלָה

I should have known! I should have seen it!

Darash chided himself as he walked the streets of Samaria, not sure where he was headed.

Bagad is connected with the cult of Molech! Moreover, he is most likely the same priest Jada's mother served. That is who told her of Jehiel's deception. This is the link we were missing.

Of course, it was possible Simon the Sorcerer had been referring to some other brothel owner, but the scars Darash had noticed on Bagad's arms when he and Ethan first visited the man now confirmed Darash's suspicions. Though Darash had never witnessed it, he had heard that cult followers sometimes cut themselves along their arms and chests during certain cult rituals. The letting of human blood before heathen gods had once been common among the Canaanites, Ammonites, Moabites, and others.

He recalled a story from the Torah about the prophet, Elijah, and his challenge to the four hundred and fifty priests of Ba'al and the four hundred priests of Asherah who sat at Queen Jezebel's table. They met on Mount Carmel near the Mediterranean Sea and built two altars. All day the heathen priests chanted before their god, dancing around their altar as they pleaded with the evil beast of darkness to send fire from Heaven to consume the sacrifice. When he did not answer, Elijah began to taunt them. Is he a god? Perhaps he sleeps! Perhaps he is too busy or is traveling!

In desperation to gain their god's attention, they wailed even louder and began to slash themselves with swords and spears. They cut deep into their bodies until the blood flowed freely. Still, neither Ba'al nor Asherah answered. Their mouths had been closed.

Finally, as evening descended, Elijah took his turn. First, he told the people to repair the old altar to Adonai, which had been torn down. They placed wood and a butchered bull on it as an offering. In this way, the preparations were similar as those made for Ba'al. However, Elijah went further. He told the people to dig a deep trench around the altar. Next he had them fill four large jugs with water and pour them over the altar. A second time he told them to fill the jugs and drench the altar, and then a third. The water soaked the offering, the wood, filled the trench, and ran across the ground.

Then Elijah prayed.

"LORD, the God of Abraham, Isaac and Israel, let it be known today that you are God in Israel and that I am your servant and have done all these things at your command. Answer me, LORD, answer me, so these people will know that you, LORD, are God, and that you are turning their hearts back again."

He only had to pray once.

An intense fire streaked from the sky and fell upon Elijah's sacrifice. In an instant, it consumed the bull and wood. The stones themselves melted in the intensity of the flames, the water evaporated, and even the soil beneath the altar burned until only a smoldering crater remained.

But though the people stood nearby, not one of them was injured.

This was one of Darash's favorite stories.

He loved the simplicity of Elijah's prayer and the prophet's desire to see the God of Israel recognized for Who He was. He loved the challenge and the way Elijah, in complete confidence, doused his offering to prove that nothing was too difficult for the true God. And Darash's heart burned with excitement and awe of the fire that burned hot enough to consume stone… but did not harm a single man, woman, or child.

Surely the same God reigns in Israel today! Surely He still desires that people know He is the one true God. Molech cannot be allowed to receive any more sacrifices! Not today.

Darash turned north and found a street that angled around the Roman stadium and opened into the main road that led out of the city by way of the North-East Gate. He traveled the road Ethan had showed him for a little while, but then he cut to the right and scaled a small hill. He did not want to be seen approaching the high place ruins—not by Bagad, the other cult members, nor by the Roman soldiers that would soon be heading that way.

The way was difficult, for deep shadows now hid the stones and pits in his path.

I must hurry, or I will get lost out in these hills and not be able to find my way back until morning. If that happens, all will be lost.

Despite the descending darkness and the lack of a trail, Darash picked up his pace. He topped the small hill and started down the far side, intending to skirt around behind the mountain where the high place rested. If he headed straight to the high place itself, there would be nowhere to hide. However, if he could approach from the southeast, he would likely not be seen, for the high place rested in a northeastern alcove near the top of the mountain. The only possibility to observe the ceremony from a safe place would be to watch from above.

Darash made it safely past the first hill and began scaling the second. It was even harder this time, as the darkness moved in swiftly. If his estimation was correct, he still had to get to the other side of this hill and then up the back of the next mountain, before angling northeast across the mountain's crest. But each step became more precarious than the last. As the ground before him merged with the darkness, his sandals began to slip on small pebbles. Halfway up the second hill, he thought he heard voices echoing across the hills. Excited, he lunged forward to try to find out where they were coming from. A spray of pain shot through his right foot. He had stubbed in on a rock and had to stop and take deep breaths to squelch his desire to cry out.

The voices reached him only intermittently, distant and muffled. He started out again, still following them but needing to feel his way up. Reaching forward in the darkness, he was able to distinguish the dark masses as he approached them. A bush, a stone, a thicket of thorns.

"Ow!" he muttered, losing his battle with himself to remain silent.

Now nursing two wounds, a hand that stung and toes that throbbed, Darash moved more slowly, heading into deeper and deeper black, gaging his position only by the incline of the terrain. Finally, he reached the top of the second hill. He stopped catch his breath and to try to identify his location by the landscape. Though he strained his eyes to make out the terrain, he saw only distant, looming shadows. The voices had silenced.

I will never make it!

Darash sat down and rubbed his sore toes with his good hand. A few moments later, though, as the cold crept through his robe, he stood again and inched toward the northeastern slope.

If I do not try to find them, people may die.... Children may die.

Darash felt the path with his feet as he moved in the direction he believed to be correct. A thin tree aided him as he used its trunk to balance himself at the crest of the hill and find safe footing down the first steep decline.

Darash let go of the tree and stretched his foot toward a dark mass he thought was a stone. It was not.

Stepping into a thick patch of brambles, Darash reacted to the pain and lost his balance. He felt himself falling forward into darkness. He reached out to break his fall only to find nothing there but gravel. The gravel slipped, cutting into his palms and knuckles. His body pitched forward. Rocks and branches beat at him for a few terrifying seconds before a final blow to the head flung him into oblivion.

XVIII

The Brazen Altar

Darash blinked. At least, he thought he blinked. It was hard to tell if his eyes were open or closed. He had never experienced such deep blackness. New moon nights were always deathly dark, despite their significance as the beginning of something new—something good. Tonight marked the beginning of the first of Shevat—a new month which would bring with it new blessings. Even now the priests in Jerusalem would be making sacrifices and calling the People to worship.

Darash tried to move. He groaned as pain attacked him from all sides. He discovered he had landed on his side on a patch of rocky soil. His head throbbed loudest of all, but his entire body ached from so many injuries he could not tell one from another.

How far did I fall? And how long was I unconscious?

Darash pushed himself to a sitting position, and rested his head in his hands for a few moments, willing the ache to subside. He felt thick, slippery moisture on his brow. Blood.

I must not have been unconscious very long. The blood is still flowing.

Still, Darash had no way of determining his location. Though he undoubtedly lay in the valley at the base of the mountain where the high place resided, he could no longer tell which way was northeast of his previous position.

Thankfully, though his body had been bruised on all sides, he did not detect any serious injuries—no broken bones, at least, though a sharp ache on his right forearm demanded attention as the throb in his head lessened.

Darash pulled his robe about him, thankful it had remained attached to his body in the fall. He pulled his legs to his chest and hugged them to his body to regain his warmth.

I am stuck here. I will never find my way out of this valley in the darkness. I was a fool to even attempt such a thing. I might have broken my neck!

Darash buried his head in his arms, atop his knees. There was nothing to do but wait. He sat for a long time, shivering in the cold and listening to the night sounds. Crickets chirped in the brush nearby. An owl hooted from a nearby tree. Low, rhythmic drum beats rose in the distance.

Drums!

Darash lifted his head and turned his ear toward the sound. Indeed, deep, steady beats rose from the back side of the mountain to his right. That meant the hill he had fallen from was on his left. He knew where he was.

Darash stood and faced the sound. The ceremony had begun. Undoubtedly, the followers of Molech had filled the flat, stone platform on the far side of the mountain and now waited for their god to show up. First, they would have to get his attention… by offering him the blood of the innocent.

As Darash faced the sound of drumming, he realized something else. He could see—just a bit. A light had risen from the top of the mountain. They had lit the fire and had begun heating their idol of bronze—the image of their god—an altar to his lust.

Though Darash still stood in darkness, he saw the direction he must head if he still hoped to observe the ceremony and see if, indeed, children were slated for sacrifice.

Despite the aches in his bones, the cut on his arm, and the bloodied knot on his head, Darash moved toward the mountainside and began to climb toward the light and sound.

סֶ֑לָה

At least forty people stood in a semi-circle around the image of Molech, which sat atop a blazing fire. The branches that had once hidden the false god now served to warm him. Red and orange flames licked the base of the idol and cast flickering shadows across the solemn faces of the worshippers. Large bowls of burning incense flanked their smoldering god punching thick plumes of musty-sweet smoke into the air.

Darash watched from behind a boulder overlooking the old high place from the southern ridge. He sat above them, almost directly behind the idol itself. To see the altar itself, he had to stand and look over the top of the boulder. However, not wanting to be spotted in the thin light cast his direction, he kept low to the ground and watched the faces of the people. Staring eyes, barely parted lips that moved in a rhythmic hum. If they were chanting actual words, Darash could not make them out.

He is not there. Bagad is not among them. Perhaps I was wrong about him, after all.

A line of men sat together to Darash's right—the far side of the high place from the path they took to get there. These men hugged wooden, leather-topped drums under their left arms and pounded them in unison with their right hands. Slow, steady, deep beats filled the night and unified the people in a kind of stupor as they gazed into the burning eyes of their god.

To Darash's left a hooded man approached, his hidden right profile to Darash. He was tall, compared to the rest of the people. He moved to the middle of the stone floor and stopped to face the gathered worshippers.

"Welcome my sons and daughters," he began. "Tonight we come together to celebrate the new moon and to honor the one who protects us from darkness—the great and horrible Molech!" He swung an arm toward the idol.

The people let out a loud cry and dropped to all fours, bowing low to the ground so their foreheads touched the dusty stone floor. Seven times in unison the people swayed up on their arms to look at their god, then down again to touch their faces to the ground.

Seven times. They are fully devoted.

As the people bowed, Darash noticed a line of animals behind them, tied to stakes and rocks. The evening's sacrifices had been chosen. Thankfully, Darash did not spot any human children among the beasts.

"Yes, my children," the priest said, lifting his arms over them as they completed their ritual of submission. As he did so, his long sleeves slipped down on his arms revealing scars—much like those Darash had seen on Bagad's arms. "Oh, Molech, the great and horrible," he began chanting in a sing-song voice, "come to us tonight! We welcome you!"

Again, he repeated the words, and as he did so, the people joined in. Together the cult members chanted together. Over and over again, they said the same thing. As they chanted, their voices grew in intensity. As their voices grew more pitched and feverish, the drummers picked up the rhythm, pounding their instruments harder. As the sound of drums increased in passion, the people swayed back and forth, dancing for their god and crying out for him to hear them.

"We ask for strength!" the priest shouted, cutting through the din.

"We ask for strength!" the people echoed in a great shout.

"We ask for wealth!" he cried.

"We ask for wealth!" they clamored.

"We ask for power!"

"We ask for power!"

"We ask for health!"

"We ask for health!"

"We ask for virility!"

"We ask for virility!"

"Protect us from our enemies!" he shouted, changing the rhythm of his voice to match the words.

"Protect us from our enemies!" the people repeated after him.

"Smite all who oppose us!"

"Smite all who oppose us!"

"Make this land yours once again!"

"Make this land yours once again!"

The hairs on the back of Darash's neck stood on end as he watched and listened to their ritualistic chants. His heart pounded in his chest. He could not tell, but it felt like the darkness around him had deepened, despite that the flames around the idol had grown.

He cowered next to the rock and wondered why he was there. He had seen only adults in the crowd—no children at all. And, so far, he had not recognized anyone. And, though, the chanting and heathen supplications put a terror in Darash's heart, none of the cult members had done anything illegal, despite the rumors against them. If Quintus Arrius arrived now, he would find no reason to arrest anyone. Indeed, his own religious festivals were likely similar.

Darash turned from the ceremony below, leaned his back against the boulder, and closed his eyes. A distaste had risen in his mouth and throat for everything he had witnessed and for his own foolish involvement. He would be stuck on this mountain until morning, and morning was yet a long way off. His head ached. His body burned with pain. His right sleeve felt stiff with dried blood, and his arm rebelled when he tried to move it.

Drumming and chanting and wailing continued to fill the night. The priest made loud supplications and demands of Molech, and the people repeated his words with fervor. At one point, the rhythm of the drums changed, and the people joined together in a strange chorus.

"Molech is our god! He alone do we serve! Look how well we serve our god! He will grant our requests!"

From the sound of sandaled feet against the sand-strewn stone floor, the people must have been participating in some kind of dance. Darash did not bother to look. The ceremony below put a knot in his stomach.

Many of the people below were Jewish—at least, in part. How could people, who had heard of the true God of Israel, think that some other, lesser being could help them? Darash's mind turned to the many rituals the priests performed in the Temple in Jerusalem. They, too, offered sacrifices on a bronze altar. But the similarities ended there.

The altar of Elohim was situated in the main courtyard of the Temple on a raised platform. In order to make a sacrifice, the animal first had to be lifted up to God. Four horns projected from the four corners of the top of the altar.

For the Jew, the slaying of an unblemished, sacrificial animal and the act of offering it upon the altar signified the need for the shedding of perfect blood before a sinful man or woman could approach a holy God. It was an act of humility.

However, if the rumors about the cult of Molech were true, and they did, indeed, sacrifice human children, they did so with a completely different attitude and for a wholly different purpose. Their willingness to kill—to take innocent, human life—was intended to prove their devotion, to show the lengths to which they would go to serve their god. For their god was not a god of love and mercy, but a god of hatred and destruction. They feared him—not because he was great—but because he was evil. They believed that, by proving their willingness to offer him the destruction of the innocent—something he craved beyond all things, their god would be compelled to grant their desires. In this way, they believed they could control and manipulate him. Their sacrifices were not born of humility, but of pride.

As Darash considered these things, the sounds in the rocky alcove beneath suddenly came to a halt. The sudden silence created an eeriness more intense than the drums or chanting had. Darash moved so he could again watch what was happening.

The priest and all the people had ceased their singing, dancing, and drumming. They all looked in the direction of the path Darash and Ethan had first traveled to find this place. Darash, too, looked that direction, and though he could not at first make out any motion in the darkness, he heard the sound of someone moving toward them.

Quintus Arrius and his men! It must be them. They will come, find nothing of interest here, and be forced to return empty-handed.

Darash peered through the shadows. Gradually, he began to make out bodies moving closer along the pebble-strewn path.

Odd, I expected they would ride their horses up here.

To Darash's surprise, the first figure to emerge from the shadows was not a Roman soldier. It was a woman.

Jada!

The light-haired young woman walked forward in confidence toward the group of devotees, a look of solemn determination on her face. But she was not alone. Holding her hand and walking a bit behind her, came a young boy.

XIX

The Substitute

"The sacrifice has arrived!" the priest said, holding his arms up again. "Tonight Molech will finally hear us!"

A cheer rose from the crowd.

The priest turned toward the idol. He removed his hood and knelt before Molech. As the light from the fire splashed upon the priest's face, Darash recognized him.

Bagad! I knew it! This Esh'Molech is Bagad!

"Tonight," Bagad cried, extending his knife-scarred arms toward the idol, "I will offer Molech the most valuable sacrifice of all! My own son!"

Jada stepped forward pulling the little boy with her. The child, though, had become fearful at being the center of attention, of the blazing idol, and of the strange words. He tried to pull away from her and, when she did not release him, he cried out. At the sound of his wails the line of drummers started up again.

To Darash's surprise, Bagad waved Jada and the child back.

"But all in due time. …First, we have other sacrifices to offer." He turned toward the crowd and said, "Bring the sacrifices to the altar!"

The crowd parted. One of the men moved to a place out of Darash's line of sight near the line of tethered animals and returned with a sack. He handed it to Bagad.

The priest of Molech took the sack and turned to the idol. He placed the sack on the ground before the bronze god and knelt. The people mimicked him, kneeling together as they had before.

"We first offer you a sacrifice of grain, oh mighty Molech," he cried. "The produce of this land is yours. We freely give of our labor and of that which sustains us."

Priest Bagad bowed low to the ground seven times, touching his forehead to the dirt before the blazing idol. When he rose, some of the filth stuck to the sweat on his face, but he did not appear to notice. The crowd, too, peered with white eyes from smudged faces.

Bagad took the sack of grain in his hands and nodded toward a man who had moved to stand near the line of drummers. He came forward, a metal rod in his hands, and approached the idol. Carefully, and standing far enough back to avoid the worst of the heat, he used the rod to open the compartment in the belly of Molech's torso. Bagad approached and tossed the entire sack of grain inside, and the man closed the compartment again.

The drummers picked up the beat, the people swayed, danced, and chanted. Molech had been fed his first course.

Next, a man approached carrying a cage. Inside, two terrified turtle-doves fluttered around, sending feathers flying into the night air to float silently to the ground. Again Molech placed the cage before the idol and knelt. Again he prayed, offering the birds freely to his god. Again the man with the metal rod approached and opened the idol's belly.

Bagad did not bother to open the cage. He tossed the entire thing inside. The door closed again. Flames picked up inside the beast and licked through the cracks around the edges of the bronze door. The birds became Molech's second course.

The next offering to be brought forward was a ewe. After another round of prayer and bowing, Bagad slit the animal's throat, dipped his hand in its blood, and flung it across the crowd. They cheered in crazed fervor, many of them licking the blood from their lips and fingers. Bagad's son, still held tightly by Jada, cried in fear at seeing the animal slaughtered and again when they pushed the body of the animal into the burning belly of Molech. No one bothered to comfort him.

The ewe became Molech's third course.

Next they brought forward a ram. It pulled against the rope and had to be dragged forward.

Where are the magistrate and his men? Why have they not arrived yet?

Darash's heart pounded in near panic. Though he found it difficult to judge the hour, surely Quintus Arrius and his soldiers should be on their way by now. If they did not arrive soon it would be too late. Besides the ram, Darash saw only a calf and an ox left. Then it would be the child's turn.

The ceremony continued. Despite the lateness of the hour, the people did not tire. In fact, their energy increased with each progressive sacrifice. Some of them danced erratically, heads back, eyes rolled back in their heads, as if overtaken by some trance.

Bagad slit the ram's throat. By now the ground at Bagad's feet ran with thick, red blood. When he knelt and stood again, his face dripped with it. His sleeves and robes soaked it up. Darash had never seen anyone more terrifying.

The ram became Molech's fourth course.

Come, Magistrate, please come now!

A man untied the calf and drew it forward. Shadows danced across the worshippers' bloodied faces. The drummers hammered away, maintaining the frenzied sound. When Bagad drew his long knife again, Darash turned his eyes away. He heard the bronze door open and close again and the cry of victory and bloodlust from the crowd. Molech feasted on his fifth course.

The ox snorted and made a sound of protest but, from the sounds below, Darash knew the moment of death. He could only imagine the amount of blood that now ran across the ground.

Where is the magistrate? Perhaps he got turned around at the hidden path. Perhaps, in the darkness, he missed the symbol of the serpent on the rock! They could be wandering these hills looking for us even now, but I have no way to signal them!

Darash felt his panic rise. Time had run out.

I must do something, but what? If I give myself away, they will come after me. But if I do nothing, the child will die!

Darash tried to think of some way he could ensure the child's safety, but nothing came to mind.

"And now," Bagad cried, "it is time for the most valuable sacrifice of all. Human blood!"

The crowd cried out in ecstasy.

"Draw your swords and daggers, my sons and daughters. Join yourself with this sacrifice by letting some of your blood."

The people drew knives and swords of various kinds from their robes and, in unison with Bagad, bared their left arms and drew the blades across their skin. Soon their arms dripped crimson. Their sleeves stained red.

"Now… bring my son forward!" Bagad cried.

"Yes, Esh'Molech," Jada responded, her voice emotionless, but the child, who had been crying and whimpering, now began to scream in fear.

No, no, no! This cannot be happening! But nothing I can do would stop them!

Jada struggled to pull the child forward. He fought her, crying and trying to get away.

"Bring him!" Bagad said again, extending a hand toward them. "It is time to offer mighty Molech his seventh and final sacrifice! A human child! My own son!"

The crowd cheered.

Jada finally managed to pull the little boy to the center of the floor where the people could see him. Bagad grabbed the child's arm and pulled him closer. He turned, still gripping the boy and faced Molech. He began to pray.

"Oh, great and horrible, Molech! I—your priest and the first of your people—offer you my own child as a sacrifice, my only son! I give him freely to you, that you might see my devotion and bless me!"

The drummers picked up the beat, and the people responded with a loud chant as Bagad finished his prayer. As he finished, he raised his arms, only able to lift his left arm as far as the child could extend his. As he did so, the child's right arm was exposed. The light of the fire revealed a club-shaped birthmark on the boy's arm.

That is not Bagad's son! That child is Ikaiah, Hazaiah and Eliana's son! He has substituted a stolen child for his own!

In Darash frustration and desperation, he turned away from the sight. He leaned hard against the rock… and felt it give just a bit.

Suddenly, Darash knew what to do. He positioned himself behind the boulder, braced his back against the stone and his legs against the rocky embankment, and pushed. He felt the massive rock give a little more. Darash pushed harder. The stone slid several inches, but then stopped. Darash pushed again. Nothing.

Please, Adonai! Please give me strength! Please stop these evil men as you stopped the priests of Ba'al and Asherah in the day of Elijah!

Darash stood and rocked the stone back and forth. The boulder budged a bit more. Darash pushed with all his might. The pebbles near his feet shifted. Small stones moved aside and headed downhill in a small shower toward the gathering, but the drums drowned out the noise.

Suddenly Darash felt the boulder give way and move away from him. He let go just in time to fling himself back and catch his balance against the hillside. The boulder rolled downhill, crashing through bushes and smaller clusters of rock and picking up speed and sound. Several worshippers noticed the large object heading toward them out of the darkness just as it launched into the air.

Bagad turned and, seeing the massive stone appearing from the shadows, cried out and moved out of the boulder's path, pulling the child with him.

Darash could not have planned nor even anticipated the perfection of the boulder's trajectory. It left the embankment and crashed into the image of Molech, smashing a giant dent in the idol's back, toppling the glowing beast, and sending a shower of flame and coals upon the worshippers. The entire mountainside shook, sending showers of smaller rocks sliding down in a shower that filled the air with dust.

The drumming stopped. Men and women cried out in terror—suddenly awakened from their demonic stupor—and then coughed in the silt-filled air. Several slapped themselves to rid their clothing of burning embers. Giant pieces of burning logs and red hot coals sizzled in the blood on the stone floor. One of the incense bowls had been scattered. Molech himself lay with his face in a puddle of blood. One of his arms lay in a broken, twisted heap to his right. The smell of the roasting animals in his gut—fur and all—filled the air. A giant, red and glowing plume of smoke rose above the high place.

Bagad looked upon the destruction of his work, a look of dismay and rage on his face.

"Who has done this?" he cried in a voice filled with fury. "Who has desecrated Molech's image and destroyed his temple?"

Bagad moved forward again and looked toward the hillside where Darash sat. Now that the bronze image had been shifted from its place atop the fire, the flames blazed higher, sending a splash of light up the mountain.

He sees me!

"There!" Bagad cried, pointing toward Darash. "There is someone on that hill! Bring him to me!"

Six men pulled away from the crowd and headed for the embankment. Darash turned and tried to move again up the hillside in the dark.

I must get away! But the child! The child is still in danger!

Within what seemed like only moments the men were closing on his position. Darash picked up a stone and launched it at them. It hit one of the men in the head. He lost his balance and slid back down to the ground below.

"Get him!" Bagad screamed.

Darash threw another stone, but missed. A third hit a man in the chest, but did not stop his ascent. Darash scrambled across a patch of loose rock, lost his balance, and slipped closer to his pursuers. He grabbed a branch to pull himself up higher, but felt a hand wrap around his right ankle.

"Let go!" he cried. "Let me go!"

Another hand grabbed his left leg, and he felt himself being dragged down the mountainside. No matter how much he struggled, he could not escape them. They pulled him down the embankment and dragged him to stand before Bagad, his arms firmly held by bloody-faced men.

Bagad scrutinized the skinny youth before him with wide eyes. The whites of his eyes glowed ominously from a face covered in blood.

"I know you," he said, recognition on his face. "You were with Ethan—the betrayer!"

Darash said nothing. He tried to pull away again, but the men's fierce grip on his arms held him fast. His right arm seared with pain as strong hands gripped him right over the wound he had sustained in his fall. The smoke and the pain made his mind feel foggy.

Bagad turned to his people.

"This man has destroyed our sacred image! He has interrupted our ceremony! He has desecrated the temple of Molech! Tell me, what should be his fate?"

"Death!" the people cried in unison, loathing and hatred on their faces. "Death! Death!"

They chanted the words together, growing louder and louder. The drummers took this as a cue to start up again, adding their rhythmic melody to the fray.

Darash trembled with fear as Bagad again turned his eyes on Darash's face.

"Indeed," he said, an evil smile cutting through the filth of his countenance. "It looks like your fate has been decided." Bagad turned to Jada. "Come take the boy!" He handed Ikaiah off to her and then turned back to Darash. He pulled his blade from his belt—a long, curved knife already stained with blood. He took a step forward.

Darash fought to get away but felt his feet sliding easily across the bloody ground as the men pulled him toward their priest. Bagad stepped forward, his face so close Darash could feel his breath. The musty sweet smell of incense mingled with the sour, metallic smell of blood.

"No, no!" Darash cried.

"Only by your blood can this act be erased!" Bagad hissed. He raised his knife to Darash's throat. "Then we will sacrifice my son! If you thought you would save him, you have failed!"

"He is not your son!" Darash cried as loudly as he could. Looking to the crowd he cried again, "The boy is not Bagad's son! He is the son of another man! Your priest has been lying to you!"

The drummers stopped and the people grew silent.

"That child is not the son of your priest!" Darash cried again. "Check his arm! He has a birthmark. Bagad's son does not. Surely some of you must know this!"

"Lies!" Bagad cried.

The people glanced toward the boy but then back to Darash and Bagad. None of them moved.

XX

The Romans

"Check his arm!" Darash cried, desperation rising in his voice.

Bagad leaned down and put his face in Darash's face and stared him in the eyes. He smiled.

"Can you not see?" he oozed. "These people belong to me. Nothing you can say or do will ever change that." He rose again and lifted his knife. "And now, for the glory of Molech," he cried, "you die!"

The sound of hooves and jingling bridles arose from the path at Darash's back. Bagad glanced up.

"Halt! In the name of Caesar Tiberius and the Roman Empire, stop what you are doing!"

Magistrate Quintus Arrius, followed by at least a dozen Roman soldiers, rode their horses into the middle of the ancient high place. At the sight of them the people scattered. Some attempted in vain to hide in the thin scrub brush or behind rocks. Others flung themselves down the rocky hillside into darkness. Several of the men, still holding their weapons, foolishly fought back. Bagad pushed Darash out of the way to defend himself against the Roman invaders.

Quintus and his men dismounted, swords drawn. Darash landed hard on the ground. He scrambled out of the way of the horses' hooves and backed up against the embankment to avoid being trampled.

Where is the child? Where is Ikaiah?

Darash searched through a sea of legs, both human and animal. A soldier passed in front of him to stab a sword-wielding cult member through the abdomen. The criminal cried out in agony as he fell. Swords clashed, women screamed, and men shrieked as they felt the full brunt of Rome's power. Another soldier and horse passed before Darash and, as they moved out of the way, Darash finally caught a glimpse of the child. He lay unmoving on the ground on the opposite side of the stone floor from Darash.

Oh, no! No!

Darash's eyes landed on Jada. She no longer looked anything like the girl he had seen at Ethan and Photina's meeting of believers. Blood stained face, hands, and clothing made her fierce to look upon, and she evidently had no intention of staying around to see how the battle would end. She took one last glance behind her and slipped out of sight down the rocky embankment toward the valley below.

A broad-shouldered, heavily muscled Roman soldier caught sight of Darash and seized the youth by his left arm, dragging him to his feet. He raised his sword to dispatch him.

"I know the magistrate!" Darash cried. "I am not one of these people! I know the magistrate!"

The soldier hesitated just long enough to hear Quintus Arrius say, "Wait!"

The magistrate approached, leaving his other men to the work of chasing down the few who had escaped. Otherwise, the brief skirmish ended almost as swiftly as it had begun.

"Darash, is that you?"

"Yes, it is I," Darash squeaked.

The soldier lowered his sword, but did not loosen his grip on Darash's arm.

A look of anger crossed the magistrate's brow. "I thought I told you to stay away from here! I should let this man run you through for your disobedience!"

"Forgive me, but I had to—"

"You had to what? Do you have any idea what you look like? How are we supposed to tell you apart from these murdering fiends?"

Now that the magistrate mentioned it, Darash realized he must look a sight. His sleeve had been soaked in blood from his fall and the cuts he sustained. After having been flung to the ground by Bagad, he too was covered in blood—no different from the Molech worshippers themselves.

"Well, uh… they are all cut on their left arms. I am cut on my right."

The magistrate stared at Darash with a look of exasperation. Finally he just shook his head and walked away. "Let him go," he ordered over his shoulder, "but we will take him back with us."

The large man let Darash go and followed the magistrate to help tally the bodies.

"What will we do to those who ran?" he asked.

"Track them if we can… arrest them for participating in an attempted murder…."

Darash let Quintus's voice fade into the background as he approached Ikaiah's huddled body. The child lay with his face buried in one arm, knees pulled up to his chest.

Oh, no! My God!

Darash put a hand over his mouth. He felt an intense grief welling inside his chest for the poor, slain boy. He moved to the boy's side and knelt on the ground next to his body.

"Oh, no!"

At the sound of Darash's voice, Ikaiah raised his head.

"You are alive!" Darash gasped, joy and relief instantly replacing his fear and sorrow.

Ikaiah gave Darash one look and screamed.

The cry drew Quintus Arrius's attention once again. He walked over and picked the child up from the ground and into his arms. Though the child fought, Quintus did not let him go.

"It is alright now, little one," he said. "Do not struggle. You are safe now. All the scary men are gone." He glanced at Darash. "Well, except that one."

סֶ לָ ה

Once again, Darash found himself in the company of Artorius, the same man who gave him a ride to the scene of Ikaiah's kidnapping a little over a week earlier. This time, at least, Darash was given a mule to ride by himself. The child rode with Artorius on his horse, too frightened of Darash's appearance to ride with him.

A servant walked ahead of them carrying a lantern to lead the way across the rocky trails. Their progress was slow and, now that the night of horror was over, Darash felt his many aches returning. His head throbbed. His ribs ached with every step of the mule took. His right arm had started bleeding again. The blood crusted on his face and clothing grew intolerably uncomfortable, but there was little he could do about it.

Darash had no idea what time it was when they finally made it to the North-East Gate and Artorius ordered the guards to open it for them. As they passed beneath the torches, Darash saw that Ikaiah had fallen asleep against the soldier's chest. He wondered what his mother, Revayah, would say if she saw a Roman soldier cradling a sleeping Jewish child in his arms.

"The magistrate told me to take you back to the acropolis," Artorius said, as they continued past the gate toward the main city, "unless you would rather go somewhere else."

Darash's head felt foggy again. Ethan and Photina would be asleep… so would Zuar and Mitchah. He had no idea whether Zephath and Phoebe would be at Zuar's home or at Jehiel's place.

"I… I…."

"The acropolis it is," Artorius said. "You will be able to bathe and have a meal, if you want it. There will be a bed for you both, as well. The magistrate will decide what to do with you in the morning."

סֶ לָ ה

The next hour passed in a fog. They arrived at the acropolis and someone took charge of the mule Darash had been riding. Someone else led him into a building—he had no idea which one—and to a tiled room with a stone bath built into the floor. Warm water already filled it. Two male attendants removed his clothing and left the room. Another scrubbed him clean. A fourth—or perhaps he was one of the original two—entered with fresh clothing, treated and bound Darash's wounds, and helped Darash dress again.

They offered him some food but, for the first time in his life, he turned it down. By the time Darash made it to the bed offered him, he could barely stand. He lay down, let a servant pull a blanket over him, and fell into a deep sleep.

סֶ לָ ה

Morning came and went. When Darash opened his eyes the sun had crawled high into the sky and begun its descent again. His dreams had been dark and fretful. Constant drumming. People screaming. Blood everywhere. Twice he had awakened with a start—once when Bagad flung him off the mountainside into darkness, again when a Roman soldier had run him through with a sword.

Darash groaned when he tried to sit up. Though his body had ached the night before, he could now barely move. He lay on his mat staring at the whitewashed ceiling of a room he did not recognize.

Where am I?

He had no idea. For a long moment he lay on his mat trying to identify anything in the room that looked familiar. Nothing did.

Again, Darash gathered his courage to again try to move. He finally managed to raise his left arm to his head, where he detected a skillfully applied bandage. Another bound his right forearm, and there were more. His ribs, too, had been tightly wrapped, making it difficult to take a full breath.

Glancing around the room from where he lay, he saw that his borrowed bed was one of many in a long, narrow room. At least a dozen other beds neatly lined both walls, each with a wooden box at its foot and a small stand with a lamp at its head. A series of simple, rag rugs ran along the center of the floor. The back wall bore a series of pegs—all of them empty at the moment—and a narrow window near his head overlooked what sounded like the street. Otherwise, the room was empty. Despite the simplicity of the slave quarters, the room was nicer than the one Darash shared with his sister in their home in Jerusalem. Undoubtedly, in a home wealthy enough to be located in the acropolis, this was just one room of many reserved for the servants.

Darash had no idea if anyone other than himself had actually slept in that room the night before. If they had, they were about their duties at the moment.

It took Darash a full ten minutes to work himself into a seated position on his mat. In the process, he discovered so many bandages, he felt like a corpse about to be placed in its grave. As he sat staring in horror at the condition of his aching body, the small door to the servants' quarters opened.

A skinny young man entered and smiled upon seeing Darash awake and alert.

"Ah… uh, shalom," he said, using the Hebrew greeting, despite a thick Grecian accent. "So good to see you awake and looking so well!"

Darash smiled back at him, appreciating the effort. He thought he recognized him from last night as one of the servants who had helped him bathe, but he was not sure.

"Shalom," Darash said and dipped his head. "Do I have you to thank for binding my wounds?"

"Oh, no, that was our physician, not I. I bathed you and dressed you. And, I washed your clothing." He indicated a cloth bundle he carried, lifting it slightly. He knelt next to Darash and placed the bundle on the bed. He added, "I am Spiro."

"Thank you very much, Spiro," Darash said. He watched as Spiro unfolded the bundle to reveal his own clothing. Not a single blood stain remained, and several tears had been skillfully patched and mended. "Amazing!" Darash said. "They are so clean! I thought these clothes were ruined for sure."

"Oh, no! Spiro can wash anything and fix anything!" He patted his chest and gave Darash a toothy smile.

Darash chuckled. "I believe you."

"No need to change, though. You can take the clothes you are wearing. They are yours now." He rewrapped Darash's clothes as he spoke. "The physician will be in shortly to check your bandages. And then I will take you to get a meal."

Darash nodded his appreciation, then asked, "Where is the boy who was with me last night? The child, Ikaiah?"

"Oh, he is just fine! He slept with the female servants in another room. He woke up a little while ago and has already eaten. One of the servants is watching him."

"Is he alright?"

Spiro took a moment to respond, and bobbed his head back and forth as he considered. "He is… getting better." He paused again, then explained further. "He cried when he awoke surrounded by strangers in a strange place, but Mina is very good with children. She was able to calm him and get him to eat something. Now she has him in the gardens, playing. You can see him, if you like."

"Oh…. I might wait a little on that," Darash said. "He was frightened of me last night."

"We were all frightened of you last night," Spiro said, his levity returning.

Darash chuckled.

"I suppose I looked pretty terrible."

"Nothing Spiro cannot handle." He smiled again. "I was just glad most of the blood was not yours. But it took a good deal of scrubbing to be sure."

The door opened, and another man entered. He, too, was a slave or servant, but an older one. He carried a satchel. Spiro rose to get out of his way as he approached.

"Ah! Good to see you sitting up," he said to Darash. "I am the physician."

סֶ לָ ה

An hour later, Darash sat with a full belly of lamb stew, watching Mina playing with Ikaiah. Indeed, the older, Greek woman was very good with children. She even had him laughing, drawing funny faces in the dirt with a stick and then copying them by scrunching up her face and crossing her eyes.

Ikaiah did not seem to recognize Darash at all, which Darash found to be a great relief. Mina drew another silly face in the dirt. Its ears stuck out and the eyes crossed. The tongue stuck out at an angle. Mina tried to copy it by tugging on her ears, crossing her eyes, and sticking out her tongue. Ikaiah laughed loudly at her.

"Now you," she said in stilted Hebrew, pointing to his chest.

Ikaiah tried to imitate her, and she squealed in delight and clapped her hands at his effort. He glanced at Darash and pointed.

Darash pulled his ears far out from the sides of his head, stuck his tongue out to the left as far as it would go, and rolled his eyes back in his head. Ikaiah and Mina clapped and laughed at the result.

"I see you are back to your normal self," a voice boomed from the porch.

Darash turned to see Magistrate Quintus Arrius coming toward him down the tiled steps. Mina rose and scooped up Ikaiah to take him somewhere else to play. The magistrate joined Darash on his stone bench.

"I came to let you know," Quintus began, "you can travel back to Jerusalem with my men and I, if you like, but we will not be returning for another week. You are welcome to stay here until then."

"Thank you, but no. Some friends of mine will be traveling back soon. In fact, I should go to them. They will be wondering what happened to me."

"As you like. Then perhaps you can take the boy to his family when you go. No sense making them wait."

"Certainly. We would be happy to."

"What happened last night, after I left?" Darash asked.

"We arrested thirteen of the cult members for attempted murder of a child and a man—you, in case you were wondering. This morning we counted twenty-three dead on the mountain and four more dead in the ravine. The rest escaped."

"And Bagad, the priest? What of him?"

"Unfortunately, he is among those who got away."

A cold feeling passed through Darash's chest. Bagad's bloody, rage-filled face flashed before Darash's mind. The large, white eyes, the fist holding a long dagger.

"My men are searching for him now," Quintus added.

"I know where he lives," Darash said. "I can tell you, in case—"

"No need," the magistrate interrupted. "We already have that information. We went there this morning. The house was deserted."

"What about the inn—the brothel, that is—that he owned?"

"We searched that place, too. The whole place should be burned to the ground, if you ask me. But he was not there. Just a few drunks and whores." He raised a hand before Darash could make any more suggestions. "He will not be coming back to the city. We know what he looks like and our guards watch every gate. I also have a man at each water source in this entire area. We will find him eventually."

Darash nodded. "Very well." He paused. "There was a girl," he said. "She had lighter hair than most. She was young. I saw her flee down the mountain in the dark when the fighting began."

"Yes. We have her. She was one of the four bodies we found in the ravine."

Oh, no! ...So Jada is dead. ...Jehiel will be heartbroken.

The magistrate rose. "I can show you how to get to the front door, if you like," he said. "I am going that way."

"Yes, thank you," Darash said, rising and following Quintus back toward the porch. Darash had not yet figured out how to navigate the Governor's massive home. "And thank you for making arrangements for me last night."

"Ah, well, it was nothing—seeing as how it was you who made it possible for my men to find the location of the ceremony."

"Really? How did I do that?"

"By rolling that boulder down the hill and smashing the idol," Quintus said. "My men and I were nearby, but were having trouble locating the temple. The sound of the drums kept bouncing off the other hills, making it difficult for us to pinpoint their precise location."

"What about the stone with the serpent on it?"

"We must have missed it in the dark, for we did not find it." Quintus led Darash down a long corridor of arched doorways and then to the right. "When that stone smashed the idol, it made a loud noise and set up a spray fire. It showed us the way." He paused. "It was you who did that, right? At least, that is what the prisoners are saying."

Darash shrugged. "It was all I could think of to do... but it almost got me killed."

"Indeed. A very foolish thing to do!" Quintus barked, but then his tone changed. "But, if you had done nothing we would not have found them when we did. And the child would be dead."

They passed through a courtyard with a private well and headed down another corridor that opened into a wide room, richly decorated with tapestries, decorative jars, and elegant wooden, cushioned benches.

"The Governor is very pleased with me for the results," Quintus added, as he nodded to a servant to open the far door. It opened upon an outer courtyard. Darash saw the main gate beyond. "So I suppose I have you to thank for that."

"Well, I have you to thank for saving my life... for a second time."

Quintus looked at him. "That is true."

XXI

Soothing Samaria

Darash walked away from the acropolis, moving slowly to avoid further irritating his aching muscles. He still wore the simple servant's tunic he had been given, glad it was not a Greek or Roman toga. He carried his bundle of clothing under his left arm. He had left Ikaiah behind in the care of Mina for now, knowing the child would be safe and happiest in her care until it was time to take him to his own family.

How will I tell Jehiel his daughter is dead?

Darash decided to head to Zuar's home first, to make sure Zephath and Phoebe had not given up on him and gone home. As he approached the home, he ran into Zephath leaving by the front gate. The older man smiled broadly and wrapped Darash in a painful embrace.

"Darash, Darash! You are alive! We were very worried when you did not return. Then we heard rumors of last night's massacre on the mountain! Phoebe went to Ethan and Photina's house to pray for your safety and for Jada. There are a great many people there praying even now. Even Jehiel is there."

At the mention of Jada's name, Darash took a deep breath and looked down.

"What is it, my young friend?" Zephath prodded.

"Jada is dead, Zephath."

Zephath's eyes grew serious and he shook his head. "Oh, no…. That is very bad news, indeed." He paused, then put a hand on Darash's left shoulder. "Come. Let us present you to Zuar and Mithcah so they know you are well. Then we will walk to Ethan's home and meet the people there. We must tell them what you have heard."

Darash sighed, not looking forward to the grim task ahead, but he nodded.

סֶלָה

When Darash and Zephath arrived at Ethan and Photina's home, they discovered a great many people squeezed together in the small shop, sitting on the floor, leaning against walls, and standing next to shelves of decorative items, trying as best they could not to knock anything over. All heads turned toward Darash and Zephath as they entered, and a host of whispered praises arose from the group.

Ethan, with Photina on his heels, moved toward them, moving between those on the floor as best they could.

"Darash! You are alright!" Ethan said, relief on his face.

"What happened to your head?" Photina asked. "And your arms and legs are bandaged as well, I see."

"I tumbled down a hillside and bumped my head," he explained, "as well as a few other places… but I am alright now. The Roman soldiers rescued me and took me to the acropolis where they bandaged my wounds."

"The Romans?" someone in the crowd said, incredulity in his voice.

The sentiment was mimicked by several others.

"We have been praying all night for your safe return," Ethan said. "We were afraid for your life when you did not return last night."

"Forgive me," Darash said. "I had no idea. I should have sent you word somehow."

"No, no! It is alright. Prayer is never wasted!"

"Indeed," Photina added, "perhaps our prayers kept you safe."

Darash smiled and thanked them. His eyes found Jehiel, sitting on some cushions where Ethan and Photina's adopted daughter usually played. He still looked weak, but now more from sorrow and worry than from the illness. The room grew silent as Darash read the unasked question in Jehiel's eyes.

"I am sorry, Jehiel," Darash said. He paused, but decided the best way to give bad news was to just state it simply and honestly. No use avoiding truth, no matter how painful. "Your daughter was at the ceremony. When the Romans arrived to arrest the people, Jada fled. She fell from the cliff in the darkness. She did not survive."

The people gasped. Many covered their mouths and heads. Some of the women cried. Jehiel lowered his head into his hands and wept.

Darash spotted another face in the crowd—Melchi. His face was stricken with something more than sorrow—absolute shock.

סֶֽלָה

As evening approached, Darash sat with Ethan and Photina on a low couch in their home during his final night with them. Zephath and Phoebe intended on starting their trip back to Gophna in the morning. Nimrah would be going with them, as would Darash and Ikaiah.

"You have a long journey ahead," Ethan observed. "I suppose you will stay tomorrow night in Shechem and arrive in Gophna the next evening? Then on to Yerushaláyim the day after that?"

Darash nodded. "That is the plan."

"I wonder if you might be willing to deliver a message for us," Photina said. She glanced at her husband, who rose to retrieve a small scroll from the back room.

When Ethan returned, he explained. "We are writing to the Followers of the Way in Yerushaláyim. We are a growing community of believers, but we lack full understanding of what it means to believe in and follow Yeshua—the Messiah. Our letter asks for someone from there—perhaps someone who knew Yeshua well—to come to us and answer our questions. Our interaction with Him was impactful, but brief. He stayed with us only two days. We long to know more." He extended the small vellum wrap toward Darash.

"Certainly," Darash answered, taking the scroll and tucking it in his belt. "I am not a member of their group, but I know where to find them."

"Wonderful," Ethan smiled and took his seat again. "You have helped us greatly!"

And I may have just sealed my own fate, if Imah finds this letter.

"Will Jehiel be alright?" Darash asked, switching topics.

Ethan sighed and exchanged a glance with Photina. "He is heartbroken, of course," Ethan said. "Jada's betrayal took him—took us all—by surprise. And then, to have her die as she did, without the chance to reconcile.... Well, it is very hard. But, Jehiel has a great many friends here. We will keep caring for him, checking on him, and praying for him. This life often brings trouble, but he will find joy in the next."

"And Melchi?"

"He is young. He will find another woman to marry." Ethan paused. "He mourns her death, of course... but he was also very surprised to hear of her involvement with the cult. I think he is realizing he did not really know her and, for him, at least, that will help him recover from her loss."

"None of us knew her, it seems," Photina said. She spread her hands in a motion of defeat. "Some of us suspected she might have been dabbling in dangerous things... but we had no idea she was capable of... of...."

"Such treachery," Ethan supplied.

A moment of silence passed.

"You know," Photina finally ventured, "I realized something through all of this. "I used to think of the God of the Jews as cruel—particularly toward my people. You see, I have ancestors who are Jewish, but I am also descended from Assyrians and Canaanites. I grew up not knowing which gods to follow, so I tried to follow them all. But, after today— recognizing the horrible things these lesser gods demand—I am now thankful that Adonai will not stand for it. As I become more familiar with the Torah, I see that He requires strict devotion to Himself alone—not because He is cruel—but because He loves us. He knows the suffering these other gods create, and He loves us too much to see us destroyed by them."

Ethan nodded in agreement. "I recently realized, in reading about the old wars for the Promised Land, that, though Adonai gave the land to the Israelites, the Israelites did not attack any of them first. They offered peace. The war was started by the wicked, idolatrous peoples—people very much like the Molech-worshippers you ran into last night." He leaned back and continued, "In this way, the Israelites maintained their innocence as non-aggressors. Additionally, God gave them strict and specific boundaries. The Israelites were not empire-builders, intent on expanding their borders across the globe, like the Egyptians, Assyrians, Babylonians, Greeks, or Romans. They were simply returning to the land they had once inhabited—this land—and were satisfied with what God had provided."

Now this is something Imah would like to hear. ...Of course, she would be shocked it came from someone like Ethan and Photina. Not only are they Samaritans, but they are also Way Followers.

"Amazing, is it not?" Photina said, looking at her husband, a small smile playing about her lips. "That despite the loss, God shows us His ultimate purpose—and it is for our benefit. He is good and holy and loving. He simply cannot share space with what is evil, unholy, or treacherous." She paused. "That has been true enough in my own life. When Yeshua came and spoke to me, He showed me these things. And, each day, as the wicked places in my heart are identified and expelled, I grow more and more free."

"The same is true for me," Ethan said, now smiling as well. "As a younger man I did everything I could to add pleasure and security and joy to my life. But all my efforts were wasted, because my desire was for this world and the things of it… things that do not last. But when I met Yeshua, He showed me something that does last. Now my desire is to know God. Now, other things that bring joy—my wife, my daughter, the believing people of Samaria—He has added to my life."

Darash tried to absorb this, finding it difficult to imagine either Ethan or Photina ever having lived different lives or being any less compassionate and generous.

Photina rose and returned with cups of warm goat's milk that had been simmering on a metal grate over a small indoor, portable firepot. She handed one to Darash and then to her husband.

"Thank you," Darash said with a smile of gratitude. He took a sip of the creamy, warm liquid. He detected a hint of honey as the smooth fluid filled his mouth and slipped down his throat, warming him all the way to his middle. "Ah..." he said, smiling at the sensation. "This is delicious. Thank you."

Photina smiled. Her eyes twinkled in the light of the oil lamp on a table nearby, as she watched and appreciated Darash's enjoyment of the drink.

"I hope you know you are always welcome in our home," Photina said.

"Yes!" Ethan added enthusiastically. "If you or your family ever come to Samaria again, you must stay with us."

Darash dipped his head in gratefulness and said, "Thank you. I will," but he could not imagine his mother ever being willing to eat with a Gentile, let alone sleep in their home.

סֶ לָ ה

Darash went to bed early that night, despite having slept so long into the day. His body ached incessantly, draining his energy. He lay down on the thin, straw mattress belonging to Ethan and Photina's daughter. They had taken the child into their room so Darash could have a private place to rest.

"I, for one, will sleep much better tonight," Photina had said, before bidding him goodnight, "knowing that little boy is safe and will soon be returned to his mother's arms."

"You have done a very brave—a very noble thing," Ethan had added. "You offered your life for someone else—someone you did not even know. Yeshua, your Messiah, did the same thing for you... and for all of us."

Lying there, staring up at the ceiling of wood beams, mud, and straw, Darash considered the things he had seen and heard. Was Yeshua truly the long-awaited Messiah? Others had come, claiming to be the Messiah, only to fail. Others, like Bar'abbas, had sparked rebellions against the Romans and raised the hopes of the people—only to be quickly squelched. What made Yeshua different?

Darash remembered Jehiel's story and his subsequent dream—seeing Yeshua's eyes as he cast the demon out. He remembered hearing Yeshua speak on a hillside several years ago with his father. He remembered the stories of sightings of Yeshua after his crucifixion. He had even seen the empty tomb.

As Darash watched the shadows deepen in the corners of the room, he realized part of him wanted to believe. But he still had too many unanswered questions. If Yeshua was the Messiah, how could he let the Romans kill him? Why did they still rule over the Jews?

And what did Ethan mean that Yeshua gave his life for mine?

I wonder… before Abba died, did he come to believe Yeshua was the Messiah?

The thought had never occurred to Darash until now, though he had known of his father's fascination with the unusual teacher from Nazareth—something he kept hidden from Revayah. But how far Tuwr had taken his interest, Darash could not say.

Darash readjusted himself on the mattress, as best he could, to alleviate the worst of his aches. His eyes grew heavy but, upon closing them, images of the day ran through his mind. He tried to push away the darker images, but Bagad's face continued to flash before him.

He is still out there somewhere. Is he looking for me? The one who destroyed his idol and exposed his lie to his followers?

Darash shuddered and pulled the thick wool blanket up around his neck. As long as he remained in the city, he was safe. He believed the magistrate would diligently guard the entrances.

But tomorrow we travel to Shechem… along the same route he has attacked before …when he and his followers killed Hazaiah's three servants and kidnapped Ikaiah.

Darash would not be travelling alone, of course but, as he thought of each of his traveling companions, that fact did not offer much comfort. His companions included a drunk, a woman, a nitwit, and a child. What could any of them do against a man like Bagad?

Perhaps he has already left the area. The magistrate said his home had been abandoned, his wife and real son gone. They probably met up with him, and are in some other city even now.

Thinking of this possibility made Darash feel a little better. But then he realized that it was equally possible that, upon hearing of her husband's disastrous exposure as a liar and a hypocrite to his own followers, Bagad's wife might have realized the danger she and her son were in and simply fled without him.

And, even if they are in some other city, that city might be Shechem.

XXII

The Road Home

The cart creaked as Zephath moved his thick frame onto the drivers' seat. He reached down to give Phoebe a hand up. She tucked her hair behind her ears, adjusted her head-covering snuggly around her head, and positioned herself primly on the wooden bench next to him, hands resting in her lap. Darash, Nimrah, and Ikaiah sat in the back, amongst the bundles and baskets and nearly empty wine jugs.

Zuar and Mithcah, Ethan, Photina, and their daughter had accompanied Darash to the inn to see the motley group off. Zephath's cart and horse had remained lodged at the inn during their stay, since it was so close to the city gate. Horse carts were not allowed deeper into the city, for the narrow roads and alleys could not handle the congestion. Their small group of friends waved as Zephath pulled away.

"Ah, it is good to see them together," Phoebe said to Zephath as they moved out of earshot of their new friends.

"Why do you say that?" he asked.

"Because Mithcah has very much wanted to join our small believer's fellowship to learn about Yeshua, but Zuar has been against it."

"What makes you think he will agree?"

"Because Ethan and Photina can be very convincing." She smiled.

Darash sensed an awkward pause—awkward on Zephath's part, anyway. Then the man said, "You know, there is no believer's fellowship in Gophna."

Phoebe turned to her husband, smiled, and patted his hand. "Oh, do not worry. There soon will be."

"I was not worried," he said, but then muttered, "at least, not until now."

The cart creaked along for a spell at a reasonable pace, first having no difficulty navigating the valley surrounding Samaria, until the path began a steep ascent again into the hills beyond.

"Alright, everyone!" Zephath called, bringing the cart to a halt. "We must all get out and walk for a while. My poor horse can only handle so much. As I warned you before we started, we will ride on the downhill and flat places, but we will walk the uphill places."

No one complained as they disembarked. Zephath and Phoebe hopped down first, and Phoebe came around to the back so Nimrah could hand the boy to her. Darash moved the most slowly, willing his aching muscles to obey. Zephath offered him a hand, which he gladly took.

Perhaps a walk will do me good... help me loosen up a bit. Besides, the cart shakes so much I cannot distinguish its movements from the throbbing in my head.

Zephath took the reins, pulled them forward, and led his mare up the incline. Phoebe held Ikaiah's hand as they walked, asking him to point out interesting plants or rock formations along the way. Ikaiah, looking to have slept well the night before, bounced along next to her, answering her questions, but every once in a while interrupting their seek and find game to ask about his mother.

"Imah will come?" he asked for the tenth time, looking up into Phoebe's face for reassurance.

"We are taking you to her, remember?" Phoebe told him. "Your Imah and Abba are waiting for us in Gophna."

"We will see them tonight?"

Phoebe shook her head. "Not tonight. Gophna is very far. But we will see her tomorrow. Just one more sleep. We stay in Shechem tonight. And Gophna tomorrow. Can you say, 'Gophna'?"

"Gophna."

"Very good, Ikaiah!"

Darash and Nimrah walked along together, having no one else to walk with. Nimrah no longer complained about leaving Samaria, but kept his head and eyes down, saying nothing to anyone. Darash, having said nothing to the awkward, lanky man since the day Ethan dragged him out of the brothel, had even less interest in speaking to him now.

Darash paused to stretch his aching back. Out of the corner of his eyes, he noticed movement along the road behind them. A lone traveler walked in their direction, traveling south.

Nimrah let out a loud sigh as Darash joined him again.

An awkward moment passed.

Another soulful sigh.

"Uh..." Darash ventured, trying to figure out how to address Nimrah, "are you thirsty? There is a wine flask in the back of the cart."

Nimrah was likely a good decade Darash's senior, but had never married, nor even participated in many social events, despite his mother's unreserved and out-going nature. His hunched shoulders, oversized nose, and pock-marked face were the least of his troubles. Darash had seen far uglier men happily married. But Nimrah failed to understand, let alone apply, the finer points of appropriate social behavior, such proper eye-contact, the ability to contribute confidently to a conversation, and what to do with one's hands.

Nimrah did not answer Darash's question, but sighed again.

"Perhaps you would like to stop for a while and—"

"It is a terrible thing!" Nimrah cried, clenching his fist and startling Darash.

"Wh-what is?"

"To be a Jew in a country where the Romans take whatever they want!"

Darash nodded. Indeed, the Romans had stolen much from the Jewish people.

"They take our land! Our homes! And now they have killed my bride! Cursed be the Romans!"

Darash furrowed his brow in confusion. Even Zephath, from where he walked several paces ahead, leading the mare and cart, overheard Nimrah's outburst. He glanced back, exchanged a look with Darash, then turned back to the road, shaking his head.

Darash decided contradicting Nimrah with facts would likely not end well, so he held his tongue.

The group made it to the top of the hill and piled back into the cart. Even going downhill, they moved barely above walking pace, but Darash found it agreeable to take the weight off his aching legs again—even though the jolting of the cart aggravated his headache.

Morning evaporated into noon, after several moves between riding and walking. Darash found the frequent changing of positions helped manage his aching muscles. At one point he fell asleep in the cart and, when they woke him to eat their noon meal—packed for them by Mithcah, Darash felt a good deal better.

Hmm…. The other traveler is gaining on us.

Darash gazed north toward the direction they had come as he chewed his meal of bread spread thickly with cheese. Though they had lost sight of the man for a time, he now approached at a steady pace, evidently not stopping to eat. And he was far closer now. He was tall, thin, and walked with head down, taking rapid steps despite a slight limp. He wore a long, white robe with a head covering that effectively kept Darash from making out his features. He walked with arms crossed, hands tucked in the opposite sleeves for warmth.

Something about the way he walked and his steady, determined approach unnerved Darash.

"Zephath, could we get moving again?" Darash asked, standing and moving to the front of the cart where Zephath had anchored his mare to a large stone.

"Why the hurry?" Zephath asked from his spot on the ground where he sat next to Phoebe with Ikaiah on his lap. "We should get to Shechem before sundown, and Adonai has blessed us with fair weather."

Odd how spiritual he sounded now that Phoebe was with him. And he had not touched his cart wine yet.

"I am just eager to get this trip over with," Darash said.

"The young man has been through a great deal, my husband," Phoebe said, putting a hand on his arm. "It would be good for him to have a nice long rest this evening before we have to start again tomorrow."

"Ah, very well," Zephath said, motioning of the child to rise from his lap and then struggling his fat frame to his feet. "The young never let the grass grow under their feet, I suppose."

Phoebe smiled as he reached down to pull her up.

"Thank you," Darash said with a nervous glance over his shoulder. The mysterious traveler was now only a stone's throw away. The man glanced up, looking straight at Darash and his traveling party. Still, Darash could not make out the man's face, as the hood obscured his features.

Darash lifted Ikaiah into the cart and hopped in after him, forgetting the aches in his body. He gritted his teeth in frustration as he waited for Zephath and Phoebe to settle themselves on the seat. Zephath had to choose that precise moment to take his first swig of wine.

"Just a bit… to wash down the bread," he said to Phoebe, who watched him with suspicion.

The man was nearly upon them when the cart finally got rolling again. The traveler stopped, appearing to watch in disappointment as they pulled away.

He is definitely following us!

Darash felt his heart quicken at the realization, but breathed a sigh of relief as he watched the distance between them and the traveler increase. But the man started walking again, as if determined to reach them.

There were several inns in Shechem, and it might take time for the man to locate the same one Zephath would choose. Still, he would find them eventually, and Darash could think of only one person who would bother to seek them out—Bagad.

Once we are in Shechem at the inn, there will be many people around. It will be harder for him to get to me… but not impossible.

Darash wracked his brain for a way to protect himself against the wicked priest, but nothing came to mind.

סֶלָה

"You know," Zephath said, as they walked up another steep incline, "your description of that enormous idol of Molech got me to wondering."

Darash had moved to walk alongside Zephath and Phoebe, leaving Nimrah to follow along behind. The traveler had once again faded into the distance, allowing Darash to breathe a little easier, but he still found Nimrah a poor traveling companion. In another hour or so they would see the town of Shechem coming into view.

"Oh? Wondering what?" Darash asked.

"About where they could have found a metalworker with a forge large enough to make such a thing."

Darash pondered for a moment. "The forge at Gophna," he finally said, remembering how unusually large it was.

Zephath nodded, concern crossing his brow. "I cannot be sure, of course, but I think so. I have long suspected something strange was going on in Gophna… something connected to the murmurings about cult activity in the region… but your description of the idol gives me serious reason to be concerned."

"What will you do?"

"What can I do?" Zephath looked at Darash and shrugged. "I have no proof, and the man is a friend of mine."

They entered a narrow stretch of road with large boulders on either side.

"You can always pray for him," Phoebe said, having overheard from where she walked on the other side of the mare, holding Ikaiah's hand.

"Yes, of course, my wife," Zephath said, nodding and smiling at her, but he shot Darash a look.

Nimrah let out a moan of frustration. "Are we there yet?" he asked.

"Almost," Zephath called, trying to remain cheery. "We need only make it across this hill and the next, if memory serves."

"I am tired of walking," Nimrah complained.

"As are we all," Zephath said, gritting his teeth ever so slightly. "You managed to make it all the way to Samaria. Surely you can make it home again."

"But I had a horse then."

"What? A horse?" Zephath looked back at his nephew. "Why did you not say? Where is it now?"

"I sold it in Samaria to help pay for my lodgings."

Do you mean to tell me—"

"Patience, my husband," Phoebe interrupted, patting his arm. "There is no use discussing it now."

Zephath groaned and shook his head. "You are right, of course," he whispered back to her, and pursued the conversation with Nimrah no further.

Phoebe stepped aside and let the cart roll passed her so she and Ikaiah could join Nimrah at the back of the cart. Once the cart passed, she started walking again, and turned to Nimrah, "Here, Nimrah. Put Ikaiah in the cart and let him ride. He is getting sleepy."

"I want to ride, too," Nimrah complained.

"No, only the child can ride for now. We are still moving uphill, and he is very light."

"I am light, too."

"Nimrah." Phoebe's voice changed.

"Oh, all right." Nimrah picked Ikaiah up and, as they walked, he set the child in the back of the cart.

Suddenly, Ikaiah let out a terrified scream.

All eyes turned to the child, and Zephath drew the cart to a standstill in the road. Ikaiah stood in the middle of the cart, wide eyes transfixed. Darash and the others followed his gaze to see a man stepping out from behind one of the boulders just ahead. His clothing was stained with darkened blood and dirt. He held a long, curved dagger in his right hand.

The man stood looking directly at Darash, eyes wide and unblinking, a look of abandoned determination and merciless loathing on his face.

Bagad.

XXIII

The Suspicious Traveler

Ikaiah dropped to the bed of the cart and hid himself under some bundles. Nimrah moved to the opposite side of the cart, took one more look at Bagad, his blood-stained clothing and sharp knife, and ran away toward Shechem without looking back. Zephath swung an arm in front of Phoebe and pushed her back so he stood between her and their assailant. Darash remained frozen to his spot.

"You!" Bagad cried, hatred dripping from his tongue. "You ruined everything!"

He moved toward Darash with slow steps.

"Stop right there!" Zephath cried, moving forward a step.

"Stay back, or you die first! Then I will kill your woman and that boy, as well!"

Zephath took a step back again as Phoebe moved aside, which brought him close to the front of the cart. He reached in and grabbed hold of a jug of his cart-wine. He held it up like a shield, as if intending to block any knife thrusts Bagad might wield at him.

"Now, I said stop, and I mean it!" Zephath cried again attempting to move between Darash and the approaching attacker, holding his clay jug in self-defense.

Bagad turned steely eyes on Zephath. Molech's priest now stood only a few paces from the winemaker of Gophna. Bagad moved forward swiftly bringing his knife down on Zephath. Darash moved forward and Phoebe screamed as Zephath effectively deflected the blade with his jug. But Bagad followed up with a left hook to Zephath's chin, which sent him sprawling backward, tripping over his own feet and landing hard on the ground with an 'oof.'

Bagad wasted no more time with Zephath and refocused on his true target—Darash.

Darash backed away, but Bagad moved in swiftly. He grabbed Darash by the front of his cloak and pulled him close. "You robbed me!" he seethed. "I lost everything because of you!" The strain of Bagad's rage made every vein, every tendon in his neck visible. "My wife and son deserted me. I am an exile from my own city. My followers have turned on me. Molech himself may even strike me dead." He brought the knife near Darash's face. His knuckles whitened as he gripped the handle, eager for the kill. "But before he does, I have one more sacrifice for him."

Darash sucked in his breath as Bagad pulled back to drive the blade into Darash's chest. A strange sound escaped Bagad, and he stopped as if paralyzed—blade held high, his fist still gripping Darash. He staggered and Darash pulled away.

Bagad's eyes stared strangely, and he teetered and moved to the left. He tried to take a breath but only gasped and choked.

A figure emerged from behind Bagad—a stranger in a white cloak with a look of pure hatred on his face.

Bagad fell to the ground. A knife protruded from his back, and a bright red stain appeared and spread through the darker blood and dirt stains on his robe.

The stranger stood over Bagad watching as the life slipped from the wicked man. Darash suddenly recognized him as the traveler who had been following them.

"That is for making me sacrifice my son," the stranger said to Bagad's corpse, "but being unwilling to sacrifice your own!" He barely acknowledged Darash, though he had just spared his life. Tears of rage made their way down dusty cheeks. "You hypocrite! You deceiver!" He took in a ragged breath, choked with emotion. "Hear me now—and be sure to tell Molech when you see him—that I will never serve you or your wicked, deceiving god again!"

סֶ֫לָה

"Darash," Zephath said, handing him the reins of his mare once they reached the inn of Shechem where they intended to stay for the night. "Start unloading the cart. Phoebe can help you once she gets the child settled."

"There is no need," Darash answered. "I can do it."

"Are you sure? You look pretty shaken up."

"The work will do me good."

Zephath nodded. "Alright, then." He pulled his robe tighter around his rotund frame and cinched his belt. "I will go in search of Nimrah." He groaned and rubbed the back of his head. "I admit, I am tempted to forget about him altogether."

Zephath headed back out the inn's outer courtyard as Darash reached for the first bundle of goods. The innkeeper at this establishment had not seen or heard of Nimrah. Zephath intended to visit every inn he could find until he located the young man.

Once again, we find ourselves looking for Nimrah!

Darash shook his head.

If Nimrah had any sense at all, he would have run directly to the Roman governor to report the attack. Then he could have waited for us at the first inn at the city, letting the Romans know where we could find him.

Of course, Nimrah had no sense.

And, thanks to his skewed memory of what happened in Samaria, he now has even less reason to seek help from the Romans—even to save our lives!

No, Nimrah had disappeared once again. This time, though, Darash had no intention of looking for him.

Tomorrow was Yom Ha′shee′shee, the sixth day. Dusk would mark the beginning of Shabbat. They would have to make it to Gophna by then, lest they be caught traveling on Shabbat. He had no desire to make camp for an entire day on the road.

I wish I was home already. Imah will be worried about me by now. I will have been gone a full two weeks by the time I get back. I told her I would only be away for one.

Darash had more reasons to want to be home than his mother's concern. Truth be told, Revayah was unlikely to worry much. She was used to Tuwr's travels taking longer than expected. The life of a merchant's wife—or mother—demanded flexibility. Darash missed his own bed, his little sister, and Nib'haz—the blind basket seller who always knew how to help him sort out his troubles. Today, he had so many troubles. ...But Darash also wanted to find out how Amah fared. Had she settled in? Was she getting along with Tsarah? Making herself useful to Imah?

Suddenly, two days seemed like an eternity.

סֶ לְ ה

To Darash's surprise, Zephath returned a couple of hours later, with Nimrah in tow. What did not surprise Darash was that Zephath found the young man at a brothel near the Roman Acropolis of Shechem. Neither wanted to discuss it.

"I spoke to the magistrate of Shechem," Zephath told Darash after dinner that night, "and informed him of what happened on the road. He told me he would send someone out to collect the body, but he did not extend any promises about locating Bagad's killer." He shrugged. "Personally, I consider the matter closed."

Darash nodded in agreement.

"That man had been following us all day," Darash said. "For a while, I thought he was Bagad."

"Why did you not say anything?"

"I intended on telling you once we reached town. I did not want to alarm the others unnecessarily. Besides, we were in a cart, and he was on foot. I thought we had lost him."

"Good thing we did not," Zephath said.

סֶ לָ ה

They rose before the sun the next morning, ate a hurried breakfast, and paid for their lodgings. Zephath pulled his cart out of Shechem as the first rays of sun played along the eastern horizon. The road improved the closer they got to Jerusalem. Ikaiah quickly went back to sleep, resting in Phoebe's arms. She sat in the back of the cart amongst the bags, cradling him. Nimrah sat opposite her, nodding off. He finally put his head back against the jolting wooden sideboard, and fell asleep, his mouth wide open.

Darash had joined Zephath on the seat up front. He glanced behind at the others.

"How can he sleep like that?" he asked Zephath, staring at Nimrah.

Zephath glanced back and smirked. "He is like his father. He can sleep through anything."

The second day of travel passed without incident. They continued to disembark from the cart whenever they came to a hill, but the road here was smoother and the traveling easier. Still, they all smiled and gave a sigh of relief as they rounded the last bend and Gophna came into view well before dusk.

"You will stay with us at our house," Zephath told Darash. "But first we have very important business to attend to." He glanced back at Ikaiah.

Zephath drew the cart to a stop in front of the inn of Gophna. Ira came out the front gate as Darash's foot touched the ground.

"Zephath, young Darash! It is good to see you back!" He took a double-take at Darash. "You looked better when you left, though. You will have to tell me all about—" He stopped mid-sentence, seeing Phoebe climbing from the back of the cart, bringing a child with her. "Phoebe! You have returned! And is that…? It cannot be! Is that the missing child?"

"He is missing no longer, thanks be to Adonai," Phoebe said, a smile spreading across her face. She smiled warmly on Darash. "And to Darash."

"I will get his parents!" Ira cried. "They had nearly lost hope and were planning on returning home in the morning, since Hazaiah has mostly recovered from his wound. But this will finally bring a smile to his face!" Ira darted off, raising a shout within that all could hear. "He has been found! Hazaiah and Eliana! Your son has been found!"

The sound of cries of joy erupted from the inn as Zephath, Phoebe, Darash, Nimrah, and Ikaiah crossed the yard. Eliana burst from the front door, her face contorted with joy and relief so intense she wept aloud. Instantly, her eyes found her son. She swept him into her arms and held him tightly, kissing him over and over again as she wept.

Hazaiah, too, came outside, walking as fast as his weakened state would allow. Ira supported him on one side, and another guest supported him on the other. He cried aloud in praise to Elohim as he encircled both his son and his wife with his arms. Tears ran freely down his cheeks to disappear in his beard. He stroked his son's head and kissed him again and again.

Ira and his family and all of his guests surrounded the young family and cheered. Someone burst into an impromptu song of praise, a psalm of David. Others quickly joined in, clapping, dancing, and lifting their voices with gusto. People from the nearby homes heard the sound and came over to find out what was going on. Soon the entire town of Gophna celebrated in the streets for the son who had been lost, but now was found.

סֶ לָ ה

Night crept upon the celebrating city, sending people back to their homes, smiling, whistling, and chattering about the amazing story they had heard and the miraculous reunion they had witnessed. Hazaiah and Eliana sat with Ikaiah in a corner, watching him sleep with awe like that of new parents. Eliana wept, purging the sorrow and fear of the past weeks to make room for joy.

As Phoebe, Nimrah, and Darash prepared to take their leave, Zephath embraced his old friend, Ira. "Thank you, again, my friend, for taking such good care of these people." He glanced at the family. "They have been in good hands with you."

"It was my pleasure, of course," Ira responded, smiling. He turned to Darash. "I am only glad their story ended as a happy one… thanks to this young man."

Darash colored. "Well… I only delayed things. It was the Romans who stopped the evil men."

"You found the boy and led the Romans to him," Ira countered, having paid close attention to every detail Zephath had shared. "No.

Without you, the child would not be here tonight. And we would not be celebrating."

Darash felt a hand touch his shoulder from behind. He turned to look up into the face of Hazaiah. Hazaiah's face contorted with emotion as he spoke.

"Ira is right," Hazaiah said. "We owe you everything." He had to pause to gather his emotions enough to form the words. He took Darash's hand and placed something in it. "Please, take this. It is not enough to repay you for what you have done for us, but I insist you have it."

Darash glanced at the small, leather bag of coins. Undoubtedly, this was the remainder of the silver Magistrate Quintus Arrius had returned to them after his men found it in their burned out cart—having been overlooked by Bagad in his desperation to steal their son from them.

"Oh, no," Darash said, pushing it back to them. "I cannot—"

"You must!" Hazaiah took Darash's hand in both of his and squeezed Darash's fingers around the bag. "I will not take no for an answer! May God deal with me ever so severely if I do not give you all I can! What you have given me is far, far more precious to me than silver or gold."

סֶ לָ ה

Phoebe took one step into the home she had left three and a half months earlier and stopped in the doorway.

"My heavens!" she said, staring at the filthy floor, the unwashed dishes, and the piles of soiled clothing and blankets. The house reeked of filth and alcohol. "Now I know how Nehemiah felt when he returned to the ruins of Yerushaláyim after the seventy years of exile were over."

XXIV

Gone

Darash spent Shabbat in Gophna, then he and Nimrah headed home early on the morning of Yom Reeshone, the first day of the new week. Darash led a well-rested Nekoda, loaded down with his purchases and the wine Zephath gave him. He carried the silver he had acquired in his belt.

The two young men traveled mostly in silence, for which Darash was thankful. He had heard enough of Nimrah's moaning about Jada, his imagined betrothal, and the evil of the Roman Empire. Darash's mind was full of thoughts of home, seeing Tsarah again, making sure his mother was well, and talking with Nib'haz. But, most of all, he wanted to see Amah.

As they neared the city, the road grew more congested with travelers—Romans heading off to parts unknown on horseback or riding in the back of a chariot, families traveling together, and fellow merchants leading camels, donkeys, or mules. Darash was so eager to get home that he refused to stop to eat the snack Phoebe had packed for them, insisting they eat as they walked. The gates of Jerusalem came into view just as Darash and Nimrah finished the olives and flatbread. Phoebe had apologized for the simplicity of the meal, having had no time to prepare something more elaborate, but Darash found it perfectly filling and delicious. Anything tasted good to a hungry young man of fifteen.

The welcome sounds of Jerusalem met their ears—the braying of cattle in their pens as they waited to be sold, loud discussions among those who sat at the city gate, shouted advertisements from innkeepers and merchants to those entering the city. A smile spread across Darash's face and his heart warmed.

I am home.

They traveled through the Tyropeon Valley, passing the Antonia Fortress and the western side of the Temple Mount. They moved through the original city wall into the wealthy neighborhood surrounding Herod Antipas's palace before entering the Upper Shuk, within the Upper City. Darash ran into his old friend, Chaphash, but only stopped to talk briefly, promising to visit him soon.

They continued down the embankment and through another set of gates into the Lower City and the Lower Shuk, where Darash usually did business. He was anxious to be rid of Nimrah and worried the man might disappear on him again before he could deliver him to his parents.

When they neared the dyers' booth, Nimrah grew hesitant, dragging his feet.

"We should not delay," Darash said. "Your mother and father will be overjoyed to see you."

Nimrah said nothing, but continued forward. Before the colorful dyers' booth even came into view, someone must have spotted Nimrah and Darash as they walked through the market and run off to tell Millah and Obed, for they came around the corner arms wide and rushing forward toward their son. Darash moved out of the way as Millah enveloped Nimrah in a strong embrace and Obed put an arm around him, patting his back. Darash noticed that Obed did not look at all ill, after all. Though Nimrah stood a good head taller than either of his parents, his severely stooped shoulders allowed them to reach him.

"You are home! Praise Adonai, you are home!" Millah cried and kissed him repeatedly on both cheeks, which Nimrah merely tolerated. Then she stood back, keeping a hand on each of his arms, and looked up at him, her expression changing from one of joy to one of irritation. "How could you do such a thing to your poor mother?"

"And father," Obed added.

"Do you not know how worried I have been?"

"As have I," Obed said.

"Why did you not tell me where you were going?"

"Or me?"

Nimrah hung his head, then finally looked his mother in the eyes.

"If only you knew the great trouble I have had," he said in a sorrowful voice.

"Oh, dear!" Millah said. "You must come home at once and let your Imah cook you a good meal." She turned to lead him away. "Then you can tell me all about it."

"And I, as well," Obed said, following his wife and son back to their home behind the sales booth.

Several curious neighbors followed the trio, hoping to overhear details of Nimrah's misadventures. Darash had no doubt Nimrah's skewed version of the events in Samaria would become Jerusalem's next choice piece of gossip within a matter of hours. He watched them go, having not drawn so much as a look from any of them.

Happy to be rid of Nimrah, despite having received no reward for the fool's safe return, Darash continued through the shuk, passed the well at the center of the marketplace, and headed toward the alley where he knew Nib'haz would be hard at work making and selling baskets.

"Ah, Darash! You have returned!" Nib'haz, though blind, always knew the sound of Darash's approach. He called to him, a smile of anticipation on his weathered face and a half-finished, reed basket in his lap.

"Shalom, Nib'haz," Darash said, smiling. He took the man's extended hand in his own, then leaned down to kiss his mentor on both cheeks.

"When did you return?" Valad, the cheese-seller, asked with a smile.

"Just now. I have not yet been home."

"Oh, then you must go and set your mother's mind at ease," Nib'haz said. "She will be worried about you."

"I will in a moment," Darash moved a stack of baskets aside and made a spot for himself to sit next to his old friend.

"Tell us all about your journey," Nib'haz said, picking up his basket again so as to work while he listened.

"As you know," Darash said, "I only intended to be gone a week—maybe a week and a half—to resupply and sell a few items in Gophna and to the merchants who happened to be traveling through."

"From the looks of your donkey," Valad said, "it looks like you have done well for yourself. Are those jugs of wine or oil?"

"Wine," Darash answered. "The best that can be had."

"Ah!" Valad's eyes lit up.

"What kept you so away so long?" Nib'haz asked.

"Yes, and why are you so beat up?" Valad added. "You are covered in bandages and bruises."

"As I left town, I was asked to track down the dyers' son, who had run off."

"I heard of that," Valad said. "They asked almost everyone in Yerushaláyim if we had seen him. Whatever happened to him?"

Darash sighed, unsure how much to tell.

"He went to find himself a wife… but things did not work out well for him."

Though Valad probed further, that was all Darash was willing to say about Nimrah and was glad when Nib'haz returned to the original subject.

"Tell us of your time in Gophna."

"I ran into a couple whose son had been stolen from them on the road to Samaria. The husband, Hazaiah, had been stabbed, his wife knocked unconscious, and their servants and animals slain."

Nib'haz's hands stopped moving across the dry reeds as he listened. He shook his head. "Horrible," he said. "We heard rumors about more attacks on the road, but I did not hear that a child had gone missing."

"The winemaker of Gophna, Zephath, invited me to go with him to look for Nimrah, so I agreed. We first went to Shechem. Then we went on to Samaria."

"Samaria?" Valad asked. "That far? And to those people? Do not let your mother find out!"

"Once in Samaria, things became much more complicated than I ever imagined."

Darash recounted his adventures to his friends, who listened with rapt attention to every detail, then asked for more. It felt good to share with them. The terrible memories felt a bit lighter as he finished up his tale.

"I have never witnessed evil like that," Darash said, finally. "Not up close."

Nib'haz nodded. "It is a hard thing... to grow up in a world filled with such wickedness. But, know this—Elohim is yet in control. And He is not a God who will allow evil to grow unchecked. Indeed, it is the nature of evil to destroy itself in the end." He paused. "Those who bow to idols do so to gain power. Their lust for power is very great, indeed. They lie, steal, and kill to get it, believing that, by doing so, they earn the right to control the gods. But they deceive themselves. For the only real power false gods have is the power of deception. The more people try to control a false god, the more they become his slaves."

As Nib'haz said those words, Darash recalled something his father, Tuwr, had once told him, not long before he died. "The teacher, Yeshua, says the most fascinating things," Tuwr had said. "Do not tell your mother, but I find the man intriguing… and more than a little dangerous. He speaks to the Pharisees and teachers of the law as if they are children. Indeed, just the other day, he told them they were the children of the devil, rather than the children of God, as they always claim." He shook his head in incredulity. "He also told the Jews that, if they followed His teachings, they would know the truth. And the truth would set them free."

The truth will set you free.

Darash was not sure what Yeshua had meant by this, or how one could be certain of the truth. But his mind returned to the dream he had—the dream where Yeshua stood over him, calling to the demon within Darash's chest, and casting it out.

Darash, in a subconscious motion, put a hand to his chest over the scar where the knife had gone in. Suddenly, he realized something. He had not felt the pain of the wound, nor shortness of breath since waking from that dream. He had struggled on his way to Gophna and during the early days there. But later, even as he traveled long distances, ran through the city of Samaria to fetch Phoebe for Jehiel, climbed hills in the dark, and pushed a boulder down a mountainside, he had felt nothing from his old wound. The pain was simply… gone.

"What are you smiling about?" Valad asked, jolting Darash back to the conversation at hand.

"Oh… nothing." Darash stood. "I have another errand to run, and then I should be getting home. I will come back in the morning." He moved to Nekoda to untie her from the hitching post, but before leaving he turned back to his friends. "In the morning, I would like to talk to both of you about a new business idea I have—something I saw in practice in Samaria. It might allow us to finally get out of this alley."

סֶלָה

Darash remembered well the time Barus, the Greek man whose daughter was murdered, invited Darash to go to a meeting of the Followers of Yeshua—the Way Followers or Nazarites, as they were sometimes called. Darash had made an excuse to avoid attending the meeting. However, he had seen his father's old friend, Rabbi Nathan, entering the meeting and being welcomed like a regular member.

Photina and Ethan had entrusted Darash with a message for the believers of Jerusalem, which he still carried in his belt. Though he did not want to get mixed up with this strange religious sect himself… at least, not yet, he knew Rabbi Nathan was the perfect person to deliver it for him.

Darash headed down a familiar street to the rabbi's home, where he had spent many evenings as a child, visiting with his family. A short rap on the door brought a servant who opened it for him.

"Oh, young Darash," the elderly servant recognized him immediately. "The rabbi is resting. I shall fetch him."

"Oh, do not bother him," Darash said. "I do not have much time, anyway. I just stopped by to give him this."

Darash pulled the small scroll from his belt.

"What is it?"

"A message."

"From whom?"

"From friends of his… friends he does not yet know he has."

The servant frowned, but he took the scroll Darash offered him.

"Do not worry," Darash said, smiling at the old man's confusion. "I am certain he will understand when he reads the contents."

סֶ לָ ה

"Darash, is that you?"

Revayah's voice met him as he opened the outer gate of their home. She came out the front door of the house and crossed the small yard to give him a welcoming embrace, but stopped when she got within a few paces of him.

"Whatever have you done to yourself?"

"Oh… I…."

"You look worse now than you did when you left! What happened to you? Did you fall off a cliff or something?"

"Actually…."

"What?" Revayah stared at Darash, eyes wide and waiting for an explanation. "Are you telling me the truth? You fell off a cliff? What am I going to do with you?"

"It was not a cliff, precisely," Darash said. "I sort-of tumbled down a mountainside… in the dark."

"Is that how you got that welt on your head?"

Darash nodded.

Revayah's eyes narrowed. "That is it! You are not going on any trips out of the city until further notice! Do you understand me?"

Darash nodded again.

"Darash!" Tsarah's voice greeted him from the doorway. He handed Nekoda's lead rope to Revayah so he could stoop down to embrace his sister with both arms. "You are back! You are back!" She nearly danced with joy, and Darash found it hard to hold onto her.

He laughed at her exuberance and kissed her on the top of the head.

"I was only gone a couple of weeks," he said, smiling, but then glanced at his mother's cross face. "And I will not be going anywhere for a while."

"Did you bring me anything?" Tsarah wanted to know.

Darash chuckled. "Yes. New sandals. I got new sandals for us all. And a new comb for Imah." He caught Revayah's eyes. She smiled, but said nothing. "Wait till you see it," he told Tsarah. "It is very beautiful. Perhaps Imah will comb your hair with it tonight."

Revayah and Tsarah helped Darash unload Nekoda, brush her down, and settle her in the stable. All the while, Darash kept glancing at the house, wondering if Amah might come out to greet him as well. She did not.

"Are you hungry?" Revayah asked him, as she picked up a bundle of goods to carry into the house.

"I had something to eat not long ago," Darash said, "but, yes, I am hungry."

They walked toward the front door. Tsarah helped, as well, carrying a small sack. Darash carried one of the large jugs of wine he had obtained from Zephath.

"Where is Amah?" he asked his mother. "Have you sent her on an errand of some sort?"

Revayah did not answer right away. She went inside to set the bundles in a corner, then waited until Darash, too, had set down the jug.

"I am afraid Amah is no longer here, Darash," she said, looking at him and clasping her hands together at her waist.

Darash stared at her for a moment, glanced around the room, then back at his mother.

"What do you mean? Where is she?"

"I wish I knew. About a week after you left, I woke up one morning and she was just… gone. She must have gotten up in the night and left without waking us."

"Did you look for her?"

"Of course, I did, Darash," Revayah said, a hint of annoyance in her voice. "I even got Ananias to find out if she had gone back to Pertho. He asked around and discovered she had not. I asked everyone I could think of. No one knew anything. I doubt she is still in the city."

"She could be in danger, Imah," Darash said, his voice strained. "We have to keep looking for her." He walked toward the kitchen shelves then turned and paced back to where he had been standing. "What happened? Why did she go?"

"Darash," Revayah's voice was softer than usual. "You have to understand the kind of life she lived." She paused. "Sometimes people have trouble… letting go."

"But her life before was terrible. Why would she go back to it?"

"She knew nothing else, Darash. Even if we do find her again, she may not be willing to return with us. You have to prepare yourself for that."

Darash recalled what Ira, the innkeeper of Gophna, had said on the night Jehiel had shared his story. "Like Rachel who stole Laban's household gods and took them with her into her new life with Jacob, there are those who have not let go of the ancient gods. Some strongholds are not so easily broken."

No. I will not accept that! There must be some way to find her …and bring her back.

~ The End ~

~ The End ~

Character Descriptions

Amah	Pertho's young, beautiful maidservant purchased by Darash in Book I. [Amah: "female servant."] (Amah is not her real name.)
Ananias	Old family friends of Darash's family. Husband of Sapphira.
Artorius	A Roman soldier and one of Magistrate Quintus Arrius's men.
Bagad	A traveler met at an inn in Schechem by Hazaiah and his family.
Bar'abbas	A Jewish folk-hero of sorts who violently rebelled against the Romans and was captured, convicted of murder, and scheduled for crucifixion. When Pilate offered to free one of their captives—either Bar'abbas or Jesus, the Jews demanded the release of Bar'abbas, condemning Jesus to the cross.
Chaphash	A Jewish young man and the bondsman of Gabahh & Nasha. Darash's best friend.
Darash	Fifteen-year-old, Jewish boy who recently took over his father's merchant business after his father's murder. He's skinny, with stringy black hair. [Darash: "to tread or frequent, usually to follow (for pursuit or search), to seek or ask, to worship, diligently inquire, make inquisition, question, require, search, seek for/out, surely."]
Eliana	Wife of Hazaiah. Mother of Ikaiah, the four-year-old boy who disappeared.
Esh' Molech	The title of a priest of the evil god, Molech.

Ethan	Husband of Photina.
Hathal	Another former business associate of Tuwr.
Hazaiah	Husband of Eliana. Father of Ikaiah, the four-year-old who disappeared.
Huldah	A former house servant who left to find new employment when the money began to run out.
Ibnei'ah	He is a local, Jewish paver—he works with brightly colored stones to decorate the homes/gardens of the wealthy—as well as does regular stone working. He is a widower and has a six-year-old daughter named Ra'ah.
Ikaiah	Four-year-old son of Hazaiah and Eliana.
Ira	Innkeeper at Gophna.
Jada	Daughter of Jehiel, mid-teens.
Jehiel	Jada's father
Luke	A Greek physician.
Melchi	A young Gentile from Samaria who is part of the fellowship of believers there.
Millah	The dyer's wife and the town gossip. Wife of Obed. Mother of Nimrah.
Mina	A female servant in the Roman acropolis of Samaria.
Mithcah	Wife of Zuar, the leathermaker of Samaria.
Nakal	Tuwr's former business associate.

Nekoda	Darash's spotted, female donkey. [Nekoda: "Spotted."]
Nib'haz	A Jewish, blind basket seller & friend/mentor to Darash. [Nib'haz: "We shall utter (what) is seen."]
Nimrah	Son of the dyers of Jerusalem, Obed and Millah.
Obed	The dyer of Jerusalem. Husband of Millah. Father of Nimrah.
Pertho	A wicked Greek man.
Phoebe	Wife of Zephath. A skilled herbalist.
Photina	Woman of Sychar whom Jesus met at the well. Wife of Ethan.
Quintus Arrius	The Roman magistrate officially in charge of the murder investigation.
Rabbi Nathan	A Jewish rabbi and old family friend. Formerly, Tuwr's best friend.
Revayah	Darash and Tsarah's mother.
Sapphira	Revayah's best friend. Wife of Ananias.
Sergius	A Roman soldier and one of Magistrate Quintus Arrius's men.
Simon the Sorcerer	A well-known soothsayer of Samaria.
Spiro	A male servant in the Roman acropolis of Samaria.
Tsarah	Darash's younger sister, age eight.

Tuwr	Father of Darash. A merchant & moneychanger who was murdered by an unknown assailant.
Valad	Another Jewish, merchant and seller of cheese & goat milk.
Yeshua	Jesus, who eight months earlier, had been crucified, buried, and rumored to have come back from the dead. At this time, His followers are unifying, performing miracles, and boldly preaching Him as the Jewish Messiah.
Zephath	Husband of Phoebe. Wine-maker of Gophna, brother of Obed.
Zuar	Leathermaker of Samaria.

Going Deeper...

Discussion Questions

Chapter One

Read Psalm 103:6, Isaiah 1:16-18, & Luke 4:18

<u>Into the Past</u>

The Israelites were enslaved in Egypt for hundreds of years. When God finally sent Moses to free His people, God first had to convince Pharaoh to listen by sending 10 plagues. The final plague was the death of the firstborn son when the Angel of Death passed over the land. The Israelites were instructed to protect their children through a special ceremony called Passover, which is still practiced today. In what way does this story foreshadow what Jesus came to do on the cross?

<u>Into the Story</u>

When Nib'haz hears that Darash paid a great deal of money for Amah, he defends the purchase, saying, "No amount is too large to free a Jewess from slavery." Why would saying something like that be enough to silence Valad—or any Jew who might be tempted to look down on Amah?

<u>Into the Present</u>

Today, human trafficking is an enormous, monstrous problem. According to the US Department of State, in 2015, human trafficking (including labor and sex trafficking) is a $150 billion business. The 2014 Global Slavery Index reported that 35.8 million men, women, and children around the world were trapped in slavery. Over sixty-thousand of those are here in the United States. Twenty-six percent of modern day slaves are children.

What can you or your school, youth group, or church do to help the victims of modern day slavery?

Chapter Two

Read Luke 6:12-16, Galatians 3:28 & Romans 10:12

Into the Past

At the time of Jesus, bands of political rebels, called Zealots, sometimes hid out in caves and rocky areas throughout Judea. Their intent was to build an army large enough to drive the Romans out of Israel; however, they were never successful. At least one of Jesus's disciples was a known Zealot. Which one was it?

Into the Story

Magistrate Quintus Arrius, trying to make a point, asks one of his soldiers, "Are you a Jew?" The soldier reacts violently, saying, "No! I am no dog!" What does this statement show about the sentiments between Romans and Jews at this time?

Into the Present

We like to think of prejudice based on race, gender, or politics as a thing of the past, but it is an ever-present companion. No one is immune to its effects, as it is part of the culture within which we were raised. However, how does the Bible teach us to think about those who are different from us?

Chapter Three

Read Exodus 1:15-22, Ephesians 5:18, Romans 13:13, & I Corinthians 10:23-24

Into the Past

Physicians, at the time of Jesus, were mostly slaves of the wealthy who had been trained to care for the ill of that one family. Sometimes they were loaned out to others in the community. The trade of the physician, since it originated from within the slave class, was not the revered profession it is today. Midwifery, however, was an honored occupation reserved exclusively to female practitioners. Since childbirth is such a common but also dangerous experience for a woman, every community, small and large, required at least two midwives—a master and an apprentice. Physicians, herbalists, and midwives comprised the medical community of Jesus's day. The field of medicine grew in prestige as knowledge was acquired, skills improved, and more success was seen in the art of healing,. This happened most rapidly among the Greeks, who were the most scientifically advanced at that time. How many physicians and midwives can you remember from Scripture? What can you remember about their stories?

Into the Story

Who do we meet in this chapter who was a real person and biblical figure? What book did he write? Why do you think God inspired a physician to write a Gospel account of Jesus's life, including his death, burial, and resurrection?

Into the Present

The Bible shows Jesus making wine as His first miracle. Jesus also is often shown drinking wine in biblical narratives. Some years back, a rumor circulated within conservative churches that the wine Jesus made and drank was watered down (wouldn't actually make you drunk) and/or that the people of Jesus's time only drank wine to avoid contaminants in the water. Neither of these claims are historically accurate. However, the

Bible does have a great deal to say about the dangers of drinking to excess and drunkenness. What are the precautions we are called to follow when it comes to drinking alcohol?

In our story, Darash meets a drunk, who also happens to be a wine-maker. Why is this a bad arrangement? Why does this man drink? What do you know about alcoholism today and its effects on the family? Have you experienced its effects first-hand?

Chapter Four

Read Exodus 12:29-32, 20:3, Mark 1:21-28, & Romans 8:38-39

Into the Past

The Bible makes frequent references to demon-possession. Perhaps the open worship of false gods (demons & evil spirits), was the reason it was such a common phenomenon at that time. Most of the people in that region were polytheists—worshippers of multiple, lesser gods. The true God, however, commands that we should "have no other gods" before Him. Why do you think God insisted that His chosen people, the Jews, refrained from involving themselves in the religions of the people around them? What happened when they disobeyed?

Into the Story

Though Mark does not give the name of the demon-possessed man from Capernaum, whom Jesus freed, he is called Jehiel in this story. How did Jehiel first become possessed? How did Jesus free Jehiel? In our story, how did this meeting with Jesus affect Jehiel's life? What does this story show about Jesus's character?

Into the Present

Does demon-possession still happen today? Is it possible for a Christian to be possessed? What does the Romans passage above say about the power of Christ in our lives?

Chapter Five

Read Luke 8:26-39, I Corinthians 10:20, Col. 1:11-14, I John 4:4

Into the Past

Jesus cast out many demons during His earthly ministry. Read the Luke passage. How is it similar to the story Mark tells? What are the differences? In each case, what is the result?

Into the Story

Darash has a terrible nightmare brought on by Jehiel's story of demon-possession. Why do you think he reacts this way? If Darash knew the saving power of Jesus Christ for himself, what assurances would he have?

Into the Present

Jesus had the power to cast out demons and free people because He is God. He has the power to free anyone, but He typically only frees those who will choose to realize that freedom by believing in Him. Otherwise, that person would simply end up where they started and what would be the point? Are you suffering from something that is keeping you captive? Are you willing, once and for all, to trust Jesus with that area of your life?

Chapter Six

Read Genesis 34, Proverbs 16:2, & Hebrews 4:13

Into the Past

Shechem is an ancient, Canaanite city with a rich and terrible history. The Bible's first mention of it appears in Genesis 12, but perhaps the most memorable story is what occurred after the incident between Jacob's daughter, Dinah, and the young prince of that city. Dinah's brothers, Simeon and Levi, claiming vengeance for their sister, launch a sneak-attack massacre. Given that Simeon and Levi also plundered the city, do you believe their true or sole intent was to protect their sister's honor? Do you think their excuse was acceptable to God?

Into the Story

Zephath sings the story of Dinah as a bawdy drinking song. He sings of a situation that was handled very poorly, but Zephath is not handling the loss of his wife in a godly way either. What was Jacob's reaction to the news of what his sons, Simeon and Levi, did to the inhabitants of Shechem? How might this situation been dealt with in a more godly way? How might Zephath deal with his loss in a more godly way?

Into the Present

Like Simeon and Levi, we often try to excuse our own bad behavior to make ourselves look less guilty. Can you think of a time you did this? How did it affect your relationship with the people around you? How did it affect your relationship with God?

Chapter Seven

Read Isaiah 23:11, II Corinthians 10:3-5, & Psalm 94:22

Into the Past

A "stronghold" is an area where something is protected or maintained. What is a stronghold of sin? Shechem, as a Canaanite city and a stronghold of recurring idolatry, has made itself subject to God's judgment. What are the signs that a place (either a physical location or an area of someone's life) is a stronghold meant to protect and maintain a sinful way of life? What, if anything, should/could be done about it?

Into the Story

How is the city of Shechem a "stronghold" of sin and idolatry? What signs of this stronghold does Darash discover in Shechem? How does he react? Was there anything he could have or should have done differently? Why or why not? What might be the strongholds in Darash's own life and heart?

Into the Present

What strongholds of sin and idolatry can you identify in society? In your school or workplace? What about in your home or in your own life? What does God tell us to do about them? What does the Psalm passage above tell us should be our stronghold? How do we make sure that happens?

Chapter Eight

Read Deuteronomy 18:9-14, Leviticus 20:6, & Galatians 6:7

<u>Into the Past</u>

The basic premise of pagan religion is the idea that human beings are able to gain power through or over spiritual beings. This is attempted through the performance of rituals, divination, and the offering of sacrifices. The homage paid by the worshippers is not representative of a love relationship, as with the true God; rather, it is given in exchange for something—such as power, health, success, prestige, or vengeance over an enemy. Of course, those who practice sorcery, witchcraft, divination, and the like are wholly deceived. For the demons they worship desire only the destruction of humanity; whereas, God, who cannot be manipulated, desires our hearts. Have you ever witnessed these kinds of practices? What does God say about them in His Word?

<u>Into the Story</u>

Nimrah wanted a wife and was not willing to wait for his parents to help him find an acceptable match. Nor did he bother to seek the Lord. Instead, he decided to take matters into his own hands. What tactics did Nimrah employ to get what he wanted? How do you think it's going to turn out for him? What dangers is he facing by doing things his way instead of waiting on God's way?

<u>Into the Present</u>

Just as Nimrah tried to force God's hand, the basic premise of witchcraft is to try to force God or "the gods" to give us what we want when we want it. Have you ever tried to get what you wanted, even when you knew it was against God's will or timing? How did that turn out for you? How did it affect your relationship with God?

Chapter Nine

Read Acts 8:9-25, 17:11, I John 4:1-6, & Matthew 7:15-20

<u>Into the Past</u>

Simon the Sorcerer was a real person who lived in Samaria during New Testament times. According to Acts, how did Simon manage to attract a following? How did he react when Philip arrived and performed miraculous signs and wonders in the name of Jesus? What did Simon offer to buy from Peter and John when they came later? How did they respond?

<u>Into the Story</u>

At the time Darash is in Samaria, Philip has not yet arrived to explain the Gospel to the people there. How, then, did the people already know about Jesus? What did Ethan and Photina want Darash to do for them so that they might learn more? How does this scene tie into true historical events?

<u>Into the Present</u>

The Bible warns us to be on guard against false teachers and even tells us that these people could be members (or even among the leadership) in our local churches. What instructions are we given to help us identify false teachers and false teachings? What are we to do once they are identified?

Chapter Ten

Read John 4:1-42

Into the Past

The woman at the well was from Sychar, which some scholars believe is another name for Shechem—or at least is the same general area. Jacob's well is supposed to be here, too. Shechem and the well are located within the larger area of Samaria (which, to avoid confusion, is also the name of the main city there.) Most Jews refused to go through Samaria because of the deep, religious, and racial prejudices between them. However, Jesus chose to go through it. Why was it so shocking for Jesus to speak to a Samaritan woman? What was the main message Jesus was trying to explain to her? What did the woman do after Jesus spoke with her?

Into the Story

Darash meets Photina and her husband, Ethan. What does he learn about their past association with Jesus? How had their lives changed upon meeting Christ? What good things came out of the community of believers which Photina had started?

Into the Present

Sometimes to share the love and salvation of Jesus Christ, we must do things that are counter-cultural—things the world and, possibly, our own friends, families, and church will not understand or support. We must be willing to follow Jesus's example and the Holy Spirit's leading when He asks us to speak to people and love the people whom society has rejected. Can you think of an example of this from your own experience? What happened? What were the results? What have you learned from that experience?

Chapter Eleven

Read Psalm 32:5, Proverbs 18:24, Colossians 3:13, Mark 16:16, & I John 1:9

<u>Into the Past</u>

Jesus loves us, and He died to save us. But Jesus does not save people because He loves them. He loves all people, He died for all people, but He will not save all people. Jesus saves only those people who accept Him. You see, Jesus is not a bully. He has given us free will, and He is not about to take that away from us so He can get what He wants. Jesus wants our love, but love cannot be taken—it must be given willingly. Therefore, until the end, He will respect our choice—even if we do not choose Him. This is why some people will not be saved. It's tragic, but those people will be getting what they wanted. What did Jesus do to make it possible for us to have a love relationship with Him? If we accept Jesus's offer of forgiveness, how should our lives then change?

<u>Into the Story</u>

Zuar and Zephath had grown up together as best friends. Now there is a rift between them that has lasted for years—all because of unforgiveness. Have you ever experienced the break of a friendship over something silly like this? What advice would you give Zuar and Zephath? What does the Bible say about the value of friendship? What does it say about forgiveness?

<u>Into the Present</u>

Forgiving someone who has hurt you does not mean that what they did was okay. After all, if what they did was okay, there would be no need to forgive them, right? Forgiveness is simply the process by which you give that grievance over to God and let go of your right to be angry. Forgiveness will, hopefully, be the first step in a restored relationship. However, sometimes it isn't. It is possible to forgive someone but also recognize that you cannot, at least for now, trust them—even though you desire only their best. Therefore, dealing with the hurts others inflict on us can be quite confusing, and it requires that we be open to the leading of the Holy Spirit. Have you experienced forgiveness that restored a relationship? Have you experienced forgiveness that didn't restore the relationship? Share your experiences.

Chapter Twelve

Read Ezekiel 3:17-19, Luke 6:31, Luke 12:11-12, & Matthew 5:15-16

Into the Past

Though a Jew could do business with Gentiles in a limited capacity (since it was often necessary for survival), they still believed it was wrong to associate with Gentiles on a personal level. One did not eat with Gentiles, intermarry with Gentiles, or associate with them any more than absolutely necessary. If a Gentile came into your home, and you left him or her alone in a room for even a moment, everything in the room became ceremonially unclean, necessitating a lengthy ritual to get it ceremonially clean again. How do you think these cultures benefitted and/or suffered from these strict, religious and cultural rules?

Into the Story

Darash was raised to believe it was wrong for Jews to associate with Gentiles, but he justifies his dealings with them as "business," whenever possible. We, of course, know that Jesus came, in part, to break down those kinds of barriers. Jesus desires that all people be united in Him. However, what do you think of Darash trying to justify a behavior he believes is wrong? What do you think God would think of it? What should Darash do when he comes into spiritual conflicts like this one? What purpose might God have in all of this?

Into the Present

Have you ever had a good friend who did not share your core beliefs about God or morality? How did you maintain the friendship, despite your differences? How do you maintain your relationship with God without being tempted to abandon Him in order to please your friends? Are you able to share Christ's love and message of salvation with your non-Christian friends without insulting them or alienating them?

Chapter Thirteen

Read Matthew 5:21-24, 38-48, I John 4:19-20, & Romans 12:19

<u>Into the Past</u>

The mandrake is first mentioned in Scripture in Genesis 30, when Rachel bargains with Leah for some mandrakes, which she believes will cure her barrenness. The root and leaves of the mandrake are toxic and hallucinogenic, but were used in ancient times to increase fertility, as an anesthetic for surgery, and as a magical element in pagan spiritual rituals. What is the moral difference between using something for medicinal purposes vs using them for magical or spiritual purposes?

<u>Into the Story</u>

Phoebe believes Jehiel has been poisoned, and she is doing her best to save his life. Who does she think might be responsible? What do you believe motivated the would-be killer? What do you think should be done in this situation?

<u>Into the Present</u>

It's just as easy today, as it was in ancient times, to allow hatred and bitterness a place in our hearts. If someone hurts us, or if we allow ourselves to become envious of others' perceived good fortunes, we may be tempted to hate. However, what does God say about hatred? What does He say about vengeance? What does He say about loving your enemies? Is there someone in your life whom you should be treating differently?

Chapter Fourteen

Read Romans 6:1-14, II Corinthians 5:17-19 & 10:4-5

<u>Into the Past</u>

During ancient times sexual immorality was not only as widely available, as it is today, it was also an integral part of certain pagan religious rituals. Part of the reason Gentiles were not respected by the Jews was because of their habitual use of temple prostitutes—both male and female. Though we have indicated above that we should not hate those who are different from us or those who have different beliefs and lifestyles, it is also greatly important that we go through life with our eyes wide open— so that we are never tempted to compromise God's ways for the world's ways. Did the Jews manage to avoid falling into the same kinds of sin as the people around them? When they did manage to avoid it, how did they do so? When they did not, what happened? What lessons can we learn from their successes and failures?

<u>Into the Story</u>

Ethan already knows about the local brothel and indicates that he has this knowledge from personal experience. What does Darash think about Ethan as he is today? What brought about such a dramatic change in Ethan's life?

<u>Into the Present</u>

Even after we come to know Jesus, we may still struggle with the temptation to sin. Some temptations are difficult to avoid because they are all around us. Others feel impossible to avoid because we have allowed ourselves to become addicted. What advice are we given in the II Corinthians 10 passage above? Explain what you think it means to "take every thought captive and make it obedient to Christ." When trying to modify our behavior, why is important to start with our thoughts?

Chapter Fifteen

Read Genesis 22:1-19, Exodus 34:14, Leviticus 18:21

Into the Past

Many ancient cultures practiced human sacrifice and child-sacrifice. Sometimes these victims were willing; other times they were captured citizens, slaves or prisoners of war. Only twice in Scripture does God demand a human sacrifice. The first time, He demanded that Abraham sacrifice Isaac. However, how did that story end? Did God intend to start a ritual of human sacrifice or did He have another purpose?

The second time God demanded a human sacrifice, He became that sacrifice Himself on the cross. He became the first and final willing human sacrifice—approved of God—for the purpose of rescuing us from sin and death.

Into the Story

Darash is discovering that the center of the Molech cult revival is in the city of Samaria. Do you think Darash is in danger of being sucked into this cult? Why or why not?

Into the Present

Scripture refers to God as a jealous God. Why do you think that is? What right does God have to be jealous? What is He jealous of? How do you think God feels when we worship other gods or follow our own desires instead of listening to His voice?

Chapter Sixteen

Read Matthew 28:16-20, Hebrews 12:14, I Thessalonians 5:15

Into the Past

Despite the animosity between the Jews and Romans, when the Romans took control over Israel, the nation experienced a peace it hadn't enjoyed in centuries. Though the Romans could be brutal (slavery or death was the punishment for just about everything), they could also be benevolent and lenient toward cultures not their own. They allowed the Jews to worship their own God in their own Temple, to pay a portion of their taxes to their own governing authorities, and they did not forcefully conscript Jewish males for their armies. This era was called the *Pax Romana*, or the Roman Peace. During this time the Romans also built an extensive road system throughout their entire empire. Why do you think Jesus chose this time in history to come? How did the Pax Romana help the spread of the Gospel?

Into the Story

Darash goes to the Roman acropolis (like a small, fortified city within a city) to tell Magistrate Quintus Arrius where to find the cult of Molech. How do you think Darash felt, as a Jewish youth, going into the Roman acropolis alone? What did he notice about the place that made him uncomfortable? Can you think of a time you had to go somewhere that made you feel uncomfortable in a similar way?

Into the Present

The Jews had peace, even though they did not have complete freedom or autonomy. This peace came at great cost. Have you ever heard the saying, "It's better to have peace than be right." Do you agree? Why or why not? Is there a situation you can think of where that statement might be true? False?

Chapter Seventeen

Read I Kings 18:20-40, Psalm 119:105, & Romans 15:4

Into the Past

The story of Elijah and the priests of Ba'al is a fascinating one. Two opposing religious factions gather for the greatest face-off in history, with Truth as the ultimate goal and prize. Is the God of the Jews the true God? The all-powerful, all-knowing Creator? Or do the gods of the pagans have the power to bless and to save? One God or many? Elijah prays to God so that this question will be settled once and for all. What does Elijah do? What does God do? Has this question been settled? Why or why not?

Into the Story

What is Darash's favorite story from Scripture? How does that story compare with what Darash is facing now? What lessons or advice might Darash be able to glean from that story that he can apply to his present situation?

Into the Present

What is your favorite Bible story? Why? How has that story encouraged you in your walk with the Lord?

Chapter Eighteen

Read Exodus 27:1-8, John 1:12 & 29, and John 3:16-21

Into the Past

The brazen altar, situated just inside the courtyard of the tabernacle and, later, the Temple, was the place of sacrifice. Sin offerings were made there as a recognition that the penalty of sin is death; therefore, only through death can sins be forgiven. The altar served to foreshadow the cross—the place where Jesus Christ would sacrifice His life in final restitution before God for the sins of the world. God ordered the Jews to only sacrifice healthy, spotless, and unblemished animals. Why was this important? How did this practice also point to Jesus?

Into the Story

Darash is horrified when he sees the grotesque bronze altar to Molech where human sacrifices were made. However, he had seen many sacrifices offered on the altar in the Temple. Why does he react the way he does? What similarities does he draw between the two practices? What are the key differences?

Into the Present

Jesus became the willing, sinless, unblemished sacrifice for our sins. He died a terrible death on the cross to pay the death-penalty for us once and for all. However, only those who recognize and accept His sacrifice will benefit from it. Those who do not will remain in their sin, separated from God forever. Have you decided for yourself what you will choose? Will you choose to believe in and follow Jesus as the Lord of your life? If you have never done so before or aren't sure, now is the perfect time to confess your sinfulness, admit to God you need a Savior, accept Jesus's payment for your sin, and enter a love-relationship with Him.

Chapter Nineteen

Read Genesis 22:8, John 1:29-34, & Mark 10:45

Into the Past

We have already mentioned the time when God asked Abraham to sacrifice Isaac. In the Genesis passage above, what does Abraham say God will do? Does God, in fact, do as Abraham predicts?

Though God provided a ram as a substitute for Isaac's life, He provides Jesus as a substitute for ours. In fact, the mountain where God tells Abraham to sacrifice his son is the same mountain where Jesus later gives up His life for our sins. Why do you think this is significant? What is similar about these two stories of substitution and sacrifice? What is different?

Into the Story

In our story, there is also a substitution being made—one life for another. Whose life is being spared? Why? Whose life is being sacrificed? Why? Does the person doing the sacrificing and making these exchanges have the right to do so? What is motivating this man's choices? How do you think his followers will respond? How do you think God will respond?

Into the Present

Though God is the author of all life and, therefore, has the right to give life or destroy it, He chose instead NOT to punish us for our sin. Indeed sin and its natural consequences—suffering, death, and separation from God—are punishment enough. Rather, God instead did everything in His power to save us from the horrifying consequences of our fallen state. By what means did God make a way for you and I to escape the due penalty for our sin? What did He have to do to make that possible? Why did He do it?

Chapter Twenty

Read Proverbs 6:16-19, Psalm 106:34-39, & Romans 6:15-23

<u>Into the Past</u>

According to the Proverbs passage above, what are the six things God hates? Can you think of a Bible story that illustrates each of these six things and their consequences?

<u>Into the Story</u>

What happened to Jada in this chapter? What choices did she make that led to this outcome? If you could have met her earlier in the story, what advice would you give her? Do you think that she could have received forgiveness from God for her sin? What would you say to Jehiel?

<u>Into the Present</u>

We are often tempted to justify sin or to think it's not such a big deal. After all, everyone is doing it, right? But considering the consequences of sin in this chapter, and how a father's sin affected his daughter and vice versa, can we really continue to claim that sin is "no big deal?" God certainly considered it a big deal—big enough to forbid it, warn us against it, and eventually give His life to break its hold on us. Can you think of an example of when someone's sin was so destructive that it affected not only the person him/herself, but also his/her family, friends, and/or future generations?

Chapter Twenty-one

Read I Kings 13:32, 16:31-33, & Matthew 28:16-20

Into the Past

After the Hebrews were released from captivity in Egypt, they entered Canaan (the Promised Land) and eventually gained control of Samaria (the region and city), wresting it from the Canaanites. After King Solomon's death, Samaria became part of the northern kingdom of Israel (c. 931 B.C.). Tirzah was the original capital of Israel, but King Omri (father of the infamous King Ahab, whose wife was Jezebel) later moved the capital to the city of Samaria. (c. 884 B.C.) In c. 726 B.C., King Shalmaneser V of Assyria invaded the northern kingdom of Israel and laid siege to Samaria for three years. Finally, the city fell, most of the population was deported to Assyria and those who remained (or managed to return) intermarried with Assyrians. By the time of Jesus's ministry, Samaria had been made a part of the Roman province of Judea.

Why, do you think, Samaria had such a violent, traumatic past?

Into the Story

From what you saw happening in our story in Samaria, what do you think the spiritual atmosphere was like there at the time of Jesus? What were the bad things that were happening? What were the hopeful things? If you were to travel there as a missionary, what kinds of things do you think you would need to know?

Into the Present

The Jews didn't want to go into Samaria, but Jesus purposely went there and later commanded His disciples to spread the Gospel (the Good News) to all people, ridding themselves of personal prejudices. Today, who would be the people we are tempted to think of with prejudice? How are we to overcome those prejudices?

Chapter Twenty-two

Read Matthew 18:15-20, Galatians 6:1, & Ephesians 4:1-3

<u>Into the Past</u>

Today, many believe it is the man's responsibility to be the primary spiritual leader in the home, church, and elsewhere. However, the Bible has many examples of women who were spiritual leaders in their homes, in the church, and in society at large—and are commended for it. Some examples include Deborah (spiritual, military, and political leader of Israel), Lydia (first believer in her home and city), Phoebe (a deacon), Junia (an apostle alongside Paul), Priscilla (minister alongside Paul), Mary (mother of Jesus), Anna (Temple minister and prophet), Miriam (prophet & leader of Hebrew nation), and there are a great many others. How do you think the woman of Sychar (the woman Jesus met at the well in Samaria) fits into this list? Can you think of other biblical examples of female leaders?

<u>Into the Story</u>

Notice the difference between how Phoebe interacts with Zephath, how Darash interacts with Nimrah, and how Zephath speaks about the metalworker of Gophna. Phoebe intends to see some changes in Zephath's behavior. Darash, however, doesn't bother contradicting the foolish things Nimrah says to try to get him to change his opinions. And, though Zephath recognizes that his friend, the metalworker of Gophna, is likely involved in the Molech-cult, he refuses to confront his friend about it. Why do you think they have such different approaches to the idea of modifying another person's behavior? Are they making good choices or bad choices in their relationships?

<u>Into the Present</u>

Think of your friends and family members. Are any of them engaging in behaviors you believe are wrong or, possibly, dangerous? What, if anything, do you think you should do to help them? In general, should we confront other people's sin if there is no indication they want to change? What kind of relationship should we have with someone before we point out their flaws? What situations might require that you intervene, even if the person will hate you for it? How should we react if someone points out our flaws?

Chapter Twenty-three

Read Exodus 20:13, Deuteronomy 19:10, 30:19, & Psalm 10

Into the Past

In ancient times, though brutality was more commonly witnessed than it is today, outright murder was still taken very seriously. Murderers were given a trial and, if found guilty, put to death. Who was the first murderer in Scripture? What happened to him? Can you think of any other biblical examples of murderers? How were they treated by society? How were they treated by God? Is God willing to forgive a murderer?

Into the Story

Two murderers appear in this chapter. Who are they and what have they done? What motivated these acts of murder? Were either of these murderers justified legally in their actions? Were either of them justified morally? What does God say about murder?

Into the Present

In what ways do you see human life devalued or disregarded in society today? Though God gives us a choice, what choice does God ask us to make when it comes to life and death? What is the reward for a good choice? What is the consequence for a bad choice?

Chapter Twenty-four

Read Genesis 46:29, Luke 15:20-24, Mark 15:34, & Jeremiah 31:3

Into the Past

The Bible has several stories of lost sons being reunited with their fathers/families. Can you think of any? When Jesus is on the cross, how does He react as He feels the separation between Himself and God? How do you think God felt at seeing Jesus suffer and die for our sins?

Into the Story

In our story, someone is found and someone is lost. Who are they? Which story had a happy ending? What do you think is going to happen to the person who is lost? Why do you think she ran away?

Into the Present

We each have experienced times of separation from loved ones. How does it feel to be away from a loved one for a long time? What feelings do we experience when we are faced with the possibility of a loved one suffering or, possibly, dying? How does it feel to be reunited?

When we separate ourselves from God through sin, how do you think God feels? What can we do to reunite with Him? What can we do to prevent future separations from God?

Glossary

סֶלָה

Hebrew word "selah," meaning "rest" or "pause" and often used during poetic verse or musical lyrics.

Abba

The transliterated Hebrew word for "father" or "dad."

Acropolis

A Roman, fortified citadel, like a city within a city.

Adonai

The Hebrew word for "Lord."

Agora

The Greek term for market.

As

A large, bronze or copper coin worth about 1/16 of a denarius.

Ba'al

The name means "lord" and is used as a general reference to the many gods of the Canaanites (and others), but is also used more specifically of a storm and fertility god and the consort of Asherah.

Bath

A liquid capacity measurement equal to an ephah or 1/10 of a homer. Approximately, 5.8 gallons.

Ben

This means "son of" in Hebrew. So, "Darash ben Tuwr" means "Darash, son of Tuwr."

Bitumen

A natural, black, tar-like substance used in construction as a kind of cement and as a means of water-proofing.

Days of the Week	Sunday: yom rishon, the first day. Monday: yom shayni, the second day. Tuesday: yom shli'shi, the third day. Wednesday: yom revi'i, the fourth day. Thursday: yom khah'mi'shi, the fifth day. Friday: yom ha'shi'shi, the sixth day. Saturday: Shabbat, the seventh day.
Denarius	A small silver coin worth about one day's wage for an unskilled laborer or common soldier. "Denarii" is the plural form.
El	"God" in Hebrew.
Elohim	"Elohim" is plural for "El" (or possibly "Eloah"). However, it does not mean "gods," but rather incorporates within it the concept of a triune God—a God consisting of three persons, God the Father, God the Son, and God the Holy Spirit.
Eloheinu	Same as "Elohim" above, except it means "our God."
Emmaus	A town located approximately 7 miles northwest of Jerusalem.
Ephah	One tenth of a homer ($^1/_3$ – ¾ of a bushel or 12-26 liters). The ephah refers to a container which would hold an ephah of produce, such as oil, wheat, flour, etc.
Gophna	A city approximately 14 miles north of Jerusalem.
Hin	A liquid capacity measurement. Approximately 1/6 of a bath or 1 gallon.
Homer	One donkey load and the most common capacity measurement. It equals approximately 3.8 to 7.5 bushels.

Imah
: The transliterated Hebrew word for "mom" or "mommy."

Jerusalem
: "Yerushaláyim" in Hebrew, this city is the capital of Judah and the original site of King Solomon's Temple. It is located on a plateau between the Mediterranean and the Dead Sea.

Leben
: A yogurt-like dairy product.

Mishnah
: The oral law—a collection of strict, highly legalistic moral teachings, imperatives, and interpretations of Scripture followed and enforced by the Pharisees.

Pharisee
: A member of an ancient Jewish religious sect. They observed strict, traditional and written laws, such as those of the Mishnah, and felt it their duty to compel others to live according to highly legalistic requirements. They controlled the synagogues and everyday Jewish life.

Prutah
: A prutah (plural: prutot) is a small, Jewish, copper coin worth about 2 lepta. A loaf of bread was worth about ten prutot.

Sadducee
: A member of an ancient Jewish religious sect. They denied the resurrection of the dead and the existence of angels, demons, or spirits. They also rejected the oral teachings and traditions, believing the written law alone. They controlled the Temple and official religious ceremonies.

Shabbat
: The Sabbath, the seventh day of the week and the traditional day of rest for the Jews. It begins at sundown on Friday and ends at sundown on Saturday.

Shadchan
: The Hebrew word for matchmaker.

Shuk	The Hebrew term for market.
Shekel	A silver or gold coin worth 3 denarii. There was also a half-shekel coin worth 1.5 denarii. It is also a unit of weight equaling approximately .4 of an ounce.
Synagogue	The building where Jewish people met for religious worship and instruction.
Torah	The first five books of the Bible: Genesis, Exodus, Leviticus, Numbers, and Deuteronomy.
Yerushaláyim	"Jerusalem" in Hebrew.
Yeshua	"Jesus" in Hebrew.
Yom	"Day" in Hebrew.a

Research Bibliography

Adkins, Lesley and Roy A. Adkins. (1994) *Handbook to Life in Ancient Rome*. New York, NY: Facts on File, Inc.

Alexander, Pat, John W. Drane, David Field, and Alan Millard (Eds.). (1987) *The Lion Encyclopedia of the Bible*. Batavia, IL: Lion Publishing.

Anderson, Rebecca J. (1994) "The Sabbath in Ancient and Modern Practice." Retrieved May 2014 from: http://www.rj-anderson.com/docs/sabbath.html

Ariès, Philippe and Georges Duby. (1987) *A History of Private Life*: *From Pagan Rome to Byzantium*. Cambridge, MA: The Belknap Press of Harvard University.

Ayayo, Karelynne, et. al. (2005) *The Archaeological Study Bible: An Illustrated Walk Through Biblical History and Culture, (New International Version)*. Grand Rapids, MI: Zondervan Publishing House.

Baker, Warren, David Kemp, and Tim Rake (Eds.). (1994) *The Complete Word Study Old Testament*. Chattanooga, TN: AMG Publishers.

Backhouse, Robert. (1996) *The Kregel Pictorial Guide to the Temple*. Grand Rapids, MI: Kregel Publications.

Beaumont, Mike. (2006) *Holman Illustrated Guide to the Bible*. Nashville, TN: B & H Publishing Group.

ben Avraham, Yehoshua. (2003) "Hebrew Day and Month Names." YashaNet. Retrieved May 2014 from: http://www.yashanet.com/library/hebrew-days-and-months.html

Berlin, Adele and Marc Zvi Brettler (Eds.). (2004) *The Jewish Study Bible* (Tanakh Translation). New York, NY: Oxford University Press.

BibleHistory.Com. "What did Jesus think when he saw this stone?" Retrieved May 2014 from: http://www.bible-history.com/archaeology/israel/temple-warning.html

Bouquet, A.C. (1954) *Everyday Life in Bible Times*. London: B.T. Batsford Ltd.

Bright, John. (1981) *A History of Israel (3ʳᵈ ed.)*. Philadelphia, PA: Westminster Press.

Bruce, F.F. (Ed.). (1979) *The International Bible Commentary (Revised Ed.)*. Grand Rapids, MI: Zondervan Publishing House.

Carcopino, Jérôme. (2003) *Daily Life in Ancient Rome (2ⁿᵈ ed.)*. New Haven: Yale University Press.

Chinuch, Merkos L'inyonei (Pub.). (2008) Translation of the Weekday Amidah. *Chabad.org*. From Siddur Tehillat Hashem. Brooklyn, NY: Kehot Publication Society. Retrieved from http://www.chabad.org/library/article_cdo/aid/867674/jewish/Translation.htm

Douglas, J.D. and Merril C. Tenney. (1987) *The New International Dictionary of the Bible*. Grand Rapids, MI: Zondervan Publishing House.

Dowley, Tim. (1999) *The Kregel Pictorial Guide to Everyday Life in Bible Times*. Grand Rapids, MI: Kregel Publications.

Dummelow, J.R. (Ed.). (1970) *The One Volume Bible Commentary*. New York, NY: The Macmillan Company.

Elwell, Walter A. (Ed.). (1989) *Baker Encyclopedia of the Bible* (Vols. 1-2). Grand Rapids, MI: Baker Book House.

Frank, Harry Thomas (Ed.). (2002) *Atlas of the Bible Lands*. Union, NJ: Hammond Incorporated.

Freedman, David Noel (Ed.). (2000) *Eerdman's Dictionary of the Bible*. Grand Rapids, MI: Wm. B. Eerdman's Publishing Co.

Grosvenor, Gilbert, et. al. (1961) *Everyday Life in Ancient Times*. Washington, D.C.: National Geographic Society.

Grosvenor, Giblert, et. al. (1967) *Everyday Life in Bible Times*. Washington, D.C.: National Geographic Society.

Hamilton, Adam. (2009) *24 Hours That Changed the World*. Nashville, TN: Abington Press.

Harrison, Everett F. and Charles R. Pfeiffer. (1968) *The Wycliffe Bible Commentary*. Nashville, TN: The Southwestern Company.

Hart, David Bentley.(2007) *The Story of Christianity*. London: Quercus.

Henry, Mathew. (1964) *Matthew Henry's Commentary on the Whole Bible in One Volume*. Grand Rapids, MI: Zondervan Publishing House.

Howard, Kevin and Marvin Rosenthal. (1997) *The Feasts of the Lord: God's Prophetic Calendar from Calvary to the Kingdom*. Nashville, TN: Thomas Nelson, Inc.

Isserlin, B.S.J. (2001) *The Israelites*. Minneapolis, MN: Fortress Press.

Jackson, J.B. (1957) *A Dictionary of Scripture Proper Names (3rd ed.)*. Neptune, NJ: Loizeaux Brothers.

Jeffers, James S. (1999) *The Greco-Roman World of the New Testament Era: Exploring the Background of Early Christianity*. Downers Grove, IL: InterVarsity Press.

Liles, John. (2014) The Life of Jesus. *The Timeline of the Bible*. Tarzana, CA: Bible Timeline. Retrieved from http://www.bibletimeline.org/webdocs/lifeofjesus.cfm

Lynch, Joseph H. (2010) *Early Christianity: A Brief History*. New York, NY: Oxford University Press.

Packer, J.I. and M.C. Tenney (Ed.). (1980) *Illustrated Manners and Customs of the Bible*. Nashville, TN: Thomas Nelson Publishers.

Rich, Tracey R. (2007) "Shabbat Evening Home Ritual." Judaism 101. Retrieved May 2014 from http://www.jewfaq.org/prayer/shabbat.htm.

Telushkin, Joseph. (2001) *Jewish Literacy: The Most Important Things to Know About the Jewish Religion, Its People, and Its History*. New York, NY: William Morrow and Company, Inc.

Vamosh, Miriam Feinberg. (2004) *Food at the Time of the Bible: From Adam's Apple to the Last Supper*. Nashville, TN: Abingdon Press.

Vamosh, Miriam Feinberg. (2007) *Daily Life at the Time of Jesus*. Herzlia, Israel: Phalpot Ltd.

Viner, J. (Host). (2007). *Lost Treasures of the Ancient World: Jerusalem.* [History Documentary]. United States: Kultur Video. Retrieved April 2014 from: https://www.youtube.com/watch?v=oBR42_UEV5g

Vos, Howard F. (1999) *New Illustrated Bible Manners and Customs*. Nashville, TN: Thomas Nelson Publishers.

Walvoord, John F. and Roy B. Zuck (Eds.). (1984) *The Bible Knowledge Commentary: An Exposition of the Scriptures by Dallas Seminary Faculty (New Testament Ed.)*. Wheaton, IL: Victor Books.

Walvoord, John F. and Roy B. Zuck (Eds.). (1984) *The Bible Knowledge Commentary: An Exposition of the Scriptures by Dallas Seminary Faculty, (Old Testament Ed.*). Wheaton, IL: Victor Books.

Whiston, Willaim (Trans.). (1987) *The Works of Josephus: Complete and Unabridged (New Updated Ed.)*. Peabody, MA: Hendrickson Publishers, Inc.

Wood, Leon J. (1986) *A Survey of Israel's History (Revised and Enlarged Ed.)*. Grand Rapids, MI: Zondervan Publishing House.

Wright, G. Ernest (Ed.). (1974) *Great People of the Bible and How They Lived*. Pleasantville, NY: The Reader's Digest Association, Inc.

Wright, Paul H. (2002) *Atlas of Bible Lands*. Nashville, TN: Holman Bible Publishers.

Zodhiates, Spiros (Ed.). (1991) *The Complete WordStudy New Testament*. Chattanooga, TN: AMG Publishers.

Other Resources:
The Global Slavery Index. (2015)
http://www.globalslaveryindex.org/findings/

Interactive Virtual Tour at the Model of Jerusalem in the Late Second Temple Period, The Israel Museum Jerusalem,
http://www.imj.org.il/panavision/model_pre_3eng.html

Holy Land Model of Ancient Jerusalem (66 CE) Holyland Corporation http://www.holylandnetwork.com/temple/model.htm

US Department of State. Human Trafficking Fact Sheets. (2015)
http://www.state.gov/j/tip/rls/fs/2015/index.htm

Wikimedia Commons. Map of First Century Jerusalem. Adaptation of File: Meyers b9 s0200.jpg Retrieved Sept. 2014 from
www.wikimedia.org

Wikimedia Commons. Map of First Century Israel. First Century Palestine.gif. Retrieved Sept. 2014 from www.wikimedia.org

More From:

The Dramatic Pen
TheDramaticPen.com
Facebook.com/TheDramaticPen
@TDPPress

The Holy Land Mysteries Series

Darash's adventures continue with…
Book III: The Mud Flower
Book IV: The Leper's Gift
Book V: The Weeping Place
And More!

The Scrolls of the Nevi'im Series

The prophets of the Old Testament come alive with…

Book I: Habakkuk's Plea: A Prophet of Elohim

Book II: Habakkuk's Plea: Evil Persists

Book III: Habakkuk's Plea: Elohim Answers

**Interactive Mystery Party Games
for Teens and Adults
S. E. Thomas**

**Who Invited the Stiff to Dinner?
Murder at Surly Gates
Accuracy
Let Them Eat Cake**

**A Reason To Celebrate
A Full-Length Christmas Production
S. E. Thomas**

For most, Christmas is a time filled with joy. But for many, Christmas can be a difficult season. But let us consider a moment what Scripture tells us of the first Christmas. What really happened? For the first time, God Himself—the Creator of the Universe, the King of Kings, the Everlasting Father—stepped into our world! He stepped in—not to enjoy the wealth or the beauty or the joys—but to experience our suffering, our longings, and our sorrows. From the moment of His birth, He experienced far from ideal circumstances. Yet, we remember His words, "In this world you will have trouble. But take heart! I have overcome the world."

Acting Out Loud
Christian Skits for All Occasions
S. E. Thomas

Whether you are a pastor looking for a skit to help drive home your message, a ministry leader desiring a dramatic reading to speak God's love at a retreat or conference, or a youth group leader hoping to spice up a youth meeting, we have the material you're looking for! Find over thirty skits, short plays, and dramatic readings that cover the following areas: Biblical Tales, Christian Living, Evangelism, Special Events, Holidays.

Lazy Dog
carol fields brown

"The quick brown fox jumps over the lazy dog." This sentence is called a pangram. A pangram contains every letter of the English alphabet at least one time. This storybook starts with this famous pangram. The Lazy Dog and the Fox start us on an animal adventure. You can write the sentences and color the pictures. At the end of the book is a chart to help you make up your own sentences. At first you may need help, but soon you will be able to make your own. Every sentence can become a story. Do you know why the Fox jumped over the lazy dog? I wonder…. What do you think? This coloring book provides an opportunity for young learners to explore the intricacies of the English language, practice their handwriting, and explore a variety of animal behaviors in a fun and creative way. Full-color illustrations, matching coloring pages, and lines for handwriting practice are also included.

Sourdough Secrets… Revealed!
From Making the Starter to Sourdough Success!
Ray Templeton

Step-by-step instructions that will allow you to make your own starter, make your first loaf, and even learn to make sourdough bread in your bread machine.

Is My Faith My Own?
A Resource for Christian Young People
Leaving Home for the First Time
S. E. Thomas

Everything was going along fine... then you got out on your own and realized it's your   responsibility to get the rest of your life right. From here on out, if you're going to follow God, you're going to be doing it on your own. You can no longer coast by on your parents' faith, your pastor's understanding, or your youth leader's morals. Now it's up to you. And you have some questions: Is my faith real? Is it growing? Is it my own? (A *Finding Hope Resource Guide*.)

Complex Simplicity:
How Psychology Suggests Atheists are Wrong about Christianity
Dr. Lucian Gideon Conway III

In *Complex Simplicity*, prominent psychology researcher Dr. Lucian Gideon Conway III addresses the modern atheist attack on the psychological effectiveness of the Christian religion. As an expert in the science of cognitive complexity, Dr. Conway uses scientific research and personal narratives to argue that Christianity is an effective guide for reconciling the many complexities built into the human psyche. Directly contradicting what many modern atheists believe, he shows that, in approaching human

psychology from a complex perspective, Christianity meets our complex needs with complex solutions. To Christian believers, he offers psychological reasons to believe their faith yields positive benefits. To skeptics, he offers a challenge to the growing cultural belief that Christianity is both simple-minded and ineffective. *Complex Simplicity* is important reading for anyone curious about the intersection of Christian teaching and human psychology.

Daily Life in Bible Times
Small Group Study
S. E. Thomas

Workbook & Leader Guide Editions

Come face to face with the people you read about in Scripture by exploring what their daily lives would have looked like. Learn how a young man selected and courted his bride, what occupations they had and how they trained for them, how infants were cared for, and how the ancients mourned and buried their dead. We will also look at the economic and political climate, learn about crime and punishment, and even find out what they ate and how they dressed. And as you come to know the culture of Jesus Christ, you will see Him more clearly, as well. ***This is a 10-week Bible study.***

Please Visit Us Again!

Find fiction and non-fiction books, study guides, plays, skits, mystery party games, fundraising resources, free downloadable templates, writers' resources, and much more at:

www.TheDramaticPen.com

Write To Bless The World